GENTLE'S STRENGTH

THE
EVERS SAGA
BOOK 2

GENTLE'S STRENGTH

B L PARKER

Book Cover by Vivian Reiss

Editor Maryssa Gordon

1st Edition 2024

ISBN – 978-0-6459760-1-4

Also by B L Parker

To mum and dad,
Thanks for always helping me
out and believing in me
Love you xx

This book is written in Australian English, so some words may be spelled a little different.

If you would love to keep up to date on what B L Parker is doing, sign up to her newsletter at
blparkerbooks.com/newsletter
Here you can find out about new releases, freebies and her writing process.

ONE

GENTLE

I was sitting on my beautiful throne, in my beautiful dress, looking serene and lovely, but inside, I was anything but. I was bored. I had been sitting in this council meeting for what felt like four hundred years, and I was so sick of listening to their voices, but I let none of it show on my face. I may be the ruler here in Aeris Isle, but I wasn't overly involved.

"Yes, tell the shovellers they must work faster. It is unacceptable to have snow covering all our walkways well into mid-morning," Vasair said, shaking his head. The eighty-year-old dwarf had wispy white hair on top of his liver-spotted head and was always whining about something. I held in my sigh and gazed around the room again.

We were sitting in the council chambers of my castle. It was a circular room with windows lining three walls. All the windows were open, and a fresh mountain breeze was blowing through. The air was cold and crisp, but I didn't mind. With my air power, I had made a small bubble around myself that was nice and warm. I hadn't extended it to anyone else, but I had controlled the air billowing through the room, so it wasn't as cold as it *could* be. The clouds were white and puffy today, and birds flew around the mountain peaks ducking and diving. The wind carried in the smell of fresh snow that had fallen overnight.

"No bombs have been found today. I believe we may have found them all."

My attention caught, and I turned to Perrian, noting his face was redder than usual. His short black hair stuck up all around his head, and I wondered what had him so flustered.

"How many did they find all up?" I asked. It was the first time I had spoken, and I think half of them had forgotten I was still here.

"Excuse me, my lady? What did you ask?"

Raising my voice so they could hear, I repeated the question.

"Oh well, I think all up we have found four bombs inside the mountain, my lady. I do believe this is the last one. We have not discovered any for days now."

I shuddered and was thankful all over again we had discovered them before they exploded underneath us. I still woke in the night with nightmares about Bilvog blowing up the mountain and killing us all.

"I would like to see one," I said. I had wanted to see one of these destructive machines since the first one had been pulled out, but something held me back. I knew looking at them would drive home that one of my most trusted advisors and someone I had called a friend had betrayed us. But now, I was ready.

"Oh no, my lady. I don't think so. They have all been kept in the mines, and it is quite dusty and dirty down there. Not somewhere for one as beautiful as you to be," said Lomano, shaking his pockmarked face and wrinkling his nose. The air elemental was so old, his eyes were clouded as he looked in my direction. When did they all get so old?

"All the same, I would like to see it. I think it is my duty as Lady of the Air to see what was to be used against us. They have been disarmed, so there is no danger," I said

"Please, don't worry about it. We have it all under control. Isn't there a ball to attend tonight? Why don't you focus on that? We can't have the Lady of the Air looking dusty and like she has done a hard day's work in the mines when she is to be entertaining."

I clenched my jaw and focused on keeping my face neutral. I ran my hands along the front of my dress, smoothing it while my foot tapped. The only indication I was seething inside. All these men wanted from me was to sit back and look pretty. What was the point of coming to these meetings? I'm sure they would rather I stayed out, but I am their Lady, even if they don't let me rule. I gave a tight nod and looked outside, tuning out the rest of the meeting.

When it ended, the six old men stood and bowed, taking their leave. I smiled tightly at them and sat up straight till the door was closed behind the last one.

I slumped in my seat and let out the breath I had been holding.

"What a waste of time," I mumbled in the quiet room.

"I don't think so, my lady," said a deep voice behind me. I jumped in my seat and whirled around.

"Amos, I had forgotten you were standing there."

"I apologise, my lady. I didn't mean to startle you," he said as he bowed. I waved away his apology.

"That's okay. Well, it doesn't look like I will be going to see those bombs anytime soon," I said, getting up from my chair. I ran my hands along the back of the glass chair, feeling its smoothness.

"If I may speak candidly?" Amos asked, his brown eyes looking at me kindly as he stood as straight and strong as the mountains in my realm. I nodded even though I held my breath not sure I wanted to her what he was going to say. There were many things I had done, or hadn't done, lately that I wasn't so proud of.

"You are the boss here. If you want to look at those bombs, that is what you should do. No one should tell you what you can and can't do in your own realm. Least of all those old men. You are much more than a pretty face. You have steel within you. Do not bend. You are intelligent and kind, and you should tell them what you want and not ask." I stared at him while I processed his words. Most people would not speak to me like that, but Amos was different. Hearing him say those things about me made me blush. Amos had been in my service for a long time, and I knew he meant every word with kindness and not criticism.

"Thank you. You have brightened my day. Unfortunately, I think I have been a doll for too long. They no longer see me as anything other than a pretty book cover with empty pages. The realm's running nicely with them. Perhaps it is for the best," I said, sadness settling in my heart. That's not the ruler I wanted to be, but I didn't know how to change it now. I did what I could, but I wondered if it was enough.

He looked at me sadly, and I turned away from him, not wanting to see his pity and, worst of all, disappointment.

Picking up the long, flowy skirts of my pretty pink dress, I walked the length of the room to the door. In the hall, people were bustling about carrying ornaments, food, linens, and anything else needed for tonight. Everyone was preparing for the annual Night of Lights ball. All along the walls, people were wiping dust out of the sconces and the baseboards and making sure everything was in it's place. I walked past, smiling at everyone, listening to Amos's heavy footfalls behind me.

At first, it had annoyed me to have him shadow my every move, but I had grown used to it these past few weeks. My council had insisted upon it after the first bomb was found. These days, I was glad to have someone to talk to, even if he himself spoke little. Being an Alanti made him part of our elite force. A force of well-trained, highly disciplined winged men and women. Amos was our highest-ranking and most experienced soldier and had taken on the role seriously. Even though he was just past middle age for his race, he was still strong and dangerous. Out of his back, two large brown feathered wings protruded and rested against the length of his body. Each feather had a gold tip, and when spread, they glinted in the sun, beautiful and powerful.

"I'm going to my room now to begin preparing for the ball tonight, Amos. You are dismissed."

His brow crinkled as he frowned at me, "If you don't mind, my lady, I would like to come with you and check your rooms," he said quietly but firmly.

"Okay. Let's go then," I said, holding in my sigh. On the walk to my rooms, I thought about the whole ordeal of getting ready for the ball tonight. So much work. It would be worth it, and I did love doing my hair and wearing beautiful dresses. I was like a new gem polished to perfection and I wasn't ashamed to admit I enjoyed the attention sometimes.

Amos checked my rooms, and when they were all clear, he left to get himself ready for the ball. Alone in my room, I sat at my window and stared out. The breeze coming in made the massive tapestries hanging from the wall wave as they did their best to keep some of the chill out. My large four-poster bed was made with so many pillows it was tempting to climb in, snuggle down and succumb to the sleepiness the meeting had brought on. Textures of all sorts filled the room, and it was my favourite place to be.

Here, I could just be me. Colours sprung out everywhere from the hot pink armchair and the sky-blue rug. No glass was in my windows, so I could breathe in the clean, fresh air that swirled around the peaks and valleys that made up my kingdom. The mountain air cleansed my room and cleaned out every nook and cranny banishing whatever mood I was in from the day.

After breathing in the cool air, I walked to my sitting desk and moved the pile of books that had accumulated there. I had been collecting them from the library, trying to find out whatever I could about the banishment of my brother, Dread. I had been reading for the last few weeks, looking for any clue where the artefacts might be, so we didn't have to go and see the hags, but so far nothing. I had found multiple accounts of what happened, some accurate, some not, and opinions on why it was and wasn't a good idea, but nothing about what happened with the artefacts after the hags were finished with them.

Thinking about the artefacts always led me to the Crown of Glass. The crown was beautiful and had been made especially for me. It was what allowed me to feel seen. People listened to my ideas and didn't only look at my beauty. I had always thought that the day I had to hand it over to the hags for the binding ritual, was the day I stopped truly ruling my realm. When I gave it to the hags, I let them take my identity and I had been trying to gather it back ever since, but deep down I knew that wasn't the only reason. I may blame the loss of my crown, but to be honest, I let it happen. I sat around like a doll and allowed others to take over the ruling of my realm. I shook myself and put the books on the floor where I couldn't see them. I needed a distraction.

I went to my vanity and picked up the mail that had been delivered during the day. Most of the other Evers preferred to use their electronic devices, but I loved the personal nature of a letter. Most were RSVPs for the ball, and I was pleased my brother Gloom and his new partner Amelia would be attending.

I liked Amelia when we met a few weeks ago, and it was nice to see my brother happy at last. They had a bond you could practically see, and I wanted to see how they were going now. Crescent and Awe would also be there, but I wasn't surprised. Awe loved any excuse for a party and to dance with the prettiest ladies in attendance.

Even though I was disappointed Ashes and Enduring couldn't make it, I smiled, my mood lifting, excited to see my family and friends. Perhaps this is what I needed to shake this melancholy from my mind. Yes, tonight would be a good night.

I looked out the window and was surprised to see the sun beginning to touch the top of the mountain peaks. I had let my thoughts get away from me and now I needed to get ready. In my dressing room, I grabbed the dress that had been laid out for me. It was a midnight blue satin with a matching tulle overlay. The tulle was covered in hundreds of tiny little gems making it look like a night sky full of stars, perfect for the ball tonight. The skirt was full and floaty, and the square neckline reached up to two thin straps where my favourite part of the dress was. On top of the thin straps was a length of tulle fabric, almost like my shoulders had capes. The fabric touched the floor to form a train. I had been saving this dress for this ball and couldn't wait to put it on.

I had a nice hot shower and got myself pampered and ready to go. My maids brushed my long blonde hair a hundred times each until it was gleaming. Lastly, I added my circlet of sapphires and got dressed. I was right. I was perfect. On the outside, I appeared every bit the queen I wanted to be. I smoothed my dress and took a deep breath.

Tonight was going to be fine.

TWO
GENTLE

The party was really getting started as I wound my way to my brother and his partner.

"Gloom! How lovely to see you," I said as he swept me up in a tight hug. I hugged him back just as tightly. "You look happy," I said with a wink.

"Ah, thank you, sister. I am," he replied, smiling down at Amelia. I turned to her and took her hand in mine. "Welcome to Aeris Isle. It's so good to see you. I hope your leg is healing well?"

"Thanks, Gentle. Yes, it's all better now. Nothing stopping me from having a dance," she said pointedly while hip-bumping Gloom. He grimaced but I saw in his eyes he would deny her nothing.

"This dress is stunning on you!" I said to her, my eyes trailing up and down.

She blushed and looked at her beautiful emerald, green ball gown. She swayed her hips slightly so the skirts moved about her, and I could tell she was pleased with my compliment. "Thanks. I have to be careful these things don't poke my eyes out," she said, motioning to the peaks of the neckline that pointed towards her collarbone like the branches of a tree.

"The price we pay for fashion," I said with a fake sigh. "I hope your ride here was comfortable?" I gestured to the carriages at the edge of the mountain.

"It was amazing! I never thought in a million years I would be attending a ball in a carriage being pulled by Pegasus. Her brow creased. "Pegasi? Whatever they are called, this has been the wildest night of my life," she said, gushing.

Gloom and I laughed, and he tucked her closer to his body. "I'm glad you enjoyed the ride," I said. "It's definitely better than *hiking* up the mountain. Now, I better let you go. I have a lot of people to greet," I said, rolling my eyes. "I'll find you later. While you and the others are here, I want to have a chat."

Gloom's eyes sharpened, and he nodded at me before he and Amelia headed to the dance floor. I watched them for a moment in their little bubble, holding each other and swaying like no one else was in the room.

"My lady?"

My thoughts were interrupted by Amos standing behind me.

"You have got to stop sneaking up on me," I said with a smile.

"I'm sorry, my lady. Next time, I shall stomp louder," he said with a glint in his eye. Surprised by his joke, I laughed out loud.

"The ballroom is clear but me and Nathaniel will be keeping a close eye on you." He gestured to the man standing across the room.

He was partially concealed in the shadows, keeping a meticulous eye on everyone who had arrived so far. The intensity of his blue gaze meant nothing got past him, and it made me somewhat uncomfortable when turned on me.

Watching him, a feeling I couldn't quite place ran through my body. Tonight, he had on the formal outfit all the guards had to wear, but on him, it looked different. The sky-blue colour set his gold hair gleaming. It also matched the pale blue of his wings that were tucked in behind him looking smooth and soft. He turned his head, and our eyes clashed.

I quickly looked away, annoyed I had been caught looking at him. I had known Nathaniel ever since he had been promoted to Amos's second a few years ago and I was drawn to him. I couldn't for the life of me work out why. He was so buttoned up and disciplined it made him very dull.

I turned back when Amos spoke. "With us here, you will be safe."

"I know, Amos," I said, touching his arm. For as long as I could remember, Amos had been here for me to protect me and counsel me. Most of the time, he gave me the confidence boost I needed to rule this realm. Thinking about him like that made me think of someone else I had admired. Bilvog. He had nurtured me and guided me, but, in the end, he betrayed me. A sour taste coated my mouth and I swallowed with difficulty. I pushed all thoughts of him aside, determined not to let it ruin my night. It would be a long evening, and I needed to play the part of host well.

I drifted around the party, welcoming the incoming guests and making sure all had a drink, were comfortable, and everything was in its correct place. Everyone seemed happy enough. I was hoping tonight would enable the people of my realm to relax a little bit. With the bombs being pulled out of the mountain, everyone was a bit tense. I wanted to make sure everyone was happy and enjoying one night where they didn't have to worry.

The ballroom was outside and had been magically heated to keep the cold mountain air out. It had no ceiling, so you could get the full view of the lights later in the evening. Twelve lilac marble pillars reached towards the heavens, and between them, thousands of small twinkling lights made a magical vision. Between the pillars on the outside, long, white sheer curtains fluttered in the breeze, wafting the smell of jasmine through the party. Food and drink tables were around the edge of the dancefloor and laden with so much food they should have been collapsing. Beautiful music floated on the air, seeming to come from nowhere and everywhere at once.

The Night of Lights Ball was usually one of my favourite parties of the year, but tonight, I was not really in the mood to celebrate. There was a constant tension in the back of my neck like I was waiting for the other shoe to drop. I did my best to keep the stress off my face as I attended to my guests, not wanting them to pick up on my mood. It was a mask I had worn more and more recently, and I hated the feeling the deception made me feel.

Before long, the room was a buzz of talking and dancing and energy crackled in the air. I played my part and danced with anyone who wanted to, even when some of my dance partners were less than ideal. Everyone said the same things. "You look beautiful tonight, my how the dress brings out your eyes, I have never seen a more beautiful woman."

I smiled and thanked them, all the while counting the minutes till I could escape. Just once, I would like someone to have a real conversation with me. Ask about my favourite book, what I like to do for hobbies, anything other than my appearance, and how beautiful I look.

Eventually, I was able to take a seat and I surveyed the crowd of people gathered. My eyes were drawn to the dance floor, where I could see Awe spinning a woman around with a grin on his face and lust in his eyes. He had been out there for at least an hour, and each time I had seen him, he had had a different woman. Awe always had the best time at balls.

I smiled as I watched him being carefree and wished I could be like that again as well. The dark and sad emotions threatened to invade me again, but I pushed them back. I refused to let what Bilvog had done to my family define every future moment of my life. It was easier said than done.

I noticed Crescent had arrived on the other side of the dancefloor. Her dark skin made her simple white dress practically glow. She was lurking in the shadows, talking to anyone game enough to approach her. She was quiet and serious, and some people didn't know how to take her. Parties were not really her thing, and I knew she was here for me. She wanted to check up on me and see how I was doing. I was glad. I didn't see her enough, and I missed her.

Nathaniel caught my eye as he weaved through the dancers while keeping a sharp eye on everyone inside and outside the room. I could trust he knew exactly who was outside, trying to avoid prying eyes and what they were doing. Amos stopped and spoke to him, and I saw them both look at me, and I turned away quickly, cursing myself for getting caught twice looking at him. They looked at me a while longer before Amos broke away and headed toward me.

He passed me a plate of food and a glass of wine.

"Don't forget to eat, my lady. You have been on the dance floor almost as much as Awe."

I thanked him as I took the plate and began to pick at the food. It was delicious, and I was hungry.

"Amos, it looks like the lights will be appearing soon. Could you gather my brothers and sisters? There is something I would like to discuss with them before the main event. We will meet in the library."

"Yes, my lady," he said, taking my now empty plate. "I will have them there in a moment."

I nodded and stood from my chair. Keeping my head down, I walked outside the ballroom and made my way to the side door leading back into the castle. Being away from the ball, it was cold, and I hurried my footsteps, using my power to keep the snow and cold air away from me as much as I could. By the time I made it to the library, the bottom of my dress was wet, and I frowned at the untidiness that would show when I returned to the ball.

"Gentle! What a fantastic party, as always. You know, I think this is one of my favourite celebrations of the year," Awe said, his voice booming through the quiet library. I smiled, and we hugged.

"Thank you, Awe. That is quite a compliment, considering all the balls you attend. How many had there been this year?"

He ran his hand through his beard and looked thoughtful. "Oh, I think it must be about six or seven by now."

"How do you stand it, brother?" said a deep but quiet voice from the doorway. Crescent practically floated in on quiet feet, followed by her closest advisor, Shayde. Crescent wasn't beautiful in the way I was, but she was striking with her black skin and large silver eyes. "Two a year is plenty enough socialising for me."

"It's good to see you, my partner in crime," said Awe, standing and embracing Crescent. With Awe's golden colouring and Crescent's dark skin, they were like opposites, which they were. Awe was the Sun Ever and Crescent the Moon Ever. They shared the skies and, because of that, had a bond.

When he finally released Crescent, I took her hands and kissed her on both cheeks. "It's so good to see you sister. It has been too long," I said, purely happy to see her. She tended to prefer to stay in her realm and didn't venture out very much. She grinned at me before squeezing my hands and turning serious. "How are you? After Bilvog?" she asked with concern in her silver eyes.

My smile faltered, and my mask slipped. Bilvog. "I am managing. It was a shock, and I think I am still recovering, to be honest," I said, turning away to break her intense gaze. I walked to the other side of the table we had gathered at and smoothed my dress and hair with unsteady hands. I heard the door open once more and took a deep breath before turning to the others gathered.

Amelia, Gloom, Amos, and Nathaniel were entering. I took a moment to steady myself while they greeted each other and took their seats. Amos stayed near the closed doors, and I could see Nathaniel out of the corner of my eyes at the other entrance to the library.

"Now, what can we do for you Gentle? My dance card is almost as full as yours, and I don't want to leave the ladies waiting," Awe said, wiggling his eyebrows at me while the rest of us groaned.

"Okay, well, I won't keep you long. I wanted to talk to you while you are all here about the hags and our artefacts." All the fun was sucked out of the room, and everyone focused and grew serious. "I think it is time we go and see them. We need to stop Bilvog and his cult from getting our artefacts. I managed to find in one of the books here that the hags dispersed the items all over the realms. It seems to be a common theory; if anyone wanted to release Dread, finding the artefacts would weaken the power that is holding him. We need to find them before he does. We saw in his mansion the cult already has Gloom's Staff of Thorns. They cannot be allowed to get any more of them."

In the silence that followed, I tried to steady my racing heart and hoped the others would agree with me. These last few weeks I had come to the realisation I was sick of being in the background. This affected us all and I wanted to help to keep that monster locked away as he should be. Seeing Dread in the basement of the mansion scared me to my core. The thought that he could get out and continue his rampage on the innocents in the world made my blood boil and my heart hurt.

I wasn't a fool, and I knew I wouldn't be able to do the fighting and more physical things, but I was prepared to do as much as possible to try and contribute in any way I could.

"I think it is time we visit our hags and try and find out where these items are."

"I think Gentle is right. It is time to be proactive. We need to put a stop to these maniacs," Crescent said.

I was glad Crescent agreed with me. I hesitated a moment while I built up the courage to voice my plan. "I am planning to go and see Belladonna. I intend to find out where my crown has gone, too."

Without wasting a moment, the protests began.

"Well, I don't know about that, Gentle. I can go and see old Bella for you. No need for you to traipse around the mountain if you don't need to. I'll head out in the morning," said Awe with great authority. I opened my mouth to protest, but before I could, Gloom spoke up. "I can come with you, Awe. It might help to be a little diplomatic," he said, rolling his eyes.

"I don't need you to go there with me. I think I can handle Bella on my own," Awe replied, laughing him off.

"Now boys, I think I am probably the only one who hasn't offended her, and she will probably be more open to me," Crescent said. I stood there and watched them dismiss me. Arguing back and forth, I was forgotten, and what I wanted was no longer important. This had been the story of my whole life. Shockingly, tears pricked my eyes, and I put my head down, hoping to keep them hidden from my siblings. I wanted to give it one more try, and I opened my mouth to speak again, hoping to find an opening to butt in, but the arguing had increased, and I closed it again.

My shoulders slumped, and I accepted defeat. I glanced around the room and saw Nathaniel staring at me, but when our eyes met this time, he looked away first. Did I see a flash of disappointment in them? What did he know? Nothing.

His wings twitched, and I turned away before he caught me looking at him again. I smoothed my skirts and waited for the discussion to run its course. I saw Amos walking across the room with purpose in his step. I straightened thinking he was coming to speak to me, and my brow furrowed when he stopped at the other end of the table and cleared his throat. All conversation stopped and everyone stared at him like he had gone crazy. It was definitely not a soldier's place to interrupt the Evers, even if he was well-trusted and liked. He didn't let anyone interrupt before he launched into what he wanted to say.

"You're wrong. You're all wrong, so listen up."

THREE

NATHANIEL

Standing against the wall, I schooled my features to show none of the shock travelling through my body at Amos's words. To speak like that to an Ever was unthinkable. One of the most important rules of being an Alanti was to be invisible. Not seen and not heard. To speak out to an Ever could mean instant dismissal. My back muscles tightened and my wings twitched as I waited to see what would happen.

"Gentle can do anything you can. She is intelligent, fierce, and brave. You may not see it, but she has a backbone of steel and can do much more than she realises. She can go and deal with Bella. She will get the information you want, and there will be no arguments about it."

I held my breath as his face grew red with the force of his words. He spoke with such conviction I think we were all stunned for a few moments. It had been a long time since I had heard Amos speak with such force, and judging by everyone else's faces, they were just as surprised. Awe's eyes were so round they were practically falling out of his head. I must admit it was good to see him on the back foot for once. He was usually so confident and cocky I knew I wouldn't forget his expression for a while.

Gloom and Crescent were deep in thought. Perhaps they were actually considering this. Gloom's partner was nodding her head with a fierce look in her eyes. Even though I didn't know much about her, I liked her. She was honest and real in a way that was different from the others that hung around the Evers. She had no agenda, and it was refreshing. I sometimes thought I was the only person who didn't have schemes and plans brewing in the background, like most people that positioned themselves in the Ever's presence.

The face I was most interested in was Gentle's. My eyes, drawn to her like always, took in her long, wavy hair that had fallen over one shoulder. In the mage light that lit the library it seemed to be a light of its own. Her eyes were wide, and they were shining, wet with tears. She blinked several times, not allowing one to spill, and straightened her shoulders and stood tall. She smiled at Amos, and he came to stand next to her at the head of the table.

"I think you all underestimate Gentle. She is an Ever, like the rest of you, and she deserves your respect and confidence," he looked every person in the eye, and I was impressed by how far he was willing to go for her. "I think you forget that in this mountain, she is here, wanting to help her people and yours. She is selfless and much more than pretty dresses and beauty. Much, much more." By the end of his speech, he was practically whispering, and no one could doubt the emotion and conviction of his words. One of the reasons I had worked so hard and pushed myself to become his second was because I knew him to be a fair and honourable man. He always fought for what was right, and I myself, aimed to be like that.

"Amos, what the hell are you talking about?" Awe asked, crossing his arms tight across his body. "Gentle is in no condition to go off battling these cult people! She was lucky the last time we were there to help her. Gentle is much more suited to sitting here and ruling and leaving the dirty work to us."

I saw Gentle flinch slightly at the insult, and so did Awe.

"I'm sorry, sister, but you know it's true," his voice gentler. "You can't be out there fighting and finding your crown, wherever it is. We don't know what we will be in for. Look, if you want to help, perhaps you can go and see Bella. One of us can go with you, but you can do the talking," he said, trying to sound reasonable. All I wanted to do was go over and shake the smug bastard. Gentle cleared her throat.

"First of all," she said, turning to Amos and laying a hand on his arm, "thank you. That was very kind." She turned to the rest of the gathered group and rubbed her hands down the front of her sparkling blue dress. "Amos is right. I sit up here and watch you all run around and do great things. I want to help. I am much more than what I look like, and I want to do what I can. I *will* be going to see Bella tomorrow and I *will* find out where my crown is. Then, once we know, we can all decide if it is something I can get, or if not, I am happy for one of you to retrieve it. I don't need you to come with me, but I will take Amos, so I am protected, and you won't have to worry. I want to do this." She nodded her head as they all stared at her. Inside, I was impressed. I knew after working around her for a long time, she didn't like conflict. This was a new side I hadn't seen in a while, especially since Bilvog betrayed her.

Awe opened his mouth to speak again when Crescent cut him off in her quiet way. I shivered at her voice as goosebumps broke out on my skin. She was more other-worldly than the others. It always seemed like she could see right through me.

"Okay, Gentle. If you want to do this, we are not going to stop you. We trust you and respect that you want to help our cause. We look forward to hearing what tale you will have to tell after your visit." She gave a soft smile and turned to her advisor. They stood. "Now I think it is nearing the time for the lights. Come. That is the *only* reason I came tonight, and I won't miss them now," she said with a wink and a small laugh.

Awe shrugged his shoulders and took Crescent's arm and walked out with her and Shayde.

Gloom looked at Amos and Gentle with a small frown on his face. "If you want to do this, Gentle, I am not going to stop you. I am a firm believer in doing whatever it takes to help your people. But I want you to be safe," he paused for a moment before continuing. "There are things out there doing their best to undermine and kill us if possible. This isn't a party game. It is real. I have full faith in you, and I know you can look after yourself. Not long ago you helped to save me and my people, so I know you are capable. I worry you won't be prepared for the things you may have to do and the things you will likely see in the coming months. Keep Amos close. He will help you." Gloom leaned in and hugged Gentle and then turned and shook Amos's hand kindly.

I turned away quickly as Gloom turned towards the door, hoping he didn't see me watching their exchange. I frowned, disappointed in myself for being so sloppy and allowing myself to get pulled into their drama. I straightened my posture and stared straight ahead at the wall, calmed my mind, and refocused myself. The Evers' lives had nothing to do with me. I was only there to keep them safe. I needed to remember to stay out of it and mind my own business.

FOUR

GENTLE

The door closed, and I slumped into my chair, a slow smile spreading across my face. I had stood up to my siblings and spoke my mind. My brain tried to remind me it had taken Amos's speech to convince them, but I didn't care. I had done something I hadn't done in a long time, and I was going to take the win where I could.

To many, this would seem like such a small thing, but to me, it was huge. It had been a long time since I had spoken so strongly to them, and I felt amazing, even if my body was shaking a little. I looked up at Amos, who appeared very uncomfortable. He had stood up for me. I had no idea he thought like that about me, and my heart grew for the gruff old soldier.

"Thank you for what you said. I must admit I am glad you will be going with me. Perhaps I have bitten off more than I can chew," I said, coming down from the clouds and second-guessing myself in the quiet.

"Now that's enough of that," he said kindly. "I don't mean to overstep more than I have already today, but may I make an observation?"

I nodded curiously.

"It seems to me you have lost a little bit of your spark since everything happened. Bilvog's betrayal had nothing to do with you." My face closed down and my heart dropped like it always did when talk turned to Bilvog and what he was trying to do. "He was always an evil man, but you are not a fool to have loved and admired him. The fault lies with him."

Tears pricked my eyes. I felt like such an idiot for believing Bilvog and trusting him. Amos was right. It impacted me in a way I didn't expect. All my confidence had leaked out of me, and I had retreated and allowed others to decide things because I no longer trusted my own intuition. Sitting there in the silence, it was like a light was shining onto my head, and a weight was lifted from my shoulders.

Something about what Amos had said stirred a feeling in me I thought was gone. He was right. It wasn't my fault. Bilvog was a master manipulator and we had all fallen for it. Not only me. It was time to remember who I was before his betrayal and find some of my strength. Before I could think, I leapt up and hugged Amos as tight as I could. I heard him grunt as he patted my back.

Over his shoulder, Nathaniel was standing and watching us. He gave me a faint nod before turning away, and I wondered what it was for before I finally let go of Amos and smiled at him. He smiled back uncomfortably, and I linked arms with him as we walked out of the library and back out to the party, with Nathaniel following behind.

We arrived at the ball, and it was in full swing. People had been enjoying the food and wine, and it appeared everyone was in good spirits. Awe was already on the dancefloor with another woman in his arms, Pegasi flew overhead, and the music was lively. Amos and I separated as Lumos came up and asked me to dance. He was from a neighbouring city and had asked for my hand in marriage recently. My advisors felt quite strongly about the match, but I had put him off, not wanting to become his bride. It seemed I could no longer ignore him.

"Gentle. I have been looking for you. Where have you been?" he asked with a nice enough tone, but his silver eyes were narrowed revealing his real thoughts. His deep blue hair was pulled back in a ponytail, and the light blue of his skin was set off by the silver and white outfit he was wearing. He was an air elemental and although they didn't have much power anymore, they were still the upper class of Aeris Isle. His hand was heavy on my hips and I could feel him directing me around the dancefloor.

"Oh, just discussing the world-changing events happening to our way of life with the other Evers. We must do all we can to keep you safe," I said with a sweet smile, but I wanted to remind him who he was speaking to. I knew it had worked when I saw his eyes harden.

"Well. That is very important, but surely you will leave it up to them? You are much more suited to ruling on a throne and not running around chasing the bad guys."

I bristled at the insult but was careful not to let it show on my face too much. In my anger, I spoke before thinking, "Now let's not forget Evers are practically Gods, and even the most...pampered ones among us are much more suited to battle than the rest of you. I will be going on a mission tomorrow to meet with Belladonna the Hag." His hand gripped tighter as we spun through the dancers. I held back my wince, not wanting him to know that it was starting to hurt.

"Well, that's interesting," he said as his eyes lit up at that bit of information. "If you were my wife, there would be no need for you to traipse around meeting fey creatures. You would be safe in my castle, and your biggest worry would be planning the next party. You have done a fantastic job tonight," he said, looking around at the space. I would have agreed with him if I wasn't so angry.

"Yes, well, thank you for the dance," I said, planting my feet firmly and bringing us to a stop. "It seems the lights are about to appear," I said, pulling away from him and nodding.

As I turned to walk away, he said, "Think about my proposal, Gentle. I won't wait forever, and I know your advisors have agreed. Perhaps it would be best if you did what they recommend, hmm?"

I continued walking, but a shiver ran down my spine, knowing he was still watching me. I made a mental note to keep an eye on him and what he was up to. Something about him was off, and I didn't like it.

I walked to the front of the gathered group and stood next to the other Evers. It was a beautiful evening and the perfect night for this celebration. There wasn't a cloud in the sky, and the stars winked brightly overhead. I breathed in the fresh air and let it refresh my soul. The temperature was starting to drop now, and small goosebumps were rising on my arms. I took a moment to flick out the fabric on my arm so they trailed along on the ground neatly.

As the music finished, I turned to the crowd and spread my arms wide to include everyone gathered. "Thank you all for coming. It is always an honour to throw this ball so we may all witness the lights in the sky that will bring us good luck. To see them all together is truly special." I lowered my arms and waited for the applause to quiet before I continued. Smiling my prettiest smile, I said, "May this year be full of good luck, abundance, wealth, and friendships. I know there have been dark times, and there will likely be more." The crowd grew sombre for a moment. "But we must remember to look after each other. If we do that, nothing can defeat us."

A cheer erupted, and I sent a silent prayer I was right, and we would be okay. I smiled again as a hush fell over the crowd, and we all stared up in anticipation.

They appeared slowly. So subtle, your eyes didn't register at first. The sky turned from inky blackness to a deep blue, and it appeared to be moving like waves on the ocean. The stars appeared and disappeared as the movement brushed over them. As the seconds ticked past, the blue became brighter and brighter until you could see it like a ribbon blowing across the sky.

Other colours began to emerge. Greens like a meadow, deep jewel purple and bright pink. Orange slashes ran between them, and they rolled and slicked over the sky like they were listening to their own music and couldn't help but move. We watched and soaked in the sight for a few more minutes until, slowly, it started to fade. The colours muted and melted back into the night sky until all was still again. The stars reappeared, and calm was restored.

For a moment, no one spoke. Each person wrapped up in what they wanted this year to be and what they saw in the lights. Every person saw something different, and many people used it as a way to determine the future. Tonight, in houses, people would be writing their foretelling for the coming year. For myself, I didn't put a lot of stock in what I saw. I enjoyed watching and getting lost in the lights. It was a way for me to say goodbye to the old and hello to the new. I let out the breath I was holding, and hope filled me. We could do this. We could defeat the cult and stop Dread. We just had to work together. Anything was possible.

I turned to address the crowd when the ground beneath my feet started to move. My brow creased as my brain fought to keep up with what was happening. Everyone gathered began to also move, and I could see on the tables cups tipping over. A loud rumbling sound came out of the earth, and I looked out over to the mountainside we were sheltered under. Shock pulsed through me as I saw a crack appear and splinter through the rock with a sharp snap. People were beginning to run and scatter about, shouting and screaming. The movement increased, and when I went to run, I got caught on the hem of my dress and stumbled.

I could hear someone shouting, "Bomb!" My brain eventually processed what was happening. One of Bilvog's bombs had gone undiscovered and was now pulling my mountain down around me. With worry filling me, I watched the other Evers and could see them making their way to the exit.

Gloom's eyes met mine, and he yelled, "Gentle, get out of there!" He gave Amelia to Crescent and pushed them forward while he ran back toward me.

The crush of people was so strong, running against it meant he could hardly move. I snapped out of my stupor and moved toward the castle. By this time, I was stepping over plates, trays, and lights that had fallen from the roof and table. The ground was littered with things and was still shaking. I helped as many people as I could, knowing I could take more damage than them.

Heavy arms draped over my shoulders and protected my head. I stared into the eyes of Amos, and they were filled with worry. "Let's get you out of here, my lady."

I nodded at him and peered behind to see Gloom wave at me and turn around. He had seen Amos and decided to leave. The push of people was intense, and I could taste the fear in the air coating the back of my throat. The ground was moving and rolling underneath me. How had we missed a bomb? Rocks snapped and crashed around us. I looked at the destruction surrounding me.

Finally, I could see the edge of the ballroom. People were running in all directions, tripping over debris and other people. I stumbled again and watched the ground disappear in front of me. Someone in front of me fell and couldn't get up. I gritted my teeth knowing how dangerous it was right here but not being able to leave them behind. I bent over and helped the lady stand, pulling her ripped dress out from under a rock that had dislodged.

Behind me I heard an almighty crack. One of the twelve pillars had cracked and shattered. I saw the lady I had helped escape and I was grateful I was able to help at least one person. I tried to run, but the ground was too uneven, and I stumbled again. I watched as the pillar hurtled down, and I knew it was going to hurt. I could hear someone yelling out for me, and I turned, my eyes widening as Amos pushed me out of the way. I went sprawling on the ground, banging my knees and ripping my dress, but I didn't notice any of that.

All I saw was Amos disappearing under rubble and debris as the pillar came crashing down and the earth bowed underneath us. I saw the fear in his normally strong eyes as he stared at me until he was gone. All the air whooshed out of me, and before I had the chance to go and help him, a shattered bit of pillar fell, and all I knew was darkness.

FIVE

NATHANIEL

Chaos reigned in the ballroom.

I helped people get to safety while I tried to see what had happened. The bomb had been planted right underneath the ballroom. There was a hole in the ground where people had been dancing moments ago, and although it wasn't a full cave-in, it was devastating.

Dust swirled around me, making it difficult to see, and people were shouting directions so others could find their way through. The dust coated my mouth and made my eyes gritty, but I kept searching. People were leaving with gashes and ripped clothes everywhere. I called out to some of the soldiers, and they were organising the injured into groups of severity. The bomb had been concentrated on the ballroom, so we started taking people into the castle for safety.

My eyes searched the crowd constantly for Gentle and Amos, but they were nowhere to be seen. The other Evers were healing people as much as they could, but I knew their power was not infinite. They were trying to conserve some of their power for the worst injured.

We eventually got the main section of the dancefloor cleared, and the dust began to settle. I managed to get the attention of some of the other Alanti helping.

"Fly up and see what you can see. Captain Amos and lady Gentle are still unaccounted for. I'll stay on the ground."

Hersal hesitated a moment and I knew he was debating whether to follow my orders or not. His normally black hair and wings were now a grey colour from the dust, and he fluffed them creating more clouds of dust as he tried to clean them. I glared at him, waiting to see what he would do as the others watched our exchange with interest. I was giving him a direct order, and though he didn't like it, I was his superior, and he knew he had to obey. He sneered at me until the others took flight. I stared at him, unrelenting and he launched into the air.

Relief passed through my body. I knew Hersal resented me, but to disobey a direct order when the life of his captain and Lady could be on the line was bad even for him. I rubbed my eyes and looked over the mess in front of me. The last I remembered, the two of them were exiting the western side of the ballroom, so I would start there. I stepped out carefully, blocking the sound of people crying and yelling, and tried to focus on the sound of the ground beneath me.

My legs were tensed as I readied my wings to lift me at a moment's notice should the ground begin to move. Sharp points and edges of the broken stone pressed through the soles of my shoes, and I held my arms out to keep my balance.

Small rocks started to shift, but above the sound I heard something.

I froze, focusing wholly on that sound. I watched the ground for any small movement and, after a moment, saw a hand reach out in desperation. I picked my way over to it and pulled the rocks out of the way, my heart hammering. In the rubble, I saw a grey face peek out and heard them draw a deep, raspy breath of the clean air. It wasn't Amos or Gentle.

"Balthail," I called.

He landed next to me gently and helped me to free the nobleman.

"Here, take him to the castle," I said, and he nodded and beat his red wings, flying to the castle.

I brushed the man's blood off my hands and continued searching.

After about fifteen minutes, we had rescued five people. Some walked out unscathed, and others had to be lifted out, unable to move. I worried more than one of them might not survive. My heart was thudding, and my breath was short as fear and desperation crept up on me. What if I couldn't find them? What if the earth had swallowed them up? I cursed Bilvog and his cult for all the pain they had caused here. I cursed the search team that they didn't find this bomb. It was obvious to me the bomb had been planted for the exact purpose of blowing up on the Night of Lights. A time when it would cause the biggest impact.

I did my best to push it all to the back of my mind and relied on the warrior training that had got me through many hard times before. I shoved the fear aside and took stock of the area around me. Tables, clothing, and pillars lay stacked up and scattered around. Something caught my eye, and I rushed over to where a midnight blue dress and yellow hair poked out of the rubble like a shining beacon. My heart was beating in my throat as I carefully picked my way over to it.

Calmness ran over me, and I methodically began to move the boulders off her. There was blood matted in her hair along with the rock dust. Before I picked her up, I ran my hands along her body to make sure there were no broken bones. When I didn't find any and I slowly rolled her over to check her face. I noted one of her arms was outstretched, and the back of my neck prickled. I called Hersal, and when he landed, he was all business.

"I've found Gentle. The last time I saw them, Amos was with her so he should be here. Search for him while I get her to safety. Her arm was pointing in that direction," I said to him, then turned my attention back to Gentle.

Hersal may have his faults, but he was a good Alanti, and I trusted him to follow through if it meant helping Gentle or Amos. I could see immediately she was breathing, but she had multiple cuts on her face and body. Luckily, nothing as bad as the cut on her head. After looking her over again, I lifted her into my arms. She was feather-light, and I didn't like the way she flopped around. I had seen her defiant and confident a few hours ago, and now she was unconscious.

My brain struggled to match the two images to one person. I held her close and tried to keep her still as I spread my wings wide, catching the wind that was always howling here in the mountains. I tilted them and let the wind lift me as smoothly as possible. My back muscles bunched and stretched as my wings pulled tight. I flapped them and soared above the devastation below. I decided to take her straight to the castle and flew over the grounds to get there.

From above looking down, it seemed like so much chaos for such a small area. The only damage I could see was the ballroom, and the neighbouring mountain had a large crack in it. I made a note to get the Geo Crew onto it and make sure it was safe.

I flew over and saw many people laid out in lines. Some were crying and holding their injuries, and a few were not moving at all. Of the hundred guests, it seemed like a handful hadn't made it. I glided on the cold mountain air and pulled Gentle closer to try and keep her warm. At the door to the castle, I could see Awe directing people inside and telling them where they should go. I descended while Gentle's hair floated around us in ribbons.

We landed, and Awe's eyes grew wide. He strode over and took her from me. Annoyance flared in me that he had taken her off me so abruptly. My body was cold and empty without her in my arms. I pushed away the ridiculousness of the thought.

"I found her in the rubble over there," I said, pointing. "I don't think she has any broken bones, but there's a gash on the back of her head that's likely the cause of her being unconscious. I'm going back to find Captain Amos."

Awe nodded at me, turned away, and entered the castle. I took to the skies again and let them draw me back to the place I had left Hersal. It had only been a few moments, but I could see he had already cleared a large area and was not slowing. I landed next to him, careful not to disturb the ground too much.

"Is she going to be alright?" he asked me, panting slightly.

"Yes. She has a nasty gash on her head, but from what I could see will be okay," I replied. Then we dug. This section of the floor had partially collapsed, and I was worried we would never get to the bottom. One by one we picked up stone and broken pillars, praying the next one we lifted would reveal him.

After what felt like forever, my heart stopped. "Here," I said, urgency filling my body. Amos's arm was lying covered in blood, making his blue shirt look purple in the night. I cleared the rubble hurriedly, hoping my mentor had survived.

I picked up a stone and underneath was his face. One look, and it was clear he had not made it. My body slumped as what I was seeing sunk in. Amos was gone. Hersal was still clearing away the rubble when he saw me stop. He glanced over and seeing Amos's face seemed to give him a burst of energy. He was a madman. Throwing rocks around and ripping them away with no care to himself. I let him go, knowing he refused to believe what he was seeing, feeling numb inside. When he was finally clear, Hersal shook him.

"Wake up, sir. Wake up." He was breathing fast, his eyes wide. I took him by the shoulders and shook him.

"He is gone, Hersal. He's dead." My voice cracked, and it broke through to him. He set Amos down and muttered a prayer before he lifted into the air and disappeared, his black wings blending into the night sky.

I closed my eyes and said the warrior's prayer for my fallen captain and put my arms under his broken body. Where Gentle's body was light, his was heavy. My arms shook, but I ignored it. I lifted into the air with difficulty and wondered where I should take him. I didn't want to take him to the rest of the fallen. He was special. In the end, I took him to the castle. I flew high in the air, letting the coldness numb me further.

While flying, I let the tears trail down my cheeks where no one could see them. I remembered what a good soldier and mentor he had been. He had seen something in me no one else had, where others would have thrown me away. He took me in and gave me a life I could never have dreamed of. He had saved me, and I could not do the same for him. Bitterness and grief settled in my chest like a rock as I flew him to the ground.

<u>SIX</u>

GENTLE

A drum pounded in my head and my body was heavy like it had been weighed down with lead. The ground was hard under my back, and when I opened my eyes, I was on a table in the middle of one of my castle's sitting rooms. People were hustling around and talking, and yelling filled the air.

I groaned as I raised a hand to my forehead and tried to remember what happened. My eyes caught on my hand that had cuts and scratches all over them, and I was covered in a grey powder that clung to everything. Slowly, things were coming back to me. We watched the lights, and the ground fell away around us. I remembered trying to run away and help people. Then, the pillar landed on me.

Amos. Where was Amos?

I sat up and tried to swallow, but my mouth was coated in dust. The back of my head was sore and tender, even though it had been healed. I took a moment to stand up and right my balance. People were laid out on stretchers and mattresses, and all of them were injured in some way. I searched their faces, looking for Amos.

My eyes were darting between the injured, and I pulled my hair over my shoulder and tried to comb it through my fingers, but my hair was knotty and matted with blood.

My movements were jerky, but I couldn't stop. There was an overriding drive to find Amos. When I couldn't see him in the room, I staggered out the door and stopped in my tracks. At least fifty people were laid out injured and hurting.

Everywhere I looked, there were people with blood on their clothes, covered in the stone dust that had formed a blanket over everything. So many people were confused and in pain. It pressed on my senses. I could see Gloom, Awe, and Crescent moving between the beds, healing as much as they could, but there was no way they had enough power for everyone. I walked over to Awe.

When he saw me, his shoulders sagged in relief, and he pulled me in for a big hug. Tears pricked my eyes as I soaked in his love. Eventually, we pulled away, and he held me out at arm's length and looked me over.

"How do you feel?" he asked, searching my face intensely.

I scanned my body and really tried to acknowledge how I felt. "Okay. A bit tender on the back of my head and a bit dizzy, but good considering," I said, gesturing around us. "What happened?"

His face pinched, and his eyes hardened. "A bomb. There was a bomb underneath the dancefloor. We are lucky not more people died. Here, have some water," he said, stopping someone with a tray of glasses of water.

I took it gratefully and let the cool water wash the dust out of my mouth and soothe my sore, dry throat. I held back a moan. It was so good. I drank the cup, and by the time I was finished, Gloom, Amelia, and Crescent were there. Putting the cup down, I hugged each of them, holding on a little longer than usual.

"Are any of you hurt?" I asked, looking at Amelia. Knowing she was human, she was my main concern.

She shook her blonde head. "No, Crescent got me out quick, so other than a few cuts, I am okay."

I smiled in relief and looked at the others.

"We are okay as well. How are you? You took quite a fall," said Gloom as he put an arm around Amelia.

"I feel a lot better." I scanned the people laid out and asked, "Where's Amos? Is he alright?"

My siblings shared a look, and my stomach dropped. They hesitated before Crescent touched my arm. "I'm sorry, Gentle. But he didn't make it."

My eyes widened, and I paled. "What do you mean he didn't make it? He was right there with me."

"I know, but—" She looked around at the others like she didn't know what to say. I waited impatiently for her to continue. "The last time I saw him, he was protecting you, but a pillar came down at the same time the ground collapsed, and he was crushed by it and trapped. I'm sorry Gentle, I know you were close."

I stared at them blankly while my mind stopped. My body started to shake uncontrollably, but I didn't care.

"I want to see him," I said eventually. "I need to see him," I said again when no one moved. My voice cracked, but it was at least a little stronger.

"I don't know if that's such a good idea. He's pretty banged up," Awe said with uncertainty written on his face. I turned to him.

"You were the one who said I couldn't handle battle when I said I could. I need to see him. I don't care what he looks like." Standing firm, I knew this was what I needed to do.

"If you are sure, then. Come with me," said Gloom, and they led me to a door on the other side that led to the library.

Each step felt like walking through honey. A huge part of my mind was screaming at me. I didn't need to see him like this. I would never be able to get this image out of my head once I had seen it.

Did I want it to be the way I remembered him?

Yes, I needed to see him. He had died trying to save me. The least I could do was show him some respect by thanking him.

My shoes clicked on the stone of the floor, matching my heartbeat. I tried to empty my mind and prepare for what I was about to see.

What else could possibly happen? First Bilvog and now Amos. I ran my hands down the front of my dress and took a deep, steadying breath. We stopped at the door to the library, and the others peered at me with sympathy. I made my face hard as stone. I was strong, and I could do this for Amos. He was always the one who believed in me and saw me as more than I ever did. Now was the time to prove him right. I let out the breath I had been holding and turned the handle, leaving my siblings at the door.

The large room dwarfed him. It was cold in there, like the heat from the fires couldn't banish the sadness that seemed to fill every inch of the room. Someone had lit incense, and there was a haze around his body, hanging like a cloud. Tears were welling up in me, but I kept them at bay. I wanted him to be proud of me, and I wanted him to see I could be everything he always said I was. I took slow steps toward his body, which was laid out on a table and had been covered with a white sheet. I could see small red patches marring its brightness.

It was jarring to see it was the same table we had been sitting at only hours ago, and I had the sudden urge to move him to another. Here, he had stood up for me and risked his position to tell the Evers what he thought. It didn't sit right with me that that memory should be darkened by his now-dead body. I smoothed my hair and rubbed my face with my hands, hoping to make myself appear more presentable.

Looking at my dress, I frowned, only to realise how dirty and ripped it was. I stared at the floor a moment longer, getting a grip on my emotions and trying to prepare myself for what I was about to see.

I looked around the room, delaying the moment I would have to go to Amos's body when I was surprised to see I wasn't alone. I had been so focused on myself and my own emotions that I hadn't noticed Nathanial standing against the wall looking at Amos.

He, like everyone else, was covered in dust and had cuts covering him. His hands were the worst. They were cracked and bloody, with large slashes all over them. On his face were two large streaks running from his eyes. He had been crying and hadn't bothered to hide it. My respect for him grew. He saw me and bowed his head. I felt a kinship with him. We were probably Amos's closest friends in the castle, and it felt right that we would be in here with him.

I cleared my throat. "Your hands are injured. You should get them seen to."

He stared at them like it was the first time he had seen them. He turned them over from front to back a few times before he glanced back at me. "They are okay, my lady. They will heal," he replied.

Something about him made my heart ache. It was like looking at a small boy who had lost his father. There was a lost look in his eyes; I had a feeling it was echoed in mine. Amos had been a constant in the kingdom for over two hundred and fifty years and had left his mark on every person here.

I walked over to him, and he straightened at his post. I wondered if he ever relaxed or if he was constantly a soldier.

"Here, let me help," I said, holding my hands out to him.

He didn't move. "It's fine. They don't hurt. Please don't concern yourself."

"I am already concerned. Please, let me do it." His white and blue wings twitched and seemed to ruffle. After a second of hesitation, he held out his hands for me. I cupped my hands around his, touching them gently, and let my power flow through them. Warmth trickled out of my hands and into his, and before our eyes, the worst of the cuts stitched and knit back together. I heard him suck in a breath, and a small smile ghosted my lips. Before long, the worst of his cuts were healed, and I stopped, mindful of not draining myself.

"That's much better," I said as I removed my hands from around his.

He looked at them again and then folded them in front of him. "Thank you for healing me, I am indebted to you."

I snorted. I couldn't help it. To his surprise, he stared at me like I had grown a second head.

"Indebted? I don't think so. You have done many things for me over the years to earn some healing."

I turned and focused on Amos, and my humour vanished. My heart thundered in my chest, and I was suddenly frightened to see him. I felt like a fool. I had made such a big deal about coming in and seeing him, and now I was backing out. I willed my feet to move, but they were frozen to the floor. My hand came up and clutched at my throat, which was now blocked by unshed tears. They burned up my throat, trying to escape, but I refused to let them fall. I let out a small whimper.

Get yourself together, Namara. You are an Ever. Conduct yourself with a bit of dignity, I thought.

I pushed my shoulders back and held my head up. A second before I took a step, there was a presence next to me. I glanced, and it was Nathaniel. He had come to stand beside me, and I felt instantly better. I was a fool to come in here by myself. I should have known I would need support, but I didn't want to show weakness in front of anyone. I was glad someone else was here with me now.

I walked toward the table, taking sure and steady steps with Nathaniel beside me. I stood next to Amos's body, and Nathaniel stood opposite me on the other side of the table. My heart was beating so loudly I was sure he could hear it.

He was patient and didn't rush me as I stared at the red blotches all over the whole sheet.

"I'll need to throw this sheet out now. I could never lay on it again."

I frowned, disappointed I could think such a thing in a moment like this and nodded at Nathaniel. He took the top of the sheet in his dusty hands and started to pull it away slowly. I kept my eyes on them, trying to delay the moment I would have to look at my guard and friend.

Eventually, I couldn't put it off any longer. I clenched my teeth and looked into the face of the man who had saved me.

The tears that clogged my throat released in a rush, and a sob burst out of me. I slapped my hand across my mouth, embarrassed I had lost my composure, but I couldn't help it. He was almost unrecognisable.

The feathers in his brown and gold wings were bent and crooked and I could see chunks of them missing. His face was covered in blood, his nose was broken, and he was missing teeth. Thankfully, he was still dressed, so I didn't have to look at the rest of his body, but I could see his hands were dark with blood and bruising. I brought a shaky hand to his wings and brushed a few feathers down.

Over the table, Nathaniel's feathers rustled, and I wondered if I had done something wrong. I didn't care. Amos had taken great care in his appearance, and I hated the sight of his wings crumpled. I said a silent thank you and motioned to Nathaniel to raise the sheet again. I stepped back and peered out one of the large windows of the library. The sun was up, and the Night of Lights was over.

Some little part of me broke off inside as I thought of what Bilvog had done. As if the betrayal wasn't enough, he had to kill my people and try to kill me at the same time. He had been here for many Night of Light celebrations, and there was not a doubt in my mind he had timed this to have the greatest impact.

Looking out at the sky lightening as I stood next to the body of my friend and guard, I resolved he would not beat me. I would carry on, and Bilvog would pay for what he had done. He would feel the wrath of the air and sky like never before.

SEVEN
GENTLE

After going to my rooms, escorted by Nathaniel, I cleaned up and headed out to the sitting room to help the people there. A lot of the people who could have already left, and there were only the seriously injured people lying in beds that had been brought in.

My own healers were handling it all well and told me most people should be ready to leave in the next week. I thanked each one personally and made my way over to my family that were sitting off to the side. They had all taken the time to get changed and cleaned up as well, but they were exhausted. They were slumped in their seats with dark circles around their eyes. Gloom in his usual black pants and jacket and Amelia was in some tight jeans and a deep purple shirt with some ballet flats. Awe was much more eye-catching in a navy suit with large golden lion heads covering it.

On anyone else, it would have been ridiculous, but on Awe...it just worked. Crescent had changed into a silver floor-length dress that she somehow made look casual. In a simple black dress, Shayde's pale skin practically glowed. Her large golden eyes took everything in.

"You look much more like your old self, Gentle," Crescent said kindly. I glanced at the seafoam green dress I had put on without looking at it. The comment annoyed me, but I put a smile on my face as I walked to stand neat them.

"Thank you." I paused and took a breath. "So, I think it is best that I leave shortly. I don't really want to travel in the dark too much if I don't have to. You are all welcome to stay the night if you like."

Confusion filled their faces an they looked at each other.

"I'm going to see Belladonna like we discussed," I reminded them.

"Gentle, you can't be serious? After what has happened, I think you should have a sleep and send someone else. You were knocked out. It's probably not safe for you to travel anyway," Gloom said, leaning forward.

"A lot of other people who were injured have left. I'll be fine, it's not far. I'll take Anena. She knows the way and will make sure I am safe." I held my breath remembering the last time I had tried to speak out I had Amos by my side.

"Anena may be good, but she is a Pegasus. How is she going to save you if you get into trouble?" Gloom asked

"We agreed. It's happening," I reminded them, steeling my voice.

"Excuse me?" I heard behind me, and I turned to see Nathaniel standing there. I didn't even know he had followed me in.

"I will take Amos's place and go with Lady Gentle to protect her," he said quietly.

"See, nothing to worry about," I said to the group, trying to cover my surprise that Nathaniel had volunteered.

Awe stood and puffed out his chest, "now wait a minute. We hardly know you. I know you are one of the Alanti, but we don't just let anyone guard Gentle."

Nathaniel straightened, too, and looked Awe dead in the eye. My anger flared.

"No. *You* wait a minute. *You* don't let me do anything. Have you forgotten I am an Ever, too? Nathaniel is...was Amos's second and is more than capable of helping me when I need it. It is not your decision who I employ." A cold wind picked up and swirled around us, making Awe's hideous suit jacket flap around him and mess up his hair.

He held up his hands to me and took a step back. "Okay. If you think you can do this then fine. But I won't be there for you if you get your pretty little head into trouble, so you better make damn sure pretty boy here can look after it." Flames began to lift off his skin.

I rolled my eyes and let my wind die down. "I'm sure he can handle it. Now I hope to see you all when we get back." Before any of them could open their interfering mouths, I turned and stalked off, but not before I saw Shayde smile.

When we were out of the door, I slumped a little and turned to Nathaniel. "Are you sure you want to come with me? I will be fine. Old Bella isn't as dangerous as some of the hags," I said with more confidence than I felt.

"Yes, I am sure. Are you ready to go?"

I thought for a moment and realised I was. "Yes. I will call for Anena, and then we can go."

"I'll get her for you, Lady. You wait here."

Before I could protest, he had leapt into the sky, flapped his enormous blue wings and was gone. Every time one of them did it, it took my breath away. Being surrounded by the Alanti, I was always jealous of the freedom they had. I would love to be able to fly at the drop of a hat.

I shrugged on a large white coat and ran through my head the questions I had to ask Bella and what she would ask of me because there was always a catch. I couldn't remember the last time I had gone to her. I didn't have a lot of need for potions these days, but I knew the people from the village and all over Aeris Isle often went to see her for her tonics and tinctures.

Lost in my thoughts, I didn't notice Nathanial was back with Anena. They landed next to me, and she was all saddled and ready to go. I stepped up to her, the first true smile spreading across my face. I rubbed her nose and leaned in close.

"Anena. I have missed you, girl. We are going to Bella's tonight." She nickered at me. "I know you don't like to go and see her, but this is important. I'll try and keep the wind favourable for you." She rubbed her head on my chest, and I gave her a kiss behind her ear. I patted her dusty pink coat and ran a finger through her darker pink mane. I had had Anena since she was a new foal, and we had a bond that would be hard to break.

I stepped up to her saddle, swung myself up, and sat between her enormous wings as I adjusted my skirts, used to doing it now.

I nodded at Nathaniel, and he nodded back. I looked back to where the devastation from last night had left a scar on the landscape. People were cleaning up and I had to remind myself this was why I was going. We had to stop Bilvog, and going to Bella was one of the steps I needed to take to make that happen. I tapped on Anena's wing with my heel, and she raised her large pink wings and brought them down with a woosh. She started to gallop, and before long, we were soaring through the cold mountain air, and I was free.

The air was biting, but I welcomed it. I was accustomed to living on the cold mountain and I found it refreshing as the air raced into my lungs. We had been flying for a few hours, and I was beginning to feel uncomfortable, but we were almost there. In the distance, I could see the light from her cottage, and I signalled to Nathaniel, who was flying next to me.

I worried he might be tiring, but he seemed to still be going strong. I had tried to adjust the wind to make it a bit easier on Anena and Nathaniel, but it was still a long flight. I wriggled on the saddle and tried to get comfortable for the rest of the trip. On the way, I had been thinking about what we had yet to do. So many artefacts to find and so little time.

We all knew Bilvog was working hard to bring Dread back, and to be honest, we still didn't know exactly what needed to be done. The hags had told us they needed the artefacts, but apart from that, we had no idea how to stop him. The shock I felt when we saw him in the basement at the battle of the Horned One still crept into my body sometimes. Seeing Dread in shadow form brought back terrible memories. He had once been my brother and had played and cared for me. How he went so wrong was a question I had been asking myself, and I still had no answer.

I shook myself to clear away the maddening thoughts and focused on the meeting with Bella as her house came into view. Her house was well-lit, and I had long ago stopped trying to work out how it had ended up there and just accepted it was magic.

The wide wooden house was perfectly nestled between two cliff sides. Long ago, the mountain split into two, leaving a gap between it, and many people thought Bella did this herself so she could build her house between them. It was supported by one plank of wood that ran from one mountainside to the other. That was it. To get to her house, you either had to fly in or take the precarious staircase that ran up the side of the mountain. The path was steep and slippery, usually covered in snow and ice.

It was thousands of steps, and if you made it to the top, then you had to walk out on the plank to get to the front door of the cottage while swaying, due to the constant wind that howled through the split mountain. It was scary, and only the most desperate came out to seek Bella. Luckily for us, we could land on the side of the mountain and bypass all the stairs. Unfortunately, there wasn't enough room for Anena at her doorstep. I brought Anena in to land and then climbed off gracefully.

I smoothed my skirts and righted my hair before patting her pink mane. "Good girl. I will see you soon."

I tried to tame my hair, wishing I had braided it as I stared at Bella's house, creaking in the wind. I looked at the beam, and my stomach leapt into my throat. I hated walking out on that thing.

Nathaniel landed beside me and was waiting patiently for me to take the first step towards her cottage. I glanced at him, and he gazed steadily back.

"After you," he said, holding out his hand, gesturing at the plank.

I shook out my hands and took a step toward the plank. I used my power to still the wind to make it easier. Everything grew quiet, and I realised how much sound the wind was making, howling through this fissure in the mountain. With the wind calmer I too calmed and stepped out onto the plank. Keeping my steps quick and sure, I made it across the wood, never looking into the black, never-ending chasm below.

Standing at the front door, I smoothed my hair and lifted my hand to knock. Nathaniel landed beside me, and I had never been more jealous of his wings in my life. He was looking at me with a small smile, tugging at his lips. It took everything in me not to make a sarcastic comment, and luckily, at that moment, the door swung open.

If I didn't know Bella, what I would have seen on the other side of the door would probably have made me stumble back and fall to my death. Thankfully, I knew what to expect. The woman who answered the door was old and wizened. She was bent over at the belly, bending her body in half. Her long, grey, stringy hair was plaited messily down her back, and her stained and burned leather apron hung from her belly straight to the ground. Her hands were scarred and burned in so many places it was nearly impossible to see any of her normal skin. The skin was red and shiny in places, while in others, it was burnt black and appeared flaky. The injuries travelled up her arms and vanished beneath the sleeve of her shirt.

Perhaps the most terrifying thing was the mask. She wore an old leather plague mask. Its black, bottomless eyes gazed out like it was looking right through you. The long-hooked nose, sharp and terrifying.

She lifted a gnarled hand and used the nose of the mask to push it to the top of her head.

"Ah, Namara. I knew it was you. Only you can silence the creaks in this old house. Come in, come in. Wouldn't want you to fall and die flat at the bottom of the mountain," she said, followed by an almighty cackle. I smiled tightly as she turned and walked into her house. I never really knew when she was joking. Nathaniel raised his eyebrows in question. He had a serious look on his face, and his body seemed tense and coiled for a fight. It seemed he wasn't sure if it was a joke either. I barely shook my head and walked into her house, hoping we could keep calm and we would be walking out of there and not falling.

EIGHT

NATHANIEL

As I followed Gentle, my body was on high alert. I scanned the room without taking in any details other than the important ones. There was an upstairs and a door that led out the back to somewhere. I made note it appeared we were the only ones in the house, and I kept my ears open for any noises coming from upstairs. As Gentle sat, I stood behind her, watching the witch, ready for anything.

"Tell your guard to stand down. I can feel him practically vibrating from here," said Bella.

I stared at her as she lowered herself into her chair with a sigh. Without her mask, you could be fooled into thinking she was a kindly old granny living out here by herself. She was one of the most powerful beings in the realm and was not to be underestimated.

My hands curled into fists involuntarily. I was here to keep Gentle safe, and that's what I would do. I was Amos's second for a reason, even if others didn't think I deserved it. I wasn't about to disappoint him now.

Gentle turned in her seat, and I turned to her. For some strange reason, her lips were quirked up, and I realised she was smiling a little. At what, I had no idea.

"It's okay, Nathaniel. Bella won't harm me. You can relax." I stared at her like she had gone crazy, and her lips curled further. "If it is alright with you, I will stay standing here. My job is to protect you," I said, bowing my head respectfully. She let out a small sigh and turned back to Bella, who was watching us with a smile on her face.

"He is new. Where is the old one? I always thought he liked me, you know," she said with another almighty cackle. I tensed at her insinuation but kept my mouth shut. Amos had told me stories about meeting with Bella over the years, and I knew she could be crass when she wanted to. She liked to get a shock out of you.

Gentle's shoulders slumped slightly, and she waited for Bella to stop laughing. When she did and looked at Gentle, a seriousness came over her.

"There was an attack yesterday," Gentle answered. "Bilvog's cult members laid bombs under my mountain, and we missed one. Last night at the Night of Lights, one of the bombs exploded and injured many, killing some. Unfortunately, Amos was one we lost." Her voice cracked at the end, and I saw her wipe her eye.

I focused my eyes on the back wall, blinking and trying to keep my tears at bay. It would not look good for Gentle's bodyguard to be crying.

"I am sorry to hear that Gentle. Such ugly business," Bella said tutting as she took the mask off her head and laid it on the table between the two of them. "Right. Well, why did you come here then? I haven't seen you in years."

Gentle cleared her throat, and our leader was back. As she spoke, I took in my surroundings now I could see there was no immediate threat. The cottage was disorganised, messy, and cluttered. Looking at it made me uncomfortable, and I wanted to straighten and tidy everything. How someone could live in a place like this was beyond me. On every table, shelf, and windowsill, there were jars and containers of strange items. The only thing that seemed to have any sort of order was all the jars were labelled with small, slanted handwriting telling what was inside.

From where I was standing, I could see a jar with ogre fingernails, bog slime, eyes of newt, and lawn clippings. I wondered what sort of concoctions she would brew up with those. There were multiple cauldrons scattered around, some clean and some full of dried-up potion, and I pitied the person who would have to clean them. I was pretty sure it wouldn't be Bella.

Multiple aprons were hanging around the room, and stirring spoons and rags were everywhere. A large window out the back stared out into the darkness. I almost wished it was daylight so I could see. I knew it would be a spectacular view. I turned back to what they were talking about.

"I still have a fairly steady business. People know my potions are worth the climb," Bella was saying.

"You make the best potions around, Bella. I hope you haven't been taking advantage of the people risking their lives to get here," Gentle said kindly.

"Of course I'm not taking advantage of them! If they are going to risk their lives and make the payment I demand, why would I sell bad potions? To be honest, I am a little miffed you would suggest otherwise. When I find out who has told such lies, I will not be selling to them anymore," Bella replied, and I tensed at the annoyance in her voice. I knew behind her grandmotherly mask she was a powerful witch and could likely take us out at the click of a finger.

"Now Bella, you know no one has spoken badly about you. I just need to make sure my people are being treated fairly like always," Gentle reassured her.

Bella sniffed and fiddled with the nose of her mask on the table. "Well, good then. Now, let's get to what you are here for. I did have some forewarning from Vivian you are looking for your artefacts. Dread is fighting back, is he? I never thought he would be able to do that. He must have some powerful friends," she said thoughtfully. Her brows furrowed, and I wondered who those friends might be.

"Yes, we need to know where you hid my crown so the others can go and retrieve it."

She shifted in her seat and fiddled with some dried herbs spilt on the table, "Your crown? Well, I hid it somewhere no one would find it. I vowed I would never reveal where it was, but maybe I could...for a price. It is for a good reason, after all," Bella said with a calculating glint in her eye. I was on alert again, wondering what she would ask of Gentle.

Gentle sighed and gazed at her lap with her lips pursed. Bella was practically on the edge of her seat, waiting to see what Gentle would say. She knew we had no choice, and Gentle would agree to whatever she wanted. I hated being backed into a corner like this. I had heard stories of what hags and witches asked of people in payment for favours, and my mind raced, trying to think about what she could ask of Gentle.

Her soul?

Her firstborn?

Her voice?

It could be anything. I knew about how tricky the Others could be and knew that although Bella appeared human, she was most definitely Other. Even though we were in a magical realm, many here had never had a lot of dealings with the Others, and they didn't realise to be wary of every word that came out of their mouth. I knew that better than anyone.

Gentle lifted her head and pinned Bella with her eyes. I could see Bella practically salivating, knowing Gentle was going to give her what she wanted.

"What is the price, Bella? I want to know where the crown is and a fast and direct way to get there and back."

I smiled inside, impressed with her forethought. Making a demand of a hag was very risky. I was glad to hear she had added the transport clause as well. Who knows where she hid the crown? Speed was important in this quest.

"I think to make a potion for transport, the price will have to be a *tiny* bit higher." She brought a gnarled and scarred finger to her chin and tapped a wart growing there. "Three hairs from your head, three tears, and three drops of blood. Some will be used for the potion, and some will be used...at my discretion."

"You will not sell my items or the potions my items are in. I won't have someone else have power over me. That is my condition."

Bella leaned her ancient body back in the creaky chair, and it was her turn to look down in thought. I studied both women sitting across from each other. One young and beautiful and one ancient and scarred. Both were some of the most powerful people in the realm, and I wondered who would win and what the outcome would be.

Bella pinned Gentle with her eyes. They stared at each other in a silent battle for a moment and then Bella stood and held out her hand. Gentle was composed and showed no surprise at all. She also stood, her green dress pooling around her feet in soft waves.

"I need to hear it, Bella. You will tell me where the crown is and provide transport there and back, and you will not sell my items or the potions made from them. I need to know. Do you understand that?"

Bella sighed but didn't drop her hand. "I will tell you where the Crown of Glass is, I will provide transport there and back, and I will be the only one with your donations…it is so agreed."

Gentle nodded and shook Bella's outstretched hand. A deal struck. A shiver ran down my back as the power of the Others' magic exploded in the air. It had been a while since I had been near an Other deal being made, and the power of it surprised me. I was worried about the items Gentle had offered up. I knew as well as she did that those items could be used for all sorts of things, and I was concerned about what that might mean for the future, but there was nothing that could be done now. The deal was made. I only hoped we would come out on top.

NINE
GENTLE

The whoosh of power rushed over my skin when the deal was struck. A queasy feeling in my stomach demanded to be noticed, but I pushed it away. I knew I had made a dangerous deal, but I needed to do dangerous things if I wanted to defeat Dread and his cult. I would worry about what she would do with the items later when I could be honest with myself about how worried I was.

Once the deal was made, quick as a flash, her twisted hand shot out and pulled three hairs from my head. I held back a yelp of surprise. Before she could pull her hand back it was gripped with strong fingers with cuts covering them. Nathaniel was gripping Bella's hand, and my stomach sank.

"You will not touch the lady unless she says to," he said quietly, and I could sense the menace ripple off him. With my mouth slightly open, I stood there as his eyes flashed. Before I could recover from my shock, he released her hand, and I risked a look at Bella.

Surprisingly, she was smiling. That scared me more than I thought it would. Still gripping my hair, she pulled her hand away from my face, and Nathaniel straightened and stood next to me.

"Such a brave boy. You do know what I could do to you in the blink of an eye, don't you?"

Nathaniel refused to back down, but I did see his throat bob.

"I think you know better than most," she said before she turned back to me. I wondered what was going on between them, but Bella spoke.

"Well, it seems like I have some information to give you then." She cleared her throat, and a small smile floated across her lips. Was she...enjoying making me work for this information? I thought so. I stared at her, trying to keep my face blank so she wouldn't get the satisfaction of seeing me annoyed.

"The Crown of Glass is in the Others Realm. In the Gleaming Grove, to be precise," she leaned back in her chair and rested her hands on her stomach. "It will be dangerous and extremely difficult to get there. I won't be able to transport you right to its location. Magic is...strange in the Others Realm and especially in the Gleaming Grove, but I'm sure you will be fine, dear. Just show your pretty face, and you'll have all the Others lords bowing at your feet." She let out another cackle and rummaged around in a basket next to her chair.

"Thank you, Bella, but I won't be going. I think one of my brothers will go," I told her.

"Oh no, I don't think so. In order to get you there, I will use your donations. The potion will only work with you. Sorry," she said, not looking up while she put random jars and bottles on the table.

My stomach dropped. I couldn't go to the Others Realm. I hated dealing with them. I wasn't like Gloom. He had a relationship with the Lord and Lady of the Forest, and they had an understanding. I didn't have any connections, and I wasn't sure I was up to fighting off beasts and monsters. I had always thought of myself as a backup. A support person. Not a front liner.

"Surely you can do something, Bella. Ashes or Awe would do much better in the Others Realm."

"I'm sure you are right, dearie, but that's the way it goes. Now we have made a bargain, so hold out your hand. I need some blood and tears from you." She reached out her hand, and something glinted in the sun shining through the back window. A needle. A very large needle. I reluctantly held out my hand while the other one bunched my dress, knowing this was likely going to hurt. She snapped hold of my hand and jabbed my finger deeply with the needle. Tears sprung to my eyes, and a strong wind blew through the building, making it creak and moan again.

As she pulled the needle out, a perfect red drop was dangling off the end of the sharp tip. I had the sudden urge to reach out and take it back, unease settling in my stomach, knowing the hag now had it. I thought of all the ways she could use it against me, and there were many, but it was too late now.

A deal had been struck.

Bella licked her lips with greed in her eyes, turned my hand over, and squeezed two more drops out and into a small saucer she had pulled out of the basket. I yanked my hand back as soon as she released it and put the finger in my mouth, and sucked, hoping to stop the flow. My hair lifted off my shoulders, and I tampered down my power. The creaking settled again, and she handed me a small vial.

"Now the tears," she said, watching me closely.

I took the vial and held it in my hands, warming the cold glass. I didn't want to cry in front of them. I wriggled on the seat, sighed, and tried to squeeze out a few tears in the most elegant way. With my eyes closed, I tried to relax, hoping that would bring the tears forth. I let my mind wander to the memory I had been keeping at bay. I thought back to the explosion the night before and all the people who had lost their lives.

I let the disappointment and anger surge through me. I had invited them there for a social event and had implied they would be safe and have a great time and I had failed them. I could still hear the screams and feel the dust in the air clogging my throat. My heart beat sped up, and my breathing became choppy at the memory. I began to feel light headed as I relived the horrible night.

So many people I didn't keep safe. How many children lost a parent? Or parents who now had to bury their beloved children? Lastly, I thought of Amos. Kind and trustworthy Amos. He had been by my side for over a hundred years, and I had listened to his council almost every one of those days.

Since Bilvog had left to go and advise Gloom, Amos had been my constant. To think about going on and ruling without him at my back made my stomach clench and the tears leaked out of my eyes. I bit back the sob rising in my throat and held the vial to my cheek, catching the falling tears, being careful to only catch the three I was obligated to.

I opened my eyes and watched my tears slide along the side of the jar and I inhaled deeply, hoping to steady myself. I held out the jar to her across the table, and she took it from my hands, holding it carefully and looking at it almost lovingly. Another wrinkle of unease ran though my body, and I wondered if I would grow to regret the deal I had made.

Once she had all the ingredients, she turned and pulled on the mask again as she started humming an old melodic tune. I sat at the table and composed myself. My knee was bouncing, and I couldn't stay seated there. I stood and focused on the shelves behind me. There were old bottles that had been cleaned and decorated nicely. I read some of the labels and wasn't really surprised at what I saw. Love potions, fertility tonics and revenge tinctures lined the wall. People would take any kind of shortcut to get what they wanted out of life. I'm sure Bella had no shortage of people battling up this mountain and buying her potions.

"Is she the only one here?" Nathaniel whispered to me. I could see him surveying the room closely, his eyes drifting to the stairs and the ceiling.

"No, she has a few girls to help her to gather herbs and ingredients. They are probably upstairs asleep at this hour. The biggest threat to us is Bella and we now have a deal. You can relax...slightly," I said, looking him up and down.

He appeared like he was carved from stone. I wondered if he had ever been relaxed in his life. I was glad he was dedicated to his job of protecting me, but it put me on edge to have him always on alert. I stepped away and continued to browse the walls and things Bella had in her house. Eventually, I made it to the large circular window that took up most of the back wall. Looking out, I saw that it was black and endless, and I had nearly forgotten we were suspended between two mountains. I took a step back and shivered.

"My lady, perhaps we should think about what sort of things you will need with you in the Others Realm. It is not a place like this, and you will need to be prepared for anything."

"Yes, I suppose I will have to think about it now that it appears I am the one to go there." I smoothed my hair again and thought of the enormous task ahead of me.

How was I supposed to get the crown when I didn't know where it was? I wasn't a fighter like my brothers. Even Crescent would be more suited to this mission than I am. I made a list of the obvious things I would need, like weapons, fighters, clothing, and food rations. I didn't want to risk eating their food if I could help it, even though I was an Ever.

We might be half Gods, but I still didn't trust the food would leave us unharmed. I would need to do a bit of training, too. It had been a long time since I had been in a fight, and I had been rusty in the fight with Bilvog when I went to help Gloom. If I was going there, I needed to be better. I should probably have a guide as well. Someone to show me the ropes and steer me in the right direction. My head was spinning from thinking about it for only a minute. I couldn't believe the organisation I would have to pull off to plan the whole thing. And I only had a day or two to do it.

My hand was shaking as I brought it to my forehead, the overwhelm soaking me. "I have no idea how I am going to do this. I would ask my brothers and sisters to help, but they should really be looking for their own artefacts. The faster we do this, the better." I shook my head, seeing the concern in Nathaniel's eyes, "I'll worry about this stuff when we get back, and I get a chance to talk to the others. When I said I wanted to help, I didn't realise it would mean going to another realm and possibly fighting my way to my crown." I pinned down the question that had been floating around my head and voiced it quietly. "Does that make me a coward?"

He stared at me for a moment, and the same feeling washed over me I got in the library when I was healing his hands. Instinctively, I knew he was a true and honest person, and I relaxed a little. This was someone like Amos who would always tell me the truth.

After a beat, he replied, "I don't think it makes you a coward. I think it makes you intelligent. It would be foolish to walk into unknown territory and not be prepared. I have found fear can sometimes be very useful in a battle or fight. The trick is knowing you can get over it, even when, in the moment, you don't think you can. This is not an impossible task. You can do it, my lady. You are much more than you give yourself credit for."

I stood there stunned. My stomach fluttered with butter-flies, and I swallowed.

"Th-thank you, Nathaniel. I needed that," was all I man-aged to get out. Something about what he said settled within me and warmed me. People had encouraged me and said nice things to me before, but the way *he* said it pierced through, and I believed it.

Unfortunately, the moment was shattered with four little words. "Your potion is ready."

TEN

GENTLE

After collecting the potion, Nathaniel and I returned to Anena and took to the dark skies. Luckily, Nathaniel could read the stars and keep us on track. I didn't tell him Anena also knew the way home. While flying, I held the vial up to the moonlight and watched the liquid inside. The potion was a bright gold in colour and swirled and bubbled all on its own. I repeated what Bella had told me so I didn't forget her instructions.

"When you drink this potion, it will take you to the Others Realm. Now, I put the crown in the Gleaming Grove, which is in King Thallan's realm. He can be capricious and tricky, so be on your guard. His one weakness, if you can call it that, is beauty. Luckily for you, you have that, so be sure to use it to your advantage if you meet him. If you're lucky, you won't have to. Once you have the crown, drink the potion again, and it will return you to where you drank it the first time. It will transport anything you are wearing or holding. You could use it to transport one other person, but I wouldn't get carried away, or you might end up with half of what you took if you understand."

She cackled as she handed it over, and I shivered at the visual.

"Well, good luck, dearie. You are doing the right thing here. I'll deny it if anyone asks but between the three of us, I don't want Dread coming back. He was bad for business, killing off half my clients. The longer he is put away, the better. I'm not sure if the rest of my coven will feel that way," she shrugged. "But now out you go. I need a nice long sleep after that." She ushered us out of the house.

I held the vial tightly and thought about the journey that lay ahead for me.

We landed outside my castle walls, and I climbed off Anena. I still clutched the vial in my hands as I walked towards the open door of the entryway. Stepping inside the hall was a relief from the biting wind that had picked up outside. Goosebumps broke out all over my skin, and my runny nose tingled as it was hit with the warm air the fires provided. I shed my large coat, and Nathaniel and I headed deeper into the castle.

We walked the halls of white stone, our footsteps muffled by the carpets of midnight blue. Dotted on the walls were lights that threw out a warm golden glow while above us hung huge chandeliers that lit the centre of the rooms and walkways. The doors were arched, and each door frame was carved with flowers, clouds, and other images.

Still clutching the vial in my frozen hands, we made our way to my personal sitting room, where my brothers and sisters were still waiting. Before we entered, Nathaniel turned to me. "I will take my leave now if you agree, my lady. I have many things to organise for Amos's burial and I need to check on my soldiers before an early start in the morning."

"Of course, Nathaniel. Thank you for accompanying me. Rest well," I said as he bowed and turned away.

I opened my door, unsure if the others would have gone home, but I was happy to see them and to fill them in on what we had learnt from Bella. As I entered, my body relaxed from being in the warm and inviting room it was so used to. Against the far wall was a large stone fireplace that had a huge mirror above it. There were five deep burgundy couches arranged around a large round coffee table that always had fresh flowers placed upon it. Lining the walls were portraits of me dressed up for the many functions I had held here over the years, looking stunning in each.

I made my way to an empty lounge and sat while I loosened my thawing fingers from around the vial. I sat the potion on the table and noticed it had left an imprint on my hand from holding it so tightly. I rubbed out the imprint and wondered if the potion would have a more permanent effect on me.

"So, how did you go? I see you have a potion. What did you have to give up for it?" Awe asked. His outlandish suit jacket was unbuttoned, and he was holding a glass of whiskey while a faint glow emanated from him. It must have been approaching dawn.

"I had to give what I had to give. Nothing for you to worry about, brother," I said, hoping I was telling the truth. "This potion will transport me to the Others Realm and then return back here. Bella put the crown in the Gleaming Grove, but the potion won't put us there. There will be a bit of travelling," I said with a sigh as I slumped back in my seat.

The events of the last twenty-four hours were catching up with me, and now I was warm, sleep was coming to claim me. I lifted my legs under my dress and curled up on the couch.

"The Gleaming Grove?" Gloom asked. "I have never heard of it. Would you like me to ask the Forest People in Toleran if they know where it is? They are part of the Others Realm, even if they prefer the forest in my realm. They might know the location or provide a map."

"That would be very handy, I think. Any extra information we can get before we enter would be a good thing." I stifled a yawn, my eyelids heavy.

"Right, well, it looks like Gentle needs a nice long sleep, and I could use one too," Crescent said. "Thank you, Gentle, for going and seeing Bella after everything that has happened. We will meet tomorrow and discuss who will be going and how many troops to take." She rounded the others to standing and practically pushed them out the door. Bella's potion limitation sprang to my lips, but I decided I was too tired to tell them I would be the one going. I didn't want to get into it right now. She was right. I needed a long sleep and some time for my emotions and body to rest after the collapse and meeting with Bella. I had a lot of things to do in a very short time.

Once they had left, I walked into my dressing room and peeled the cold and slightly wet dress from my skin. I let it puddle on the ground in such a way I knew my laundress would be cursing me, but I didn't care. I looked up at the hundreds of floaty and beautiful dresses I had in the wardrobe. One less wouldn't hurt.

Naked, I padded my way to the large shower that took up half of the bathroom. I didn't have the energy to run the tub tonight, so I turned on the water till it got hot enough to scald me and stepped in, careful not to get my hair wet. I was cold and dirty, with dust and Pegasus hair covering me. I stood under the hot jets of water, letting it pour over my skin, making it tingle with pins and needles all over.

I cleaned myself, and it wasn't long before the smell of jasmine filled the air and coated my skin. I let the smell calm me, as I tried to centre myself and not get overwhelmed by what I had agreed to. Once I was a little more relaxed, I dried myself off and slipped into a satin nighty. It was a dusty pink colour and was amazing against my pink, clean skin. My hair was knotted, and I ran a brush through it, wincing at the snags. The events of the last twenty-four hours had worn on me, and I wasn't used to being anything but immaculate.

Exhausted, I climbed into my large four-poster bed and laid my head on the pillows. The twinkling fairy lights shone down on me as I drifted off to sleep, hoping tomorrow would be an easy day.

ELEVEN

GENTLE

"I can't possibly see why you would think you can do this, and no less alone. No. I am sorry, my lady, there is no possible outcome where this happens." Councillor Lomano shook his head and scowled at the table.

I clenched my fists in my lap, and a biting cold breeze picked up in the room. A warning I was displeased. However, it seemed my counsellors hadn't picked up on it, even if my siblings had. Councillor Vasair stood next, his liver-spotted head barely reaching my shoulder.

"There must be some other way to circumvent the potion. Perhaps we could give it to one of the alchemists, and they could modify it?" he asked the gathered council and a few nodded at his suggestion.

"I wouldn't go altering Bella's potions if I were you. She is tricky and four times as old as you, hard to believe as it is," Awe said as he slouched in the very expensive chairs in the council chambers. "You would likely find yourself stranded or in the belly of a beast if you tampered with it."

He was right. There was no way I would be taking the potion if someone changed it. Bella and I might be on good terms, but I knew better than to alter her work. I rubbed my eyes and sighed. Why did I think this would be a good idea?

This morning, I woke up a little more refreshed and decided I would tell all the necessary people about my upcoming quest at once. Then, I would only have to have the argument once instead of twice, so I called a meeting. Crescent and Shayde had already left, and I was a little disappointed. I had a feeling Crescent would have sided with me faster than the others, but I wasn't surprised. Crescent liked to socialise, but she also liked her quiet. Maybe I should take a leaf from her book and live in a cottage and never invite visitors.

The argument was raging in front of me, and I was sure they had forgotten I was still sitting there. All I saw were a bunch of old men who thought they were the rulers and could choose what they wanted. Anger fizzed through me. I had been passive for too long. Amos would always tell me to stand up to them. That I wasn't only a doll or figurehead. I was an Ever and held the power. The shock of his death and others had put a lot in perspective for me, and as I watched these men decide my future and not listen to me, a switch clicked in my head, and I stood.

I stood so fast that my chair went skidding across the floor and tipped over. All eyes swivelled to me, and I stared at all of them. I was sick of looking at them and letting them decide what happened in my kingdom. The problem was I had been passive for so long that I didn't know how to do it. I stood there a moment longer as my anger drained away. I lost some of their attention, and they shuffled their papers and looked away. Desperately, I searched the gathered faces, looking for some support, but all I saw was confusion or indifference.

With a sinking heart, I realised my siblings were no help.

Something inside of my twinged and I knew a trust had been broken between us. I had always thought we were all close, but their opinion of me hurt. I glanced towards the door, wondering if I should try to escape when my eyes clashed with Nathaniel's. He was staring at me, and in his eyes, I saw what I needed. Approval. He nodded, and a small smile graced my lips.

I cleared my throat to get everyone's wavering attention again.

"I have heard all your arguments, and I must say I disagree. I wouldn't advise changing Bella's potion. She is the best in the world, and it would be dangerous to do so. What has happened is unfortunate, but they are the circumstances we are in. Now, I will be going to the Others Realm, where I will retrieve the crown. I shall take one other person with me. Preferably someone with some survival and fighting skills. I can and *will* do this."

"But we need you here, my lady. What about calming the people after the bomb? You need to be here for them," Councillor Papuana said, and I glared at him. "Do you not think I would like to be here? Of course, I want to be here and support my people, but there is, unfortunately, a time limit. We need to get the crown before Bilvog. He already has the Staff of Thorns. He cannot be allowed to get another artefact. I'm sure my brothers and sisters are more than happy to help to cover my duties here. I will be leaving in the morning. I will hear no more about it."

Shock was written on all their faces. I knew it wouldn't be long before they were again trying to convince me to stay, so I moved to leave before my council regained their senses.

"Gentle, who will be accompanying you?" Gloom asked quietly.

I stopped in my tracks and came up short. I had no idea. I would need someone who knew the area. Off the top of my head, I didn't know anyone, but I was sure I could find someone.

"I will put out an announcement today and find someone. I am sure someone here has been to the Others Realm." I sounded much more confident than I felt. Still, I was on a roll, so I walked towards the door, hoping I appeared confident and in control. I had only taken a few steps when someone cleared their throat. I closed my eyes and held in my sigh.

"I will take Lady Gentle. I have been there and can provide for her while we are travelling," Nathaniel said.

I relaxed slightly. To me, this was a much better solution. I knew Nathaniel and was comfortable around him. I nodded at him. "See, Nathaniel can join me. We will be fine. The matter is settled. We leave tomorrow. Now, I will need someone to help me pack my clothes and the kitchens will have to pack our food for while we are in there. And another thing. Since Amos is...gone, we will need someone in charge of the Alanti. I would propose Nathaniel. I believe it is well-known that was Amos's intention. Does anyone have any objections?"

There was a stunned silence at my abrupt topic change, but I knew it was important to have the position filled as soon as possible. It seemed none of them were game to speak. After a short, uncomfortable silence, Perrian spoke, "I'm not sure it is wise to appoint a new captain of the elite guard and then whisk him away on a dangerous mission. I'm sure the troop will need time to adjust."

He made a good point. "What do you think, Nathaniel? Do you agree to the position?" I asked.

He paused for a moment, eyes looking at the floor, and I was worried he might refuse but when he raised his eyes, I saw a fire blazing in them. "It would be my greatest honour to become the leader of the Alanti and to become your personal guard," he said as he got down on one knee. I stood surprised for a moment, unsure what to do about this show of fealty. I swallowed the lump clogging my throat.

"Thank you. After all this is done, we will have a proper ceremony, but I am sure you understand we simply don't have time for that now. Do you think you will be able to leave the Alanti here, or in light of this new development, would you prefer to stay here?" I asked.

Without hesitation, he answered, "My job is to guard you first and foremost, my lady. I will travel with you. I shall leave Theo in charge of the Alanti's training until I get back." He bowed his head again, but before he did, I noticed a sheen in his eyes. Was he crying?

I nodded and turned to look at Perrian while Nathaniel got control of his emotions. "Perrian I would like you to draw up an official document stating Nathaniel is to take control of the Alanti after Amos. You are all dismissed."

I sighed, glad I was able to get out of that room with Awe, Gloom, and Amelia following. I went to my rooms, planning to begin packing. "I'll see you later, Gentle. I have to go and see someone," said Awe. I wondered who he was going to see but I didn't press him, glad I wouldn't have to explain myself to him. He turned and walked down the hallway, winking at all the serving girls he passed.

"How exciting. I have been wondering what it would be like in the Others Realm. I can't wait to hear all about it," Amelia said. I couldn't tell if she was serious or supportive, but I was grateful either way. I looked at her and realised I had hardly spoken to her since she had been here. I had only met her once before, but I had taken a shine to her. She was kind and strong and the perfect match for my brother.

Emotion overtook me, and I reached over and gave her a hug, whispering in her ear, "Thank you," before I pulled away.

The crease between Gloom's brows intensified, "Right, so I suppose this is happening. Gentle between us, are you ready for this? It will be very challenging. You know what the Others are like. And what about this, Nathaniel? Can he protect you? This is a little more work than escorting you to see Bella."

I could see in his eyes that he was asking because he was worried about me, not necessarily because he didn't think I could do it. A small bit of fear crept in, and I wondered if I could. I was so used to being on my throne and throwing parties that I wasn't sure if I could handle it. We had had years of peace, and this act of violence had rattled me, and I did wonder if I was up to the task. But if I wanted to rule my realm, didn't I have to do the dangerous thing and be an Ever? Not just look like one.

Like a drop in a pool, the ripples spread, and I realised that that was what I wanted to do. I did want to take a more active role in looking after the people on my mountain. I was sick of being the figurehead with all the men running things behind me. Now all I had to do was prove I could do that and that I was capable of handling the big decisions.

"Yes, Gloom. Thank you for your concern," I said, taking his hands in mine. We had always been close, and I knew he had my best interests at heart. "We can handle this. Nathaniel is more than capable of looking after me and getting us to the crown safely. He was trained under Amos, and I believe it was Amos's idea that he would eventually take over from him when the time came."

"Well, I think you will do great. You have the potion that can take you there and back. What could go wrong?" asked Amelia.

Gloom smiled at her tightly. "I'm not going to lie, Gentle. I am worried about you. You haven't been the same since Bilvog's betrayal. You seem to have lost your spark or something."

Amelia elbowed him in the ribs.

"What? She has," he said, looking at her his eyes widening.

I felt the shutters fall over my face, and my body went cold. Gloom was right. Since Bilvog revealed himself to be in league with my brother Dread, something had changed within me. I found myself laughing less, and trusting people was now difficult. I had always been a bubbly and animated person, but lately, I had fallen into a hole, and I was finding it difficult to get out of it.

One of the reasons I wanted to take more control over my realm was so I couldn't be betrayed like that again. The reason Bilvog could do so much damage was partly because he had so much control here when he was my advisor. He knew what would cause the most damage and when. I never wanted it to happen again.

Perhaps it was a good thing I had hardened my heart.

My carefree days were over, and it was now time to change. I turned my back on Gloom and Amelia and went to stand by the large window. I gazed out over my mountain and could see people working and families living their lives. A Pegasus flew by my window, and I could see off in the distance Alanti were training. I wondered if Nathaniel should be there instead of guarding my door.

"I need to do this, Gloom. You are right. Bilvog broke me, and it has changed me, but perhaps it might turn out to be for the better. Maybe I need a harder heart to rule. That is what I intend to do. Rule." I turned back to them, and I could see worry in Gloom's eyes as well as a little spark of pride.

"Okay then. Amelia and I will be leaving soon. And I don't expect you will see Awe again before he leaves. If you need anything, please let me know. I will speak to the Forest Folk and send you a message with any information. If you need help there, the Lord and Lady of the Forest might be able to assist you. I think, from some perspective, our goals align. Good luck, Gentle. You can do this. Bring the crown home." He hugged me, and my heart swelled. It was nice to know my brother believed in me. Amelia hugged me again as well. "Good luck. If you get a chance, can you bring me back some mushrooms if you find any?" she asked. I laughed. "Sure, I'll fit it in around tracking down an artefact and trying not to get myself killed."

She smiled. "Thanks. That would be great." They left the room, and I was still chuckling. It was nice to laugh. I didn't know if I would be doing any of that any time soon.

TWELVE
NATHANIEL

After the meeting, I walked out into the cold of the mountain and stood in a small patch of sun that had managed to break through the clouds. I tilted my head and let it wash over my face and warm it, my eyes seeing red as the sun tried to sneak through my eyelids.

The cold mountain air filled my lungs, and I blew it out as a smile crept across my lips. I had done it. I had finally reached my goal. I was now the leader of the Alanti and Gentle's personal guard. All my life, I had been working for this and I had actually achieved it. Amos and my parents would be so proud of me.

My smile vanished as I realised I had imagined this day much differently. I had always assumed Amos would be here with me to celebrate and pass the torch. In all my dreams, I never thought he would be dead, and I would be alone. I lowered my head as a cloud blocked the sun and I turned toward one of the few gardens the castle had.

I loved to walk in the garden and see the plant life struggle and fight to break through the rocky ground and then see if it thrived or died. I, too, felt like those small plants, but so far, I had thrived. I walked through using my booted feet to kick aside some of the snow that had gathered on the brick walkway. A few strong trees had survived here, sheltered from the wind by the tall wall surrounding the garden. They were small and had a few red leaves clinging determinedly to the branches.

On the ground, camellias and pansies were poking out, adding a splash of colour to the white snow. I stood a moment and admired them while I tried to collect my jumbled thoughts. So much had happened in the last two days, and so much more was to come. I needed to take a moment to absorb it all and plan my next action.

My heart was still hammering in my chest from the meeting, and it took a moment of concentration to get it under control. I needed my soldier focus now to determine my next steps. I turned and walked out of the peaceful garden and to one of the many launching platforms that were dotted all over the mountain, making it easy for the Alanti and Pegasus to jump off and take flight.

I spread my blue wings and leapt off the mountain, catching the air underneath me. I beat my wings, the tight muscles in my back straining as I adjusted my body so I could be the most aerodynamic. I angled around until I caught a thermal, hard to do up on the mountain, and I was able to use it to rise higher to the next small mountain range where the Alanti were stationed. I could see the soldiers out in the yard soaking in the sunshine that was peeking through the clouds between fighting bouts. I flew down and landed on the snow with a crunch. I shook the snow off my wings and brought them in tight to my body to help keep me warm. A few of the soldiers nodded at me, and we turned to watch the fight in front of us.

In the centre of the ring were two Alanti, Balthial—with his large red-tipped wings—and big Theo fighting it out.

They were using the chalk daggers we used for practice, so there would be no injuries today. They were to fight it out until one of them "pierced" the other in the heart, leaving the chalk outline as proof of the hit. They were so fast all you could see was the pale yellow of Theo's wings and the red of Balthail's as they slashed and circled each other. I knew they were well-matched, and the fight carried back and forth for so long that I couldn't tell who had the upper hand.

Balthial misjudged his footing and slipped on a piece of ice making his block too slow, and Theo managed to land the blow to his heart that ended the match. Everyone clapped, and the two men shook hands and wiped the sweat from their brows.

"Well done men. That was a superb demonstration. Take a break. I would like to see all Alanti in the food hall in fifteen minutes. I have an announcement, and we have some plans we need to make. Some big changes are ahead, and I want to get on top of them now. I'll see you all in fifteen minutes."

Without giving them a chance to reply, I turned and made my way into the Alanti's food hall. Here, we ate and trained together and rested as well. In a separate building, we had our own rooms and bathrooms for privacy, but here is where we spent most of our time. We needed to work together as a team, and what better way to do that than to live together.

I made my way to one of the small workstations and made a list of all the things I needed to get done before I left with Gentle in the morning. I had always found I functioned better with a list. I needed to know what was coming and what I needed to achieve that day. Some of the others made fun of me, but I was disciplined, and the way I did it, I knew what I had achieved.

I made my list and thought about what I wanted to say to the men today. I knew some of them would have a problem with me taking over, and I needed to find the best way to tell them. Some of the Alanti found me cold and rigid. I was going to receive some push back, and I knew exactly who it was going to come from. I saw the clock on the wall and stood up, straightening my clothes, and tried to shake the tension out of my hands, to relieve the jittery feeling in my body.

I waited at the door to the food hall, listening to the Alanti gathering on the other side. I could hear them talking and laughing, and a small seed of jealousy sprouted in me. I had never been like that, even when I was sitting out there with them. I had always been separate, and now, being promoted, I would be more isolated from them. I would be guarding Gentle and dealing with the problems of the realm. I was surprised that it bothered me so much. I had always been on the outside but I was starting to get tired of it. I wanted to belong.

Before I fell to deep into my feelings, I shoved the jealousy aside, deciding to deal with it another day, and opened the door and walked to the front of the room. Looking out I saw about fifty Alanti all sitting on stools that allowed for their wings to be unrestrained. Wings of all colours dotted the rooms as they sat in groups and chatted. As soon as I reached the front of the room, silence descended.

I cleared my throat. "Thank you for coming on such short notice. I won't keep you long, but there are a few things happening, and they are going to be happening fast. Firstly, I would like to acknowledge the loss of Amos. Being so recent, I don't think it will have impacted us yet, but I want to say, if you need to talk, please do it. You don't have to talk to me, but talk to someone. His loss will impact us deeply, and it will take an adjustment to carry on without him. I would like to have a small memorial for him this afternoon, so if you want to attend, it will be a private Alanti memorial here in this room."

I waited a moment, giving them time to absorb the information before I revealed the next talking point.

"Now onto other business. As of this morning, Lady Gentle has appointed me as Amos's replacement. There will be an official document and announcement shortly." I had to stop as applause broke out. To be honest, it surprised, and I smiled. I didn't think it would be taken so well. I had been bracing myself for the opposite reaction.

When the applause died, and before I could speak again and thank them, I heard a voice in the back speak up, "You jumped into Amos's seat quickly, didn't you? He has barely been gone for a day, and you are already taking over."

The room went so quiet you could hear a pin drop. I controlled my face to not show the anger building up. I knew I would have to deal with this sooner or later. Also, I was a bit disappointed he had rained on my parade, but I didn't want to look at that too closely.

"Hersal, thank you for your input. Now if we could move along, I have some more news. While I am excited to take over from Amos, even though I wish it was under better circumstances, I will be gone for a few days. Lady Gentle has to go on a secret mission to the Others Realm and I am going to accompany her. While I am gone, Theo will take over your training, and I expect you all to treat him as you would me or Amos."

There was a bit of murmuring after my announcement, and I let it go before clearing my throat.

"Now I know this is a trying time, and a lot of things are happening very fast, but I need your patience, and soon we will settle, and it will be business as usual. While I am gone, I expect you to work hard and protect this mountain with everything you have." Most of the men nodded but I could see at the back of the gathered Alanti, one group of people stared on with no emotion on their faces. I stared back at them, refusing to look away when Hersal spoke.

"So, you are going to come in here, a day after our leader has died, appoint yourself our new leader and then up and abandon us? I don't know why I'm surprised. I shouldn't expect any more from you." He sneered while a few of the men around him nodded in agreement. I rubbed my eyes, not really having the energy for this but knowing I had to deal with it before I left.

"Thank you, Hersal. If you would like to stay, we can discuss your problems, but I think everyone else is dismissed. Theo, if you could stay, I will fill you in on what I expect while I am gone. If anyone else has any questions, I will be in Aeris Isle after the memorial before we leave tomorrow. Otherwise, please see Theo. I will see you all when I return."

I watched the Alanti stand and file out, all chatting before going about their business. I did notice Hersal and his group didn't leave, and I braced myself for what was to come while showing none of the weariness on my face.

Before he could open his mouth, I opened mine. "The next time you want to question me, you can do it in private or with the respectful tone you would afford a superior, which is what I am now." I couldn't help the petty thrill that ran through me being able to say those words to him.

Hersal sneered at me, "Let's not beat around the bush. We both know I don't think you should be there. There are many others more suited and who I would gladly follow. I don't know what Amos saw in you, and I'm not the only one. Who do you think you are anyway? You are just an orphan who was lucky enough to be adopted by Amos. There is nothing special about you, and you know it!" he spat viciously. I heard a roaring in my ears at the angry words he had thrown at me so many times before, and my famous control slipped.

"What? Do you think you are better? You lack discipline and respect, and the only reason you are here is because daddy paid your way in. Don't forget lots of Alanti don't make it through the training, and if I were to go and look at your records, which I can now, I would see you fell short. So, before you go hurling ugly words at people, remember who you are speaking to. I know you, Hersal. Don't forget that." By the time I was finished, I was breathing hard, and shame flooded my body. I could see in his eyes Hersal was surprised but he hid it well.

"Whatever. Let's get out of here before he kills us and takes our place as well." His insult made no sense, and he knew it as he hurried out.

I put my head in my hands and allowed myself a brief moment of feeling sorry for myself that I had stooped to his level. Hersal had never made it a secret he didn't like me. He didn't like I was no one and was faster, smarter and stronger than him, someone who had money and influence. I also knew his father didn't like it and regularly told him so. I had resolved years ago to ignore what he said, or at the very least not let it anger me. But with all the changes and everything colliding at the moment, I had let my control slip. I didn't like it, and it didn't feel good.

I allowed myself a moment before I turned to Theo.

"Ignore him, Nate. His little group are the only ones who think that. Everyone else knows you were Amos's choice to take over," Theo said.

I smiled a little at his attempt to make me feel better. He had always been the kind of person to build you up instead of knocking you down, and that is what we all needed growing up with the training and discipline needed to be an Alanti.

"Thanks, Theo," I said, not wanting to talk through my emotions. I told him what I wanted him to do while I was gone and then got out of there. I wanted to be out and away from the room where my ugly words still bounced off the walls.

THIRTEEN
GENTLE

Nathaniel and I stood in the Great Hall, bags at our feet, ready to go. I held the potion in my slightly trembling hand and went over the things I had packed, trying to think if I had forgotten anything. I had packed a few sets of travelling clothes consisting of sturdy boots, pants, and loose-fitting shirts. Basic toiletries were included, and I never went anywhere without a few nice dresses. My maids had looked a little aside at that, but it was the armour I chose to wear. Perhaps we would get into a situation where we needed to push some influence. I couldn't do that wearing pants.

A bottle of water and some food the kitchens had brought up for me were also stuffed in somehow. Nathaniel and I had gone over the plan, and we were as ready as we were ever going to be. I hefted the bag onto my back, testing the weight. It was heavy but not unmanageable, although I expected to have a sore body at the end of the day.

We were gathered with the council and other senior members of my household. Earlier in the day, we had a messenger from Gloom. He had a note explaining the Forest Folk in his realm had drawn together a small map of the area and where we needed to go. I was thankful they had managed to help us in the short time period we had, but I was also worried about the condition. I now owed them a favour to be called in when they needed it.

I frowned when I read that. I didn't like the idea of an open-ended favour owing, especially to the Forest Folk, but we were desperate, and if the map worked out well, it would be worth it. Nathaniel had the map and had taken a bit of time examining the landmarks and warnings the Forest Folk had put on there to help us.

The day had been spent packing and in preparation, and I knew Nathaniel had been busy with his Alanti. Readying them and informing them of what was to come. He had mentioned they had had a service of sorts for Amos, and while I was curious, looking at him made me bite my tongue. He seemed raw and...fragile in a way I never thought I would see him. He had been quieter than usual, and I respected that, letting him have his space. I, too, was distracted. Anxiety about what we were about to face was a beast in my body. Even now, I was trembling slightly, and I took a few steady breaths, trying to calm myself.

I waited until everyone we needed were gathered, and we were ready to leave. I took the chance to speak to my council.

"As we leave today, I don't know when we will be back. While I am gone, I expect you to rule Aeris Isle as if I were here, always putting the people first. If needed, the other Evers are available to help and can be called on. Upon my return, we will have an occasion to formally mourn the people we have lost, but for now, my efforts need to be on stopping my brother and preventing his followers from doing any more harm to innocent lives. But when we return, we will have the crown back in its rightful place upon my head and not on Bilvog's!"

An applause went up in the room, and my chest fluttered with pride, anxiety, and a tiny speck of excitement. They believed in me, and now I needed to believe in myself. I nodded to the gathered people and held my hand out to Nathaniel. He had strapped his bag across his body and was looking out at the crowd as well. He turned to me and took my hand in his. The calluses on his hand were rough, and for some reason, I was strangely self-conscious about how smooth mine were. I shook it off as I lifted the glass bottle to my lips with Bella's potion in it.

The closer it got, the dryer my mouth became until it touched my lips. A silence had fallen over the group as I took a mouthful, careful to leave enough for the trip home. The liquid was unexpectedly hot, and it splashed along my throat, searing it. My tongue burnt, and I coughed as the heat expanded in my chest. Nathaniel gripped my hand tighter.

"Are you alri—"

His words were cut off. The room around us zoomed past as the floor collapsed under us. I squeezed the bottle in one hand and Nathaniel's hand in the other, so I didn't lose either. My hair whipped around my body, stinging where it lashed me. We were in a free fall.

A scream was ripped from my lips, but no sound emerged, snatched away in the wind. Suddenly, large arms wrapped around me from the back as Nathaniel had managed to grasp me and was holding me to his chest.

I could hear Nathaniel's heavy breathing in my ear, and I was sure he could hear my heart thumping. I swallowed and willed myself to look. The ground was rising up to meet us. My head was pounding. My whole body tingled with fear, but there was nothing I could do. This was my worst nightmare. I truly hated heights, especially when over wide-open spaces. We were rushing at breakneck speed to land, and there was no way I could stop it.

A thought occurred to me.

"Nathaniel, your wings!" I squeezed through my closed throat.

"It will break them at this speed," he said, the wind almost snatching the words before I could hear them. I didn't have time to react. The ground came rushing towards us. The open field was the colour of rubies and was empty of anything. I braced myself for the impact. Another scream threw itself out of my body. I braced myself waiting to be smashed and broken on the ground. Instead, we stopped abruptly.

My head cracked forward, my hair forming a curtain around it, and my stomach felt like it fell from my ears to my feet. I felt air on the back of my neck as it rushed out of Nathaniel, and his arms tightened around my middle. We hung there a few feet off the ground for a moment, but before we could process what happened, we were released, and we landed in a heap on the red spongy ground.

We took a moment, collapsed on the ground, to catch our breath.

"That was the most terrifying thing that has ever happened to me," I puffed out as my heart rate returned to normal. "Even being the Air Ever, I did not enjoy that at all."

"No, I agree with you. I hate when I can't use my wings, and that was *not* fun," Nathaniel said, looking up into the sky like he might be able to see Aeris Isle hovering above us. I followed his gaze, but all I could see was a sky during dusk. Orange and pink were fading from the sunset and were being dulled to a dark purple colour as the stars were beginning to dot the sky. I tried to convince my body we were on solid ground and had nothing to be scared of, but it was taking time to understand. I was trembling uncontrollably, and my breathing was short and choppy.

"Is there a time change here?" I asked, trying to distract myself and also trying to get my bearings, knowing it was morning when we left Aeris Isle.

"No, this is the sky permanently. Always dusk. It will make telling the time difficult but there are tricks," he said, holding up his wrist where I could see a watch strapped to it.

I nodded at him as I stood, glad my shaking legs had enough strength to hold me up. I took a moment to finger comb some of the tangles from my hair, cursing that I hadn't braided it before to prevent the knots that had formed in our fall. Once I had done the best I could I braided it tightly and flung it over my shoulder to hang down my back. I smoothed the top to settle the unruly hairs that never really seemed to lay flat and turned in a circle to see where we were.

All around was red grass. The breeze stirred up the scent of dry hay and daisies, and I smiled. I loved daisies. The breeze was cool, and it made the grass lazily wave and undulate. It was a little mesmerising, and I had to make an effort to pull my attention back to what I was doing. I could hear the wind rustling through the grass and also strange digging noises. It reminded me we weren't alone out here, and I stared through the long grass, trying to see what it was digging.

After a few minutes, I saw it. It was a mole-like creature that was a deep burgundy colour and it blended in nicely with the tall grass. It popped its head out, had a look, and went back to digging, clearly not worried about us.

Out on the horizon, towards the sun that never truly set, I could see a tree line. Something was strange about the trees, but it was hard to pinpoint why from this distance. I turned towards the moon that hung low, suspended over the earth, and could see more grassland, desolate and lonely. I was acutely aware of how glad I was to have someone with me in this strange land.

Curiosity niggled, and I wanted to ask Nathaniel about his last visit here and what he came for. I put it on the list of questions I wanted answers to when I found the right time. Now was the time to get out of here.

I turned back to Nathaniel, and he was reading the map.

"Do you know where we are?" I asked him as I walked to stand in front of him, adjusting my pack as I went.

"I'd say we are in the Boldows Meadow. We want to be heading towards those trees over there. On the other side of the forest is the Obsidian Court. On the other side of that is the Gleaming Grove, where we will find your crown," he said, folding up the map and tucking it in one of the many pockets that covered his clothes. "We should get a move on now. We can make a fair bit of ground, and we should camp in the forest by nightfall. Now, a few things to remember about the Others Realm. You must listen to everything I say and not question if I tell you to do something. It will be to keep us alive and unharmed."

The idea of taking orders from him rankled me a bit, but I knew it was for the best. His sharp eyes stared at me, and I nodded, staring right back.

"Good. Next is don't touch things if you don't know what they are. Everything here is designed to entice you and make you want to touch and stay. Don't be fooled. Pretty much everything here can and will harm you if it gets the chance. I know you are an Ever, and you and your family are like Gods in our realms, but here, there are much older and more powerful beings, and to them, you are nothing." His harsh words shocked me, and I glanced around, realising I was now near the bottom of the food chain, and I did not like it.

"Also, when dealing with the Others, looks will only get you so far. You will need to think over each word before you speak. To make a bargain with them is perilous. If it comes to that, think over the terms and consequences carefully. There is rarely a way out of the deals you make. We will want to get through the Obsidian Court as quickly as possible. I'm sure you agree we don't want to get stuck there. As we get closer, we will have to try and avoid people and being stopped by them as much as we can. We have a bit of time before we have to worry about that, but are you okay with all that, my lady?" he asked, even though he knew I had no choice, really. He was the guide, and I would do whatever he said to get out of here alive.

"Well, I suppose I have to be," I said, standing up straight in an attempt to remember who I was. "Now here are the things I expect. I expect you to get us to the Gleaming Grove the fastest possible way, and I will need you to keep me safe and help me through this landscape."

He nodded, and I realised it was his job to bring me here. I felt so foolish I had to stop myself from rolling my eyes. I looked at Nathaniel to see if he noticed my embarrassment, but he appeared as serious as ever. I found him difficult to read, which was strange to me. I had held so many social engagements I thought I could read anyone. Apparently not.

"Right, well, let's go. The sooner we get to our camping spot, the sooner we can rest and relax," I said, hoping to break the almost uncomfortable silence.

"Yes, my lady," Nathaniel said as he readjusted his bang to hang at his hip. He walked towards the trees, and I followed behind.

We walked in silence for what felt like hours. I kept my head down, looking at the spongy ground and trying not to roll my ankle on the small mounds the moles had made. The grass was easy to move through and was like feathers when I ran my hands over it. When I did look up, it was to see we were no closer to the woods, and I wondered if it was all in my head. Nathaniel walked in front of me; his blue wings appeared darker in the twilight, and he moved without hesitation and showed no signs of tiring. I, on the other hand, had been sending a tiny stream of magic to the backs of my feet where a blister had decided to pop up from these shoes.

I passed the time thinking about the fabulous dresses and the huge bath I had left behind on Aeris Isle. I highly doubted I would be getting a hot bubble bath here anytime soon.

My patience was wearing thin when I asked, "Are we getting any closer? It feels like we have been walking for hours." I did my best to keep the whine out of my voice, but I didn't think I succeeded.

"We *have* been walking for hours. The Others Realm is strange. Things that seem close are not always. It changes all the time, making it difficult to judge how long travel will take. I think we will still have a few more hours to walk. Would you like to stop for a moment?" he asked.

"Yes, thank you," I said as I slipped the heavy bag off my back. It was such a relief to not have it bearing down on me, and I stretched out my back to loosen it up. I looked at the ground and sat on a tuft of grass to try and stay as clean as possible. With no bath, I didn't want to think about what I would look like at the end of this journey. I took a drink and had one of the snacks I had packed, mindful that I had to be careful to save some for the rest of the trip, which could apparently take three times as long as I first thought.

I looked up into the sky at the still-setting sun and the moon, which was still rising. Now we were a little closer to the forest, I could see a bit more animal life. Colourful birds flew overhead and were hunting the moles that poked their heads above ground. Some were huge, and most of them I had never seen before. I hoped they were not territorial.

"How are you, my lady?" Nathaniel asked.

It was then I realised I had sighed out loud and not only in my head as I had thought.

"I am fine. These shoes are a little uncomfortable, but otherwise, I am doing okay. Do you think there will be any trouble in the forest tonight?"

"We will have to take turns keeping watch, I think. There are all sorts of animals and beasts around, and I wouldn't like to be caught off guard. I will only need a few hours of sleep if you can keep watch." Nathaniel took the light jacket he was wearing off, revealing a large tattoo on his left arm of a bright white Pegasus. I stared at it, wondering how I had never seen it before. It took up his whole upper arm and ended below his elbow. I shook myself to stop staring at it.

"I can do that. I think it's a good idea. Who knows what is out there," I said, glancing behind me, paranoid. Nathaniel stood, and I groaned inside, knowing it would mean more walking. I put my bag back on and grit my teeth, giving myself a pep talk. *You are an Ever. You are powerful and walking never hurt anyone. You are on an important mission, and you must succeed. Prove the people who said you couldn't do this wrong.*

It worked, and I walked with a little more purpose.

"You said earlier you had a memorial for Amos." I put my hands behind my back and twisted my fingers together, "How was it?" I asked gently.

He hesitated a moment before he answered with a small smile on his face. "It was nice. Simple and to the point, like him. I decided we should gather at the top of the mountain in one of his favourite spots. He used to like going there and looking at all the people he had sworn to protect. He said it reminded him of what was important. We didn't do anything fancy. Just said a few words about the man he was and the difference he made in our lives. I wasn't sure if we would make it back before they had a proper ceremony for him, so I wanted to do something."

"I think it sounds lovely. I myself thought about him a lot while I was getting ready to leave. I could imagine his voice telling me what to pack and telling me what to expect. I think he would have approved of me going. He always believed I could do more than I thought I could," I said as tears filled my eyes at the man we had lost. I wiped my cheek and sniffled.

"Yes. He always believed the best in you. He had high expectations, and I hated to disappoint him, so I always met them," he said.

We fell into silence, thinking about Amos as we marched on towards the forest ahead.

FOURTEEN

GENTLE

We finally made it to the edge of the trees. I was exhausted, but not so exhausted that I was going to ignore the beauty of what was before me. The trees were tall and had pure white trunks. They were smooth and didn't have a mark on them. That was strange enough, but when you watched the leaves, they took your breath away. Each tree was a different colour, and the leaves were all different shades of that colour. When the sun penetrated through them, they cast a kaleidoscope onto the ground. I wished it got full light here just so I could stand underneath them and watch the colours dance over my skin.

"It's so beautiful," I said as I stared up in wonder. "Have you ever seen this before?" I asked.

"No. I've heard about it, but I have never seen it with my own eyes," he practically whispered. His tone of voice made me look over at him, and his face was completely open. He was gazing, struck by the forest's beauty as I was, and I smiled at the amazement he was showing.

I had always thought he was uptight, but in the last few days I had seen emotion from him I never would have expected. He must have sensed me watching me because he turned to me and smiled. My heart skipped a beat, and

I blushed, looking away, while smoothing the top of my hair.

"Come on. Let's find somewhere to camp," he said, stepping deeper into the forest.

I followed him, crushing the coloured leaves under my feet.

It took us over an hour to find a place to make camp and gather some wood for a fire. We had managed to find a small rock overhang that created a shallow cave. Nathaniel had inspected it and deemed it safe and unoccupied, thank goodness. I rolled out my sleeping roll against the back wall, hoping for some privacy and protection.

I spent a few minutes unpacking while Nathaniel found the wood for the fire. I changed out of my travelling clothes and pulled my heavy boots off my tired feet. I hung my clothing on a tree branch outside while I sent through a small breeze to freshen them up a bit. I did not like the idea of wearing them again tomorrow but knew the chance of washing them was slim. I changed into my favourite warm nightdress and smoothed the navy-blue velvet over my body. Looking at the hem, it immediately picked up any small twigs and leaves, and I frowned while trying to brush them off.

Perhaps this wasn't the best choice.

I sighed in defeat and sat with my hairbrush and let my hair out of the tight braid I had put it in on the walk. This time, I sighed in relief as my scalp relaxed from being pulled so tightly all day. I used the brush to give it a massage as I ran it gently through the lengths of my hair.

It was one of my favourite things to do when stressed, as it always released unknown tension in me. I let it lull me as I thought about what was ahead of me. If I was honest, it was only now truly sinking in that I could be in some real trouble here. I knew this was going to be a perilous journey, but I figured we would get in and out in a day or two. Now I wasn't so sure. When I had studied the map earlier with Nathaniel, we seemed an awfully long way from the Gleaming Grove. I bit my lip and tugged hard on my hair, catching a snag.

I stopped brushing for a moment and gazed out into the twilight of the Others Land. In the quiet, while I was alone, I let the thought I had been pushing down surface. What if they had beat us to it? What if Dread already had the artefacts and was back on his way to power while we were wasting time. I knew all my family had sent out their own scouts and mages to try and find where Bilvog and his cult were hiding, but we had uncovered nothing. It made me more than uneasy about the small amount of information we knew and how we were assuming they didn't already have our items. I thought about what it had been like with Dread before.

Growing up he had been a normal boy. He was adopted after Gloom was born but he was aged in the middle between Enduring and Ashes. I had never found out where he came from and who his parents were, but it didn't matter. He was a kind brother and slipped into our family easily. I had tried time and time again to pinpoint what had gone wrong and I never could. I had asked the others once, but they didn't want to talk about him, and I had dropped it.

I shuddered, thinking about the havoc he could cause on our lives and the people of our realms. Not to mention the human world. My thoughts were broken by Nathaniel appearing at the entrance to the cave and dropping an armful of wood. I sat up and tried to brush off my nightgown, even though it was useless. He bent over and started to build a teepee with the smaller sticks.

"Can I help with anything?" I asked, walking up and crouching next to him. Absently I noticed he smelled like leather and feathers.

"No, my lady. I'm fine," he said while concentrating on what he was doing.

"Please call me Gentle. There is no need for formality out here."

"Okay then, call me Nate. I always thought Nathaniel was a bit of a mouthful."

I smiled at him. "Okay...Nate." I stood as I rolled the word around in my mouth. I all of a sudden wanted to hear him say my name.

I went to my pack, got out some tea leaves, and filled up a small pot with some water from my canteen. By the time I had walked back to the fire, it had started to really catch. I set the water beside it and sat on a rock close to the fire.

"So, when were you here last?" I asked him as he settled himself.

"Oh, a long time ago, when I was younger."

I waited for him to elaborate, and when he didn't, I pushed a little more, "What did you come here for? Was it for a mission?"

"Not really. I spent some time here when I was little. That's all."

I got the sense he wasn't going to say any more on the matter, and I was beginning to get too weary to try and push for more. We sat in silence for a bit while the tea brewed. Nate went and got some rations, and we ate, chatting about nothing in particular while listening to the creatures around us. I could hear birds in the trees, and every now and then, I caught a glimpse of one. They were small and blended in perfectly into the colourful leaves. I did notice, however, that instead of having clawed feet, they had hands with sharp claws. Nate was right. It seemed everything in here could be dangerous.

Before packing up for the night, Nate asked, "So Gentle. I realise I don't really know a lot about you. What do you like to do when you have free time? Do you have any hobbies?"

I was so surprised I couldn't speak for a moment. Hardly anyone asked what I did for fun. "Hobbies? Well, I suppose I enjoy fashion designing," I said. I didn't know why, but I was embarrassed to tell him that. It was something I never really talked about and I felt shy telling him. "Do you have a hobby?" I asked, trying to move the attention away from me.

He stretched out his legs in front of the fire. "I have always enjoyed gardening. I don't get a lot of time these days, but I love to visit the gardens around Aeris Isle. One day, I would like to have my own," he said with a smile and a shrug.

"Huh, I didn't know that. I'm sure we can find you some room around the castle when we get back," I said, smiling, surprised to learn he had such a...calming hobby.

"Thank you, I would like that," he said, smiling back.

Exhaustion washed over me, and I stifled a yawn as we packed up our items and got ready for bed.

"You go on in, and I'll take the first watch if you like," he said.

"Thank you. I think I need some sleep. Don't forget to wake me," I said, wanting to contribute wherever I could, even though the thought of waking in only a few short hours sounded terrible to me.

"Don't worry, I will. Goodnight...Gentle."

Hearing him say my name I smiled softly as a warmth spread through my stomach. "Goodnight." I walked into the cave and lay down, wondering how I would get to sleep when it wasn't dark. I didn't need to worry. I was asleep within minutes.

FIFTEEN
NATHANIEL

I kept a vigil through the night and didn't wake Gentle once. I could hear her even and heavy breathing and made the decision she needed the sleep more than I did. As an Alanti, I could go a few days without proper sleep before it affected me. Even though she didn't say anything, I knew the walk today had tired her.

Growing up, I had always heard the Evers were above us and God-like. Now I found them to be like everyone else. Except they had powers and ruled over their realms. Apart from that, they ate, slept, and lived the same as us. Of course, there could be something I didn't know, and for that reason, I never said it to anyone else.

While she was sleeping, I took the time to run through some stretches and exercises. It helped to calm me and keep me alert. While gathering wood, I had seen no sign of larger, predatory creatures, but it didn't mean they weren't out there. I kept a sharp eye on the trees around us and often walked around the camp to make sure we were safe and alone.

Eventually, I pulled out the map again and traced the path we needed to take. My eyes settled on the Obsidian Throne, and I pursed my lips. That was the last place I wanted to go. I hadn't lied to Gentle. I hadn't been *here* before, but I had been *there*. I could tell she was probing for answers earlier, but I was quite happy to keep my last visit to the Others Realm to myself.

Not long before what would have been dawn in our time, Gentle stirred. I put the pot I had prepared earlier on the coals of the fire so we could have some tea before we left. I was keen to get on the road again, knowing it would be another long walk. It looked like on the map, there was a bog right in the middle of the forest, and unless we wanted to add days to our journey, we would have to go through it. I wanted to give us lots of time to pass through it, knowing bogs were always a bit tricky to navigate.

Gentle sat up and stretched, and I avoided looking at the way the velvet of her nightgown clung to her curves.

"Good morning," I said as I stood again. "I'm going to go for a walk now you are awake. Give you some privacy."

I started to walk off into the trees when she said, "Wait a minute. You didn't wake me."

"No, my...Gentle. I thought it best you get a good night's sleep. You were exhausted."

"Even so, I am here on this journey with you and the deal was I would take half the night's watch. What about you? You didn't get any sleep?" She had her hands on her hips and I held back a smile.

"I will be fine. As an Alanti we are trained to go a few nights without sleep. Don't worry about me."

"I would still like to take my watch all the same. We need to look out for each other while we are here. Please wake me when we rest tonight."

Her face was set in stone, and I could see she meant every word. I was surprised she would push so hard, thinking she would be glad to have a longer sleep, but I was quietly impressed and decided I would do as she said and wake her when we rested next. I nodded and continued on my walk, giving her some privacy.

When I was far enough away, I found a break in the trees, and I opened my wings fully. I closed my eyes as the muscles in my back stretched and woke up and it was amazing. Sitting with them closed all the time was not good for my back, and I couldn't wait till I had some room to go for a fly. There was a tension in my back I couldn't fully shake till I had beat my wings against the wind.

After what I judged was enough time, I went back to the camp to see her dressed in the clothes she had worn the day before and her long golden hair was cascading down her back in waves. Even though it was always styled perfectly, there were always little bits floating in the breeze that surrounded her permanently. Looking into the cave, her bed roll was rolled and attached to her bag, even if it was a tiny bit crooked.

"So do you think we will get out of here today?" she asked.

"I'm not sure. There looks to be a large bog in the centre of the forest we will have to cross so we will see where we are after that. From there, it looks like a fairly straight run. It's a shame Belladonna couldn't be more specific in her potion-making," I said.

"Yes, I also thought that. It was probably her way of getting one up on me. Even though I am friendly with my hag, I know they don't always appreciate that we Evers are in power. I have heard it said more than once, they think they should be in power."

"I have heard that too. Surely, they would never revolt?"

"I don't think so," she said thoughtfully, though she didn't seem convinced. "Between us, I hope they don't. I'm not sure we would win." She had a frown on her face, and my eyebrows rose, surprised she would say that to me.

"Right, well, time to go. I'll put this fire out, and we will be on our way." I stood and used the leftover tea to put out the fire. Steam rose up through the treetops and I again marvelled at the beauty of this place.

By the time it was out, Gentle had rebraided her hair, and we were ready.

By the end of the day, I could begin to smell the bog. A sour, wet, earthy smell pushed its way through the smell of leaves.

"We must be getting close to the bog. Do you want to keep going? We could camp here and then continue on in the morning," I asked.

"I don't mind. I'm not going to lie; I could use a break, but I am happy to keep going if you want to make it there before we rest."

I studied our surroundings. "We should camp here under the cover of trees. I think it will be slightly safer than being out in the open." I lowered my pack and surveyed the area, searching for the best place to set up. Unfortunately, there were no caves or overhangs here, so we would be amongst the trees and their ghostly forms. Unease slipped through me. I didn't like the idea of being out in the open.

"Did you notice anything while we were walking today?" I asked, trying to sound casual and not worried.

Gentle stopped unpacking her bag, confusion on her face. "No. Should I have?"

I shook my head. "On the walk today, I noticed some small creatures following us. It's probably nothing, but just to be safe, I would like to stick together."

"Okay. Should we be worried?" she asked, looking around her.

"I'm not sure, but I have found it's better to be more cautious here. Let's go and get some wood and get the camp ready."

We gathered all the things we needed for a night under the trees and ate some food while we chatted about the walk. It was a comfortable and easy conversation, and it passed the time quickly. Eventually, we began to yawn, and we cleaned up, ready to go to bed. We decided to leave most of the stuff packed as we were planning on leaving early in the morning. Plus, being out here in the open would make it easier for us to make a quick getaway if things went wrong.

"I'll take the first watch if you like," Gentle offered, seating herself next to the fire.

I nodded, knowing the look on her face meant she wouldn't take no for an answer.

"Be sure to wake me in a few hours. Keep your eyes open, and don't hesitate to wake me if you need me."

"I will, don't worry. Go and get some rest," she said as she unbraided her hair and dug around in her pack, pulling out a brush.

"Okay, goodnight then, Gentle." I lay on the ground, pulling my blanket up and adjusting my wings to the most comfortable position. I closed my eyes, and after a while, my body relaxed as Gentle hummed a tune, and I drifted off to sleep.

SIXTEEN
GENTLE

"Nate, wake up," I said as I shook him. Out in the trees, I could see multiple sets of red eyes staring at us, and a humming sound was beginning to fill the forest. Even though it never got dark here, they were too far away, and I couldn't see what they were, only that they were small but fast. However, size wouldn't matter with the amount of them, and I knew we could be in trouble here.

Nate's eyes snapped open, and without hesitation, he leapt to his feet and surveyed the situation. "How long have they been there?" he asked.

"I only just noticed them. Not long." My heart was pounding in my chest, and I whirled around in a circle, trying to take in as much as I could. I put my hand to my heart and made an effort to stand still despite my body telling me to run.

"Alright, get behind me."

I did as he asked, and he bent over and got a small log of wood from the fire and tried to illuminate them a bit more. With the light, it was easier to see them.

"Pixies," Nate said.

"Damn," I muttered under my breath. I knew pixies could be a lot of trouble. They were not the cute little creatures some people thought them to be. They were territorial and liked to hunt in packs. Although they were small, they were vicious and didn't give up easily.

"I need you to use your wind power to try and keep them at bay. Go now and grab your knife and be ready to use it if one slips in," Nate told me as he counted up the pixies. "By my count, there are about twenty of them. Not overpowering but enough to be a nuisance. Hopefully, there aren't anymore."

"We should survive twenty," I said as I wiped my sweaty hands on my pants, glad I hadn't changed into my night dress yet. I picked up the small dagger I had brought with me, and Nate collected his sword and puffed out his wings slightly. He crouched in a battle stance, and I summoned my power.

The energy sizzled through my veins, and my hair lifted off my back a little. My heart no longer beat in fear but in exhilaration. There was nothing better than to release your power and see what it could do. It had been a while since I had had a chance to do that. Not since the battle with Bilvog had I had a chance to flex my wind power, and like a bolt of lightning, I realised, I enjoyed it. I loved being useful and having a different power over people. Mostly, I relied on my looks to get me by. Not something I was particularly proud of, but it had never failed, and it was easy. As my body came to life, a different sort of confidence rose in me. I didn't have time to analyse it, though. I could see the pixies starting to emerge from behind the trees.

Their mouths were open, showing long, thin teeth bared in a grimace. Their hair was matted, and they were mostly naked, with a few scraps of fabric tied around their small bodies. They peered out of slitted eyes, and their fingers ended in long, dirty nails. Each pixie was a different colour ranging from dark green, brown and deep blue that helped them blend in better to the forest floor. They flew fast with their see-through wings, and the noise they made was an eerie humming sound.

I threw my hands out and sent my power to whip around us, putting the two of us in the centre of a tornado-like gale. Coloured leaves picked up and were thrashed in the wind as they were ripped off the trees nearby. It was difficult to see through, but it seemed to have worked and the pixies had stopped their advance. Over the howl of the wind, I could hear screeching as the pixies screamed their rage at us.

"How long can you keep that up?" Nate shouted over the different noises.

"For a while. Hopefully, they will get sick of trying and will leave," I replied, keeping my focus on what I was doing.

He nodded and looked around at our feet. Out of my tornado, our packs were laying on the ground near the fire. We looked at each other, understanding what we had done.

I continued pushing my power out, but now I was more focused on what the pixies were doing. It didn't take them long to realise what we had a moment ago. The pixies noticed, packed up neatly were our packs with all our supplies in them. One pointed, and the rest darted down, and together, they lifted them from the ground.

Before Nate could say anything, I dropped my tornado and darted forward, trying to reach them.

"Gentle, no!" I heard Nate yell behind me, but I kept on going. I was not about to let them take our food and clothing and leave us with nothing. I sent out a few puffs of air to try and knock them over, but their grip was like steel around the bags.

Out of the corner of my eye, I saw movement, and I had enough time to shield my face with my hands before stinging bites and scratches tore at my skin. It was like the pixie was going to chew and rip right through my arm to reach my face. I screamed and thrashed about, trying to dislodge it, but nothing worked. My hair was whipping about, the golden strands sticking to my bloodied arm. Sharp pain speared through my head as the pixies got tangled in the long strands, and before long, it stopped attacking my arm and was trying to free itself from my hair.

I took the chance while it was distracted, and I reached out and grabbed its small muscular body and threw it away, pulling out a chunk of my hair with it. I looked down, chest heaving and checked my arms. They were torn up and bleeding, and I wondered what kind of infection I would get from their dirty nails and teeth.

Before it could come back, I grabbed my knife, but Nate had already got it. Littering the ground around us were branches and leaves and small broken bodies of the vicious creatures. Some seemed like they had been thrown back by my wind, and others Nate had got hold of. Looking around, a small pang speared my heart at the destruction we had wrought, but my attention was caught by the stinging of my arms.

"Our packs?" I asked Nate now my breathing had slowed, and I could talk.

"Gone," he said grimly. Looking up into the bare branches of the trees surrounding us. I could see two clusters of pixies flying away, our packs hanging from them. I lowered my head as tears filled my eyes and my stomach dropped.

I bent over and put my hands on my knees as my hair fell forward and hid the tears that ran freely down my face. My air power slipped away from me, and my hair flew around my head while I thought over what this meant for the rest of our journey. Nausea churned in my gut as I frantically pawed the pockets of my clothes. The potion. Where was the potion we needed to get back? I always kept it in my pocket. The familiar lump in my pocket was gone. I searched through them again.

"Please, please, please," I muttered when I remembered I had sat it inside my pack when we made camp.

The pack the pixies had just whisked away. My stomach sank again, and I groaned out loud as my brain tried to work out what that meant. How would we get home? My people needed me, and now there was a possibility we could be stuck here.

Nate was walking around the campsite, looking at the ground, his wings twitching. His face was carefully controlled, and he was pale. "Everything. They got everything."

My heart felt like it stopped in my chest, "The map? Do you have the map?"

He looked at me, and before he spoke, I knew the answer. "No. It was in my pack." He kicked a large branch across the campsite, his teeth gritted, and hands fisted. I flinched, not expecting to see him this angry. In all the time I had known him, he was always in control.

His face was red and he ran his hands roughly through his blond hair. He took a few deep breaths, but they didn't seem to help much.

"I can't believe I let them get away! What are we going to do now? This was going to be hard enough, but now..." He took a deep breath, and I stayed quiet while he got control of himself.

I tried to calm my body as I gathered the courage to tell him about the potion. "They got the potion too. I had it in my pack while I changed last night."

The mask of control slipped a little, and I saw real worry reflected in his eyes. I stopped breathing as I waited for him to tell me it would all be okay, but he didn't. He turned, looking towards where the pixies went and rolled up his bedroll that had been on the ground. I stood and wiped my eyes, my mind buzzing at the predicament we were now in and what we were going to do about it.

After the bedroll had been tied tightly, he slung it over his shoulder. "Okay, so. Let's think about our options. We can continue on with no food, clothes, map or potion," he said, ticking the list off his fingers. "We can go to King Thallan and beg for help, probably end up owing him a favour." I screwed up my face, hating the idea of owing another favour to one of the Others. It was bad enough dealing with Bella. "Or we can go and try and find our things, hoping the map and the potion have fallen out." He sighed, knowing none of them were great options.

"Are the pixies heading in the same direction we have to go?" I asked.

"Yes. They are going North. Which is the direction we had to go to get to the Grove."

"Then maybe we follow them for a while and see if we can get our things back and see where that leaves us. Maybe we will have a bit of luck for once." I knew it was a long shot, but we had to do something, and guilt was gnawing at me that I had left an item so important in my pack.

Nate nodded and I could see his eyes clear and become more focused, like his old self. "Okay then. Let's get going," he said, adjusting the sword at his hip.

He started walking, and I followed after him, braiding my hair and wishing for my hairbrush.

SEVENTEEN

GENTLE

After hours of rushing through the forest, I was exhausted. We had been chasing the pixies all day and so far had found one of my shoes, a fork, and a ribbon that had fallen out of my pack. We emerged from the trees and stared out over the bog we had been smelling for the last few hours.

About an hour ago I had resorted to tying a scrap of fabric over my nose to try and keep out the stench, but it hadn't helped much. My mood had plummeted, and at this point, I wanted to go home. I didn't want to walk all day and chase pixies. I wanted to be in my ballroom wearing a beautiful dress, dancing the night away. Clean. I wanted to be clean. Sticks and leaves filled my hair, but I had long given up picking them out because more would get lodged in there a minute later.

I stood at the edge of the bog, and my mouth hung open. Mud. Everywhere. Around the little islands of mud was murky water that, in places, bubbled and rippled. I tried not to think about what sort of creature would be under that gross water. Dotted all around were little mounds with trees that had no leaves, branches pointing to the sky like hands reaching out for help.

"Well, here we are," Nate said.

"We don't actually have to go through this, do we?" I asked, knowing the answer but hoping for a different one.

"Yes. I am afraid we do," he said, looking at me with a small smile.

For once, I wanted to wipe that smile off his face. "Are we sure the pixies came this way? I can't see them."

He bent over to my level and stretched his arm out, pointing at a tree in the distance. As he got closer, I could smell leather, and my body hummed. "See. Over there on that mound. There is another shoe. I believe it is the mate of the other one we found," he said, his breath fanning my cheek. Together, we turned our heads, and we were face to face, nothing separating us except for a few inches of space. I couldn't move, and neither did he. Standing on the edge of a bog, chasing pixies who had stolen our things, all I could do was look into his eyes.

Nate came to his senses first and he tore his gaze away and straightened. Just like that, the scents and sounds of the bog came rushing back in, and I pulled the mask back over my nose as it wrinkled. I tried to calm my racing heart and remember why we were here. I couldn't be making puppy dog eyes at my bodyguard. We were here on an important mission, and I couldn't afford to get distracted.

I cleared my throat and asked, "What are those mounds all over the place?"

"Ballybog mounds." At my confused look, he continued, "ballybogs are large frogs that are only a little more intelligent. Some of them can communicate with us, but they are hard to understand at the best of times." He looked around the bog, "They can be a bit territorial, so we will have to try and avoid them, but it might be tricky. Come on, let's start by collecting your other shoe," he said, smiling again and I found myself smiling back under the mask.

He held out his hand and helped me take my first few steps out into the bog. That was all the talking we did for a while as it took all our concentration not to fall into the sticky, stinking mud. We hopped from tufts of grass to fallen tree branches while dodging the many small frogs and insects who called this place home.

We picked our way over and made it to the island and picked up my other shoe. We stood and surveyed the area, looking for another clue as to where the pixies went, when I saw something sitting on one of the mounds.

"There!" I pointed excitedly. "Are they our packs?"

A grin spread across Nate's face, and my brain short-circuited. In all the years he had been working for me, this was the first grin I had ever seen, and it was devastating. He looked at me, and his happiness was infectious. I jumped for joy, but on the slippery mud, I lost my balance.

My stomach dropped as I landed face-first into the mud. My mind went blank as it realised I was now covered in mud and whatever other disgusting things were in the water. I wiped my eyes and flung the mud off my hands. I was about to scream my frustration when, above me, I heard a chuckle. I glared up at Nate, about to tell him off for laughing at me, when his chuckle turned into a full-on laugh.

I knelt there in the muck, with it covering my whole body, smelling like crap, and he was laughing at me. My face reddened in anger and embarrassment, and still, he continued laughing. Even bending over and wiping tears from his face. After what felt like forever, he got himself under control and held out a hand to help me up. I reached out and used it to pull myself from the sticky mud, and I managed to stand.

He was still laughing and when I glanced at myself, a small chuckle escaped my lips as well. Of course, this would happen to me. I tried to wipe off as much of the mud as I could while holding in my laughter. I must have been growing delirious because there was nothing funny about this situation.

Nate managed to get himself under control and stopped laughing. "I'm sorry, but that was the funniest thing I have seen in ages. Is there anything I can do to help?" he asked, holding in his laughter.

"Well, do you have a bath in that bed roll?" I asked, putting my hand on my hip, a ghost of a smile showing through.

"No, I don't, but how about we go and get our packs and try and find a river to clean you off in."

I nodded, and we made our way over to where our packs were laying. I groaned as I took in my muddy clothes, but there was nothing I could do about it. There was no way I was putting a hand into the bog water, let alone washing myself off in it, so I put up with the mud that was slowly drying to my clothes.

As we made it over to the island with our packs, I could see they were open, and it looked like they had been gone through. My brow creased. What had they taken? Nate threw out his arm, and I stopped as he surveyed the area. He took a step back and went to say something when a creature hopped out from behind one of the mounds.

It was as tall as a five-year-old child and was green, slimy, and covered in mud. It had two large eyes sitting on the top of its head and a large rubbery mouth that spread across the width of its face. On top of its rubbery bald head sat a crown that had been woven from reeds and stuck together with mud. Attached to it were jewellery and leaves like someone had liked the items and pushed them into the mud, holding the crown together.

"Who you?" it croaked at us.

It seemed the ballybogs had found us.

EIGHTEEN

NATHANIEL

We stood in silence for a moment wondering what to say as more of the ballybogs, all looking the same, hopped out, surrounding us, some of them carrying spears. I tensed, wondering how I was going to keep Gentle safe with all these spears pointing at us. I knew ballybogs were generally non-violent, but I didn't want to take any chances. I put my hand on my sword.

"Who you?" it said again, stepping closer to us.

"We are travellers, and it seems you have found our packs there," I said, pointing to where they were laid out. "We will just take them and be on our way." I tried to reach out for the packs but one of the ballybogs flung out its spear, blocking my way.

"These yours?" the crowned ballybog asked. "Payment."

"You want us to pay you for our packs?" Gentle asked. His watery eyes swung to her, and I saw him take in the mud covering her. Gentle looked embarrassed under the drying mud, but she stood up a little straighter.

"Yes," he croaked.

"Well, what do you want?" she asked. He looked confused for a moment, and a few of the others circled him as they discussed what they wanted in deep, croaky noises. I looked on as I tried to edge my way closer to the packs. I could see some of our clothes and food had been flung out and would now be ruined, but I couldn't see the map and potion anywhere. The creatures separated, and the 'king' stepped forward.

"We want feather," he said, pointing at my wings, "and hair." He pointed to Gentle's braid. She reached up and pulled the braid over her shoulder, wariness in her eyes.

Gentle and I looked at each other and shrugged, realising we really had no choice. There were over thirty ballybogs scattered around watching us. Too many to fight and there would be no running away in this place. A feather and some hair would be a small price to pay.

"All right. But we get the packs," I confirmed, but the king shook his head.

"One thing."

Gentle's shoulders drooped. He was only going to let us take one thing. I glanced over at all the stuff that was bursting out of our packs. I could see Gentle was disappointed as she saw her dresses and shoes scattered about. I scanned the stuff spilling out and still couldn't see the potion and the map. Those were the things we really needed.

I wondered if there was a way to get one of those dresses for her, even if they were covered in mud. I knew she would be uncomfortable having to wear her mud-encrusted clothes for the rest of the trip. I scoured my memory for a stream around here, but I couldn't remember if there was one nearby.

While I had been thinking, Gentle had undone the tie on her braid, and her golden hair still shone out through the dirt and twigs that were tangled in it. She pulled out three hairs and held them up to the light, watching them glint in the setting sun. She sighed quietly and held them out to the closest ballybog. He took them and passed them to the king. He held the hair up to the light and admired the shining strands before winding and wrapping them in his crown.

"At this rate, I will be bald by the time we get back," she said under her breath. I smiled a little.

It was my turn now. I bent my arm back, grasped one of the light blue feathers in my wing, and tugged slightly. Reluctantly, I held it out to the ballybog, and the king stuck it in his crown in the front. It looked ridiculous, but he preened and appeared quite happy with himself.

"Right, now, our turn," I said, moving towards the bags before they could stop me. A few of them croaked in surprise, but they didn't stand in my way. I went right to Gentle's bag and began pulling things out, looking for the potion. Makeup and serums spilt out everywhere, and I wondered how she fit all this stuff in when I saw it. The golden swirling potion. I closed my eyes in relief and wrapped my fingers around the bottle. I searched through my bag, full of food and essentials needed for survival but there was no map.

"What looking for?" the king croaked in my ear. Closer than I thought. He must have snuck up on me while I was distracted. A strong smell of rotting fish wafted over me and I held in my gag. "A map. We had a map," I said, as I turned my face away.

"No map. Only that," he said, pointing with a long, rubbery finger to the potion I had grasped in my hand. "One thing."

"We need the map. We can't go on without it. Please. I'll give you more hair," Gentle pleaded. Worry was clear in her eyes.

"No find map. Where you go?" he asked, and I was starting to get sick of his halting words and putrid breath.

Gentle paused for a second, and before I could tell her to stop, she blurted, "The Gleaming Grove. We need to get there as soon as we can."

I sighed inside, wondering how long it would take the rest of the Others Realm to know where we were going, now we had told the ballybogs. The ballybogs crowded around each other again and croaked. I made my way back to Gentle's side. "Here I have the potion. What do you think they are talking about?" I asked, standing closer than I should.

A small smile graced her lips. "I don't know. The best way to cook mosquitoes?"

Surprised by her answer, a small chuckle escaped. At that moment, she was the old Gentle. The Gentle before Bilvog's betrayal. I had always admired how carefree and kind she was to everyone she met. This little glimmer of her old self filled me with hope that one day, she could get back there. The air was charged. She looked at me in a way I had dreamed about. I opened my mouth to tell her how much I missed her old self when the ballybog turned around.

"We take you," said the king.

My brow furrowed. "You are going to take us where?" I asked.

"Gleaming Grove. We take you."

"Oh, I don't know about that," I said. "If you don't have the map, we will find our way," I said, backing up slightly. I was sure I could find our way there anyway. We didn't need a troupe of ballybogs marching us through the realm. The plan was to stay inconspicuous.

"I insist," the king said, and the others crept in closer, spears in full view. It seemed like they would not be taking no for an answer.

"Thank you so much for your assistance, Your Majesty," Gentle said with a gleam in her eye as she bowed her head.

She shrugged at me and tucked her potion into a pocket in her pants. The ballybogs closed ranks, and we all moved with the king in front. I rested my hand on my sword. I was not pleased about this. The creatures from this realm rarely did anything for nothing, and I wasn't convinced they were taking us where we wanted to go. Unfortunately, I didn't have a way to get out of here without offending them, and they could be nasty when they wanted to be. The tips of their spears were not only for show. They were very, very sharp.

We walked through the wet, sticky bog for hours. How much longer could it go on? I was starting to have serious doubts about where they were taking us. They seemed tireless, and although they weren't the brightest creatures, they were still alert and watching our every move. My whole body was tense and weighing on me was the safety of Gentle and the future of Aeris Isle. I couldn't let them down.

"So, who is King Thallan? You mentioned him when we were deciding our options earlier," Gentle asked, shocking me out of my spiral.

"Ah, King Thallan is the ruler of this section of the realm," I said.

"And how do you know him?"

I flashed back to my parents, standing in his castle while the people of his court poked and prodded and pulled. I shut that memory out and pushed it deep where it belonged.

"I don't really. My parents did." I let slip while I was burying the past. I realised my mistake when Gentle's eyes sharpened.

"Your parents? They were from here?" she asked, curiosity getting the better of her.

My brain gave the automatic response whenever someone asked about my past and I gave the shortest answer possible, so I didn't have to continue talking about it, "Yes."

I didn't want to talk about my past, because if I did, that would lead to what happened to my parents, where I was from, and how I ended up in Aeris Isle, and I did not want to have that conversation walking through a bog where we were probably being led around in circles surrounded by stinking ballybogs. That was a conversation I never wanted to have.

After a pause, Gentle dropped the subject, but I could still see the wheels turning in her head about my past.

"Wait, isn't that the same tree as before?" she asked, her brow furrowed.

She was right. I knew these ballybogs were tricking us. I pulled out my sword, its blade flashing in the permanent sunset.

"Where are you taking us!" I demanded. They didn't answer, and in the silence, I heard the unmistakable sound of footfalls. I spun around, looking for where they were coming from, when out of the bog walked eight tall, fierce-looking men.

King Thallan had found us.

NINETEEN
NATHANIEL

I moved to stand in front of Gentle as I held out my sword to the men. Out of the corner of my eye, I saw the ballybogs dig and burrow into the mud, leaving us alone with the men. If I wasn't so tense, I would have thought it was funny, but I was not in the mood for laughing now.

"And who might you be?" the man in front asked. His black uniform didn't have a speck of mud on it even though they had followed us in here. His brown eyes were intense as they pinned mine over his long, sharp nose. His mouth was pressed into a hard line, and his brown hair was cut close to his head in a no-nonsense way.

"My name is Nathaniel," I told him carefully, not wanting to give him more information than needed. I knew they weren't going to let us go easily, and I wanted to make it a bit harder for them.

"And what are you doing here?" The next man took a step towards us. His long red hair tied tightly at the bottom of his head, his golden eyes flashing.

"We are here to retrieve something, and then we will be on our way. We don't want any trouble," I told them, but their attention was now on Gentle.

She had taken a step around me and although her shoulders were back and chin up, a cool wind that wasn't here before had begun to swirl around us.

"And who are you?" the first man asked her.

"I am Namara, the Air Ever of Aeris Isle," she said in a clear and powerful voice. My eyebrows rose at how confident she sounded when I knew she was frightened.

"An Ever," he said as he looked her up and down, the corner of his mouth twitching. "Aren't you meant to be the rulers of your realms? You look more like a swamp witch to me," he said, laughter in his voice. My face reddened and my hands gripped involuntarily on the hilt of my sword as I saw Gentle deflate. The others were much too disciplined to laugh, but I saw a few smiles, and all I wanted to do was wipe them off their faces. My knuckles were starting to ache with the strength of my grip.

A small, soft hand rested on mine, as Gentle held my sword arm still. I swallowed and took control of my anger as she stepped forward.

"Yes, well. We have had a rather eventful few days, but if you let us pass, we will be out of here with no trouble caused. I am on a mission to save my kingdom and have no reason to cause offence to King Thallan. We only wish to pass through and be on our way."

I was watching the men, and my heart sank when I saw their eyes remain hard and unmoved by her words. There was no way they were going to let us pass.

"Now, you have come into his realm uninvited and without permission. You have been here for a few days, and not told him, and now King Thallan is, understandably, suspicious. He has requested you come with us to meet with him and discuss this misstep before it becomes an insult," the leader said, his voice soft and menacing. The men parted and waited for us to follow.

Gentle pasted a smile on her face. A smile I had seen many times at many parties. It was the one she used when dancing with someone she didn't like or when sitting through one of the many boring conversations she had to endure. I was proud that smile had never been turned on me.

She wiped her muddy hands on her muddy clothes and tried to smooth out the hair she had left unbraided. She looked at me, and I could see the apprehension on her face, so I gave her a small smile back in reassurance. I sheathed my sword but kept my hand on the hilt.

"Right. Then let's go and meet King Thallan and get this sorted out. I have heard so much about him," she said brightly as she stepped into the gap the men had made. I followed quickly behind her and kept my eyes on them as they surrounded her. They led us through the bog and into the kingdom of the person I feared most in any world.

We followed them for a few hours out of the bog and through a meadow that was filled with flowers of every colour, shape, and size. Their scent was strong and intoxicating, making you want to run and laugh forever, but we kept a clear head. Bee-like creatures fluttered about, the size of dinner plates, and I could see herds of long-legged creatures off in the distance. Gentle gazed around in wonder, but I could still see some worry etched on her face.

The guards that led us never faulted in their job. They kept their attention on where they were going, showing no emotion or interest in either of us, and I didn't know if it was a good thing or a bad thing. My muscles were beginning to ache from being tensed for so long, and my wings were twitching, wanting to launch me into the air. Each step brought us closer to the Obsidian Throne and King Thallan, and I prayed he wouldn't recognise me. It had been over two hundred years since he had seen me, but I knew he would not have forgotten my family.

During the walk, I tried to stay out of my own feelings about seeing the castle again. I had pushed it down and buried it long ago, and there was no way I wanted it brought back up now when I was to be protecting Gentle.

How had this gone so wrong! In the space of three days we had been attacked by pixies, had our things stolen, been tricked by ballybogs of all things, and now we're being marched to the one place I wanted to avoid. I was glad Amos wasn't here to see me fail like this. He would be embarrassed by me, and I felt a pang in my heart at the thought.

As we crested the top of the small hill the group stopped, and I saw in the distance the thing I dreaded.

"Wow," breathed Gentle.

Wow indeed. In front of us loomed the Black Keep. My jaw tightened, looking at it. It was unbelievably more impressive and imposing than I remembered. The castle was surrounded by a huge black brick wall that kept most things out and most things in. The huge gates stood open today, and a steady stream of people walked in and out, but there was no laughter or springs in their steps. They kept their eyes on the ground and shoulders hunched as they walked between the many serious guards scattered inside the walled enclosure.

My eyes travelled up to the black stone castle to the main element that drew my eyes. The castle was held up and off the ground by two huge stone giants. They were carved out of a deep red rock with slashes of black veins travelling through them. The giants were crouched and carved to look like they were struggling to hold the weight of the massive black stone castle they held aloft. Their faces twisted in pain like they knew there would be no relief from the weight bearing down on them. Even though they were made of stone, I felt sorry for them and pitied them for their crushing job.

The castle was tall and slender, with many spires reaching towards the sky, each one tipped with the red stone of the giants, so they appeared like they were piercing the sky and making it bleed. Everything about it was supposed to plant fear and unease, and it worked. I ruffled my wings as a tremor went through my body, thinking about walking through those gates and past those giants.

There was a small crease between Gentle's brows, and I wondered what was going through her head. Every atom of my being was screaming to take her and fly away. The last thing I wanted was to have her walk in there and King Thallan to see her. He would want to keep her, and I knew myself well enough to know what would happen if he tried. There had been a prickling on the back of my head for the past few days, keeping me on edge.

Who was I kidding? It had been creeping up on me for years. I had deep feelings for Gentle, and they weren't the type a guard should have for who he is guarding. Unfortunately, it was making me a little bit irrational when I needed all my senses to keep us safe and get us out of here in one piece. I needed to push those feelings away and do my best to ignore them. There would be no help here where every little movement would be analysed and used against us.

The guards escorting us started to move again, and we followed, walking into the looming black castle I prayed we would come out of.

TWENTY

GENTLE

Our footsteps clipped on the smooth black stone that made up the castle floor. The hallway was wide and bare with no ornaments anywhere, just black stone and green fire flickering in the sconces dotted around the walls, providing dimmed light. The tall, angular windows had smoky glass in them, keeping out whatever sunlight was trying to peek through. I looked up and could hardly see the ceiling. It was tall and dark up there, but I could see a second and third level above us with people or creatures moving, watching us make our way through to King Thallan.

"Are we going straight to the king?" I asked our silent guards.

No one looked at me, but the leader answered, "Yes."

I stared at my mud-soaked clothing, and I could only imagine what my hair and face looked like. I wiped the front of my clothes, and little chips of mud flaked off, dirtying the shiny floor beneath us.

"Surely, he would like us to be comfortable and well-presented. We are hardly in a state to see the king looking like this," I reasoned, even though Nate still appeared relatively clean in his clothes. He did not fall in the mud like me. My cheeks heated again, thinking of how embarrassing that was.

"The king wants you to be brought right to him, so that's what we will do," he said with no room for argument. These guards were more rigid and rule-following than Nate, and I didn't want to know how they got to be that way. I found it hard to believe King Thallan was a kind man judging by the image he was putting out. Eventually, we made it to a set of huge double doors carved from wood with the same serious guards standing at attention on either side.

Our group nodded at them, and we paused in front of the door so they could open them for us. I ran a hand over my messy hair as my heart started beating faster. This was not the way I wanted to greet a king. I was filthy, and all I wanted was to brush my hair. I hated being dirty in the first place, but to meet a king and try to help convince him to let us go was going to be almost impossible, looking like this. I sighed quietly, then held my breath, waiting for the doors to open.

The group of people eating dinner turned and stared at us as we were brought in. Our guards marched us towards the head of the table, and I held my head high as I walked past a room full of beautiful, elegant creatures. I was defiant, and I decided there was no way I was going to let them look down on me. None of them had been through what I had the last few days, and I refused to be embarrassed about my appearance. That's what I told myself anyway. Inside I was cringing.

The long table was lit with mage lights and covered in platters of food. The food smelled delicious but there were some things I didn't recognise, and I decided not to look too closely at it. The people eating followed us with interest, and my skin tingled under their gaze. Nate was also ignoring them, and I could tell by his body he was tense and assessing everything that was happening and who was in the room. I walked closer to him, glad I wasn't there alone. I knew he would protect me with his life, and I surprised myself by thinking the same.

The closer we got to the head of the table, the more shame washed over me because of how I looked, and by the time we were standing in front of King Thallan, I could have melted into the floor.

"Well, well, well. Who do we have here? Are these the trespassers that have been discovered on my land?" Thallan asked, his voice booming and with no warmth at all.

The leader of the guards nodded and stepped aside to reveal us to Thallan. He smiled, and a shiver ran down my spine as I remembered what Nate had told me about being careful with what you say to the Others. His teeth were white, and his lips were full, but there was no welcome in his smile. His steel grey hair made a sharp widow's peak in the centre of his forehead, and it trailed to his mid-back. His dark purple eyes were sharp and assessing, and my mouth went dry as I stressed I was about to blow it. Should we tell him why we are really here or try to keep it a secret?.

"Why don't you tell me who you are? Perhaps then you can join us for dinner. You look like you could use a good meal," he said with a laugh. His words sounded kind, but there was no warmth behind them. It was all a front, and I instinctively knew he was dangerous.

I waited a beat to clear my head and try and work out what I wanted to say. I took a step forward and focused on Nate at my back, sending me strength. Clearing my throat, I plastered a smile on my face, hoping it was warmer than his. I bowed my head, remembering he was a king after all and looked into his hard features.

"I am Namara, the Air Ever of Aeris Isle. We are on an important mission to retrieve something to help us fight an enemy that is threatening us. I apologise we weren't able to contact you, but it is a very time-sensitive mission, and we had no time to spare. If it pleases you, we will continue and be out of your realm in a matter of days." I hoped I had given enough information so he wouldn't keep us here, but I wasn't sure. If I was honest, it had been a long time since I had had to be diplomatic. I generally left that to my council, and disappointment settled in my heart. I had let that happen.

I kept the smile on my face and tried to appear confident while I waited to hear what he said. It was silent in the room, and I held his eye contact, not wanting to be the one to look away. The time dragged on, and it was starting to get uncomfortable. I was about to break the oppressive silence when he spoke.

"You are an Ever?" he said, looking me over, and my face grew red. His eyes met mine again, and he continued, "Well, I must admit, I had always heard of your beauty...and with you standing in front of me, I can see it is all true! You see, I have an eye for beauty," he waved his hand out towards the guests gathered. "And I can see under all this...muck, you are stunning. Unfortunately, being beautiful doesn't give you permission to come onto my land uninvited. And who is this man behind you?" he said, looking at Nate.

Nate bowed his head, and I introduced him, "This is my personal guard, Nathaniel."

An excited look passed over his features so fast I almost missed it, "Ah, one of the Alanti! How lucky we are to have you! I have known a few Alanti over my time, and all were honourable, not that that helped them much," he said, directing the comment to the people eating. All the people gathered, twittered and giggled and Nate stiffened beside me. Once the crowd had quieted, Thallan stood from his chair and addressed his guests.

"Well, it seems like we have some important people in our midst. Get them chairs and let them feast. We have a big night ahead of us. Tonight, we are holding a ball, and you must come. You will have rooms to get clean and presentable, and we will throw the ball in your honour."

I smiled, but I knew it didn't reach my eyes. A ball? Tonight? I didn't think I had the energy for that but how was I to refuse? I had a feeling it would not be taken well if we said no. I held in my sigh, and I could see a knowing look in his eye. He smiled like a hunter before catching his prey.

Chairs were brought out of nowhere by beautiful women, and he smiled his cold smile as we sat in them, and plates were put in front of us. I did not trust this for a second, but what could we do? We sat as our plates were loaded with food by more beautiful women wearing essentially transparent gowns. I studied my plate and wondered if we could eat any of this. Everyone knew it was dangerous to eat food from different realms.

Thallan was watching me closely as if he had read my thoughts again. "The food is safe here. You are not human, so it won't harm you," he said, eating his own food on his plate.

I nodded politely and picked up my fork to eat. I was starving, but I only ate when I knew for certain what it was. Everyone was busy eating and chatting, so I took a moment to look around the dining room when something strange caught my eye in the large black stone room. Dotted all around were the beautiful women who served us, with blank looks on their faces. They were serving the food and wine and helping Thallan, and I wondered where the servants were and if these were them. Nate was quiet beside me, and the rest of the meal passed by without any comment directed to us.

When everyone had finished eating, we were all dismissed, and we were taken to our rooms by another beautiful but blank woman. Her red hair gleamed in the mage light as it reached to the small of her back. Her skin was tanned evenly, and her eyes were an orange colour. I tried to speak to her, but I got hardly any response. Just a muttered answer, and then she was off again.

Our rooms were in the same corridor but at opposite ends. Nate looked towards me as the woman opened his door and a zing of anxiousness went through me. I didn't like having him that far away in this castle where we weren't quite welcome. The red-haired woman led me to my room, and I almost gasped at what I saw.

It was nothing like I expected.

I thought it would be another harsh black room with no warmth or character, but it was beautiful. It was lined with white stone and had a huge bed covered in soft and colourful blankets and pillows. There was a large fireplace at one end, and the tall, pointed windows looked out to a small village behind the castle. I walked and opened one of the doors on either side of the fireplace, and there was a large tub already steaming with water. I held in my squeal of excitement while I went to the other door and opened it.

Gowns of all colours and textures practically spilt out at me, and I pulled my hands back so I didn't dirty them. I spun around to ask if they were all for me, but the lady was gone. Sitting next to the lounge on a small end table was a note with my name on it. I sat on the lounge and opened the letter squinting at the cursive lettering.

Namara,

Tonight, there will be a ball at 10pm. Rosalind will come and retrieve you and bring you to me. Please make your-self comfortable and presentable with the items in the wardrobe. I am sure they will be to your liking.

Looking forward to seeing you in all your beauty,

King Thallan

I frowned at the letter and let out the sigh I had been holding. What could I expect from tonight? Would I be safe? I shook my head and walked to the door, making sure it was locked. When I had double-checked it, I made my way to the bath, stripping off my clothes as I went.

I promised myself I would have a bath, and after that, I would think about all the things that could go wrong. But for now, I would allow myself the luxury of soaking in the hot tub.

I had been in the bath for longer than I intended, and still, it was hard to drag myself out. The first few minutes had been bliss, even if I was disgusted at the colour of the water. Luckily, the water was enchanted and cleaned itself regularly, so I didn't have to look at the dirt, mud and twigs that surrounded me. I washed my hair three times and still cringed at the tangles that were firmly embedded.

A small pang of sadness hit me when I thought about the brush I had lost in my pack. My mother had given me that brush, and although there was nothing special about it, it held many fond memories of her brushing my hair, just the two of us. I dragged myself out of the bath and wrapped myself in a beautifully soft, plush, mint green robe that was hanging on the back of the door.

Walking to the wardrobe, I was overwhelmed with what I should wear. Gowns of every colour, texture and design were screaming out at me to try on. I picked through, crossing out the ones that weren't my colour or weren't quite right. In the end, I chose a silver strapless gown with a beaded bodice and a full tulle skirt. I held it up to the mirror, and the beading cast light all around the room. I smiled my first true smile in ages and stepped out of the robe and into the dress.

Once it was on, I did a few spins and swishes and knew I had chosen right. My body relaxed for the first time in days. I was clean and dressed in a beautiful gown. My happiness popped, and I frowned when I saw my hair. It looked like a bird's nest and though it gleamed after washing it multiple times, it was no longer soft. I found a brush and tried teasing the knots out from the bottom, but it was slow progress.

Before the knots made me swear, I heard a knocking at the door. I gave up brushing my hair and went to the door unlocking and opening it. Nate was on the other side, and he looked...good. He was dressed in similar clothes as the guards, but instead of black, it was a deep burgundy colour. The suit had been altered to accommodate his wings, which were now clean and gleaming in the light. They looked soft, and I wanted to feel them under my fingers. I pulled my eyes to his face and noticed his hair was still wet. He must have come right here after showering. His blue eyes were bright, and he was clean-shaven.

"I wanted to check on you. Make sure you are alright," he said, looking over my shoulder and into the room, no doubt looking for threats. With a rustle of my skirts, I stepped aside and motioned him in, closing the door behind us. It felt strange having him in my room. Forbidden almost. We had spent most of the last three days alone together, and he had been in my room at Aeris Isle before, but here it was...intimate. He glanced around the room, and I took the time to admire his outfit and him in it. My stomach was fluttering, but I ignored it.

He turned toward me, satisfied there was no one else in the room with us, and he went still. His eyes devoured me in my dress as they raked up and down, and I blushed as satisfaction filled me. I couldn't stop myself from doing a little twirl and he swallowed as he clenched his jaw. I knew that look and I was strangely pleased I had got that reaction from him.

"You look beautiful," he said, meeting my eyes again.

"Thank you," I said softly as our eyes met, and a stillness came over the room. As one, we took one step towards each other. All I could hear was my quickening breath and my heart beating. He swallowed again and I tilted my head up to look deeper into his eyes, and I parted my lips as I breathed in the same air as he was.

We leaned in, but before anything could happen, Nate broke the spell and took a step back, breaking eye contact and clearing his throat. It felt like I had fallen out of bed and hit the ground hard. I smoothed my sweaty palms along the front of my dress and tried to get my emotions under control. I walked towards the mirror, wanting some distance, and I picked up the brush and started to untangle my hair again with maybe a bit more vigour than before.

What was wrong with me? We were in a stranger's castle, possibly in serious danger and here I was lusting over Nate. I was a little smug that he, too, was affected, but still. I was an Ever and over two hundred years old. Nate approached me and cleared his throat again.

"Here I thought you might like this," he said, reaching into his pocket. He seemed shy as he pulled the gift out, and I gasped when I saw it. In his hand was my hairbrush I had lost. I reached out and took it, unexpected tears jumping to my eyes.

"I saw it when we were with the ballybogs, and I managed to sneak it into my pocket," he said, not meeting my eyes.

"Thank you," I said with a sniff. "This means a lot to me. My mother used to brush my hair with it. It was something special we did together. I really thought I had lost it." Before I could think, I stood and wrapped my arms around him, giving him a hug filled with gratitude. How did he know this was such an important thing to me? He could have taken the map or something useful for our journey, but he had risked the ballybog spears for my hairbrush. No one else would have done that. Even Amos would have chosen the sensible thing if he had the chance.

His body was hard under my hands, and he felt strong. I closed my eyes and let his warmth sink in. After a moment's hesitation, his arms wrapped around my waist, and the weight of them made me feel safe. We stood for a moment, savouring each other, and when we separated, I felt cold.

"Well, I will see you at the ball. I had better let you finish getting ready," he said, blushing. I smiled at him and nodded as I watched him leave my room. I spent the rest of the time getting ready with a small smile on my face.

TWENTY-ONE

NATHANIEL

Dresses of all shapes and colours spun on the dance floor in front of me. Apparently, when the Others threw a ball, they went all in. Everywhere, there was wine and mead flowing and food tables laden with anything you could want. There was an orchestra playing above on the balcony, and the room was draped in red velvet curtains covering the harsh black stone. The lighting was low, allowing for all sorts of things to happen behind the curtain. So far, I had seen three fistfights, a couple making love and more naked body parts than I could count. It seemed being dressed was optional here.

I scanned the room, keeping an eye on things, while Gentle sat in her silver gown in front of the room near King Thallan. All night, I had been trying to keep my eyes off her with no luck. She was beautiful, and she was practically glowing. Her hair was glinting in the low light, and her face appeared to be almost shimmering. She was radiant in a way no one else here was. She was the most beautiful creature in here, and I ground my teeth when I heard others say the same. So far, she had been sitting next to Thallan for the whole night, but I knew as soon as possible, she would have a line-up of people wanting to dance with her.

As I was watching, she turned her head, and our eyes were drawn together across the room. I looked away quickly so she didn't see the need for them. I was in big trouble. I had always admired her, and now it seemed I was falling for her. I was sure it was because we had been spending so much time together. Once we returned to Aeris Isle and I wasn't near her every minute of the day, it would pass. That's what I told myself anyway.

Standing on the edge of the dancefloor, I had been asked to dance more than once, but I had declined. There was tension in the air. An abandonment I didn't like. It was like we were on the edge, and anything could push us off. I tried to stretch my wings behind me, but the tunic I was wearing was not made for Alanti, and someone had guessed what size to cut the holes in the back, and they were restricting, making the muscles in my back begin to ache. I needed to stretch them and feel the wind under them, but finding a chance to do that was proving difficult. I rearranged them again, hoping for some relief, and my eyes returned to Gentle and Thallan.

All night, he had sat near her, leaning in and devouring her with his eyes, ignoring everyone else in the room. Even his female servants hovering around him were blank-faced and still. Jealousy was an oily feeling in my gut, and I hated it. I had distracted myself by studying his female servants, trying to work out what was going on with them. I had tried talking to the one who served me wine, but she stared right through me with her lavender eyes.

They were scattered around the room, dressed in almost nothing. It made me shiver to think about Gentle being one of his girls and I felt sorry Thallan still kept his "collection."

I couldn't remember the women around the last time I was here, but I was only small and had other things to worry about like people plucking all my feathers or wanting to experiment on me. I shook the dark memories from my head and focused back on the people in front of me. The music was lively, and without me thinking, my foot started tapping. I had always loved the music at balls, though I never got the chance to dance. I was always on the edge, watching and waiting. My eyes slid back to Gentle, and I wondered what it would be like to dance with her.

A thought speared through me. I could find out. For the first time in a long time, I didn't want to be a guard. I was a guest, and there was nothing out of the ordinary to ask Gentle to dance. My heart picked up the beat, and I squared my shoulders, straightened my tunic, and ran my hands along the front of the black pants I had under them. I walked towards her, trying to appear confident, but I was shaking inside.

She was still talking to Thallan, but her attention was wandering, and she was wearing a fake smile. I could do this. I could hold her and spin, and it would be just the two of us. I walked with renewed purpose, thinking about what it would be like to hold her in my arms and dance and not have to worry about what others would think. I stepped around the other dancing couples and waved off the servants, handing out wine.

My stomach was fluttering as I made it to the table they were sitting at. I stood quietly and didn't interrupt Thallan as he was telling her how beautiful she looked. My jaw clenched at the hunger in his eyes, and my mouth turned sour because he didn't want her for her. He wanted her for her beauty. He only wanted to make her into one of his servants so he could admire and show her off to everyone. I saw red but it calmed when Gentle looked at me. Her eyes brightened and begged me to take her away.

Thallan stared at me, his hunger replaced with annoyance. "Ah, Nathaniel. What can we do for you? I have seen you there standing all alone. Not into women, huh?" He laughed at his little joke before his eyes narrowed on me. "You know we have had many Alanti here, but you are so familiar. Have you been here before?"

I stiffened, and before I could answer, Gentle spoke, ignoring the second question, "Oh, Nate is very popular at home. But he knows when to show self-restraint," her eyes were sparkling as she teased me. I hoped she couldn't see the gratitude that was surely on my face. She had managed to answer, so I didn't have to think of a lie to tell him about my past.

"There are many beautiful women here, that is true, but I was hoping to get a dance with this one first," I said, holding out my hand to Gentle, hoping no one could hear my thumping heart. I saw the shock on her face, and my heart stopped. She was going to say no. Thallan saw it too and he smirked, but before he could say anything, Gentle stood.

"I would love to," she said softly, and my heart began beating again. Rage flitted over Thallan's face, but he hid it quickly, and he clicked his fingers for more wine. Gentle reached out her hand and a true smile lit my face as I realised I was about to have her close, all to myself, but before her hand rested in mine, the doors were flung open.

The whole room stopped with the bang of the doors, and we turned to see who was interrupting the ball. Over the tops of the heads, I could make out the group of guards that had brought us in yesterday. I could see there were people clustered in the middle of them, but I couldn't make out who they were. The people at the ball separated and let the guards march through as they did not slow their pace. By then, the room was silent, and all we could hear was the footsteps of the people approaching King Thallan.

When they made it to the table, I stepped aside and closer towards Gentle. My neck prickled, and I knew this was what I had been waiting for. Something was about to happen, and it would be bad. My body tensed as the head guard with the brown hair spoke.

"King Thallan. I have some...guests who would like to speak to you. They said it was important and couldn't wait. Should I take them directly to the dungeons?"

Thallan breathed heavily through his nose. "No, no. I am feeling generous. Let them speak."

The guard nodded and stepped back. Before I could see who the guests were, I heard a voice. A voice I never wanted to hear again, and I heard Gentle gasp next to me.

"Thank you, King Thallan. Your generosity is highly appreciated," the voice said, and I was finally able to see who it was.

Bent at the waist was a gnome with a long white beard threaded with bells and ribbons. In his hand, he held a staff that was covered in sharp thorns.

Bilvog was here.

TWENTY-TWO
GENTLE

OMENTS EARLIER

"So Namara, what are you doing in the realm of the Others?" Thallan asked, leaning closer to me. I smiled and leaned back.

"Please call me Gentle," I said, trying to sound friendly but not quite making it. "Like I said, we are here to collect an item that has been stored here, and then, we will be on our way. I realise it was terrible manners to arrive unannounced, but there really was no time," I said, trying to be the most charming I had ever been despite him making my skin crawl.

"And where might this thing be?" he asked intently. I glanced around the room and had a small drink of wine, hoping to stall so I could think of what to say. I was walking a thin line here. I could tell Thallan was a dangerous man. A cruel streak ran through him, and I shuddered to think about what might happen if I lied to him and he found out. I gazed out at all the beautiful couples dancing and, for once, wished someone had asked me to dance so I could get out of this conversation.

Nate was standing against the wall, and I had seen him turn away many beauties who had worked up the courage to ask him to dance. Every time one approached, jealousy sizzled in my chest. Now he was watching the barely clad servants serving drinks, keeping his features still, even though he was tapping a rhythm on his thigh with his fingers.

I turned my attention back to Thallan, and he was still watching me. I shifted in my seat and tried to smile, but I was beginning to get annoyed and creeped out at his attention. I took a sip of the rich wine and, while it slipped down my throat, decided to tell him why we were here. I felt like it was better to be *partly* honest, but I couldn't see why he wanted to stop us. It had nothing to do with him, really.

"Well, we are here so we can retrieve something of mine that was hidden a long time ago. An item we now need to try and defeat an enemy that is clawing his way back." My fingers tightened on the wineglass.

"And where might this item be?" he asked again, leaning closer as if he knew I didn't want to be telling him these things.

"It was hidden by Belladonna, the hag who lives in my realm. She put it in the Gleaming Grove for safekeeping. We are going to get it and return home immediately." I hoped I had told him enough to satisfy him, but judging by the look in his eye, he was thinking hard.

The people were still out dancing and when my eyes inevitably were drawn to Nate, I saw him watching me also. He looked away quickly, and I smiled a little. Thallan chuckled, and when I turned back to him, I knew he had seen the look between Nate and me. Cold spread from my stomach, making me uneasy.

"The Gleaming Grove, you say. Yes, I know it. The hags do love to keep their things in there. But how did someone like you end up on this dangerous quest, I wonder?"

"Someone like me?" I asked innocently, but I bristled inside.

"Please don't take offence, but you don't look like the sort of woman to go trampling about the wilderness. You look more like someone who hosts balls and social occasions. And rightfully so. I have never seen such beauty before."

For a moment I was embarrassed he had pinned me so fast. That was exactly the type of person I was, and it never really bothered me before. I shrugged it off, but now, it stung a bit. I didn't want to be just that. I was more, I hoped.

"I got roped in, I'm afraid. Belladonna can be tricky with her deals, and here I am," I said with a shrug, hoping he would change the subject so I didn't have to poke the bruise to my ego that had suddenly emerged.

He smiled and paused for a moment, watching me. "I have a proposition for you," he said, calling for more wine. Once our glasses were full again, he continued, "I would love it if you would stay here with me. It is no secret I think you are beautiful, and I would love to have you in one of my collections. I am getting a bit tired of looking at the others I have gathered, but I don't think I would ever get tired of your beauty. You could live here and plan parties and dance the night away every night if you wanted. Send your bodyguard home and let him take care of Aeris Isle."

I tried to hide the surprise and must have failed.

"Don't worry, you would not be like these ones," he said, his eyes flicking at the lady who had filled our glasses. "I no longer have the means to make a husk, and I'm sure you would not agree even if I did." He took a long drink, looking at me over the glass like a predator.

My mind was reeling as I tried to process what he had just said. He wanted me to leave Aris Isle and move in here to plan parties? It was so ridiculous my brain couldn't comprehend it. I cleared my throat. "I am flattered. What did you say these women are? Husks?" I needed a moment to work out how to refuse and not show the revulsion on my face, but I had a feeling what I was about to hear would make that hard.

"Yes, they are clones of a sort. Or maybe zombies would be better? But not many people like the sound of that," he said with a chuckle.

Fancy that, I thought.

"I once had a wand that, if the woman agreed to it, would preserve their beauty forever. Unfortunately, the person who created the wand added a few conditions. Like I said, it had to be agreed to; no one else could have a claim to the woman, and they would be left empty. Still able to follow orders and function, but all personality and purpose would be stripped. Unfortunately, the wand has been out of my possession for quite a few years, and I have been left with the same old husks for too long. I would love to have you around to break up the monotony. I know it is a big ask, so think about it."

I smiled in a way I hoped appeared like I was considering it when I saw Nate approach the table. I was glad for the distraction, and a true smile spread across my face as I saw Thallan scowl. Thallan spoke before I could, and I was shocked at what came out of his mouth. I don't know why.

I knew what sort of man he was, but before I could defend Nate, Thallan asked if he had been here before, and I had to admit I was curious. I knew he *had* been here before, but I still wondered why and where he had been. He had been reluctant to tell me, and despite my good manners, I was dying to know why.

I could see he was uncomfortable and didn't want to answer, so I did it for him, making a comment about his restraint as my mind turned back to earlier in my room. I knew he would know what I was talking about. He smiled at me slightly and asked me to dance. There was nothing I wanted to do more. I held out my hand, thinking about how nice it would be to get out and move my body to the music and how glad I was it wasn't Thallan I was dancing with.

As he went to take my hand, a group of people entered. We watched as they approached, and something inside of me flipped. My whole body went taut as a warning system went off and I knew whatever happened next, I wouldn't like it. As I prepared for that to happen, I heard a voice that sent a lightning bolt through my body.

Bilvog.

My body was shaking, and my hands broke out in a sweat. Nate moved to stand more in front of me and I laid my hand on his back to help me stay standing. I took a moment to compose myself before anyone noticed my distress, knowing it was dangerous to show any weakness here. Out of nowhere, a gust of wind picked up, and I watched as it swirled around the tablecloths and dresses of the husks. It didn't take long to realise it was from me, and I grit my teeth and tried to breathe and rein it in. I couldn't fall apart in front of Thallan and Bilvog. I needed to keep it together and find out why he was here and what this was about.

I steeled my spine, stood up straight, and removed my hand from Nate's back, drawing in whatever strength I could from him standing in front of me. I made myself look over at Bilvog and confront the gnome who had turned the lives of myself and my people upside down.

Bilvog was at the front of a group of people, and it shocked me that he was the same. I secretly expected him to look twisted and ugly after everything he had done, but he didn't. He was thinner but, on the whole, looked like the same person I had once trusted and relied on. His long white beard was still threaded with ribbons and bells, and he was wearing a long dark blue robe with big bell sleeves. I did notice his left hand was tucked inside the sleeve, trying to hide the shrivelled, black hand. So, he hadn't recovered from Amelia's power.

He looked around the room, his eyes skated right past mine, and a pang stabbed my heart. I berated myself internally for wanting anything from him and focused on what was happening in front of me. Nate had taken half a step away but was still close, and I was grateful I had him to stand with. Bilvog was standing with a group of his followers, all in red robes and with shaved heads with a symbol tattooed on them. Memory was niggling me about those symbols, but whatever it was, it was just out of reach.

Thallan stood with a tight smile on his face.

"Ah, more visitors. What can we do for you?" he asked.

Bilvog bowed low, his beard pooling on the ground in front of him. "Your Majesty. Thank you for allowing us into your presence. If it is possible, I would like to speak to you in private and fill you in on all the details of our visit," Bilvog replied, his eyes flicking to me. Thallan noticed and held my stare for a moment, and I knew he had picked up on my distress moments earlier.

Thallan paused for a moment, and I tried to get a read on what he might say. Would he throw him out? Grant him his audience? There really was no way to tell, but I could see he was intrigued and wanted to know what Bilvog was doing here. I, too, wanted to know, although I was fairly certain I could guess.

"Now, now, that wouldn't be very polite to leave my ball to go and speak with you, now, would it?" he said with a cold smile on his face. "I think the best course of action would be if you and your...people...joined us." He clapped, and the band started up again, and the people gathered immediately began dancing like nothing had happened.

Bilvog bowed again, not as low this time, and dismissed his followers. They spread out into the crowd, trying to blend in and failing. It was very creepy the way they watched everything so intently. It worried me a little bit when I thought of the destruction they could bring when they wanted to. We still had not worked out how they had planted the bombs underneath my mountain, and it scared me they could move without being seen.

Thallan extended a hand to me, inviting me to sit once more and the way he looked at me, dancing with Nate was no longer an option. Not that I felt like dancing, but it would put some distance between Bilvog and me, distance I desperately wanted. I held myself together and clenched my jaw while I walked around the table and took my seat again. Nate followed and stood right behind my chair, and

I could sense the anger radiating off him. I wanted to reach back and touch his hand, but I refrained. I didn't want to draw any unnecessary attention to whatever this was between us.

Bilvog took a seat on the other side of Thallan, and I turned my stiff body to look out over the dancers, keeping my gaze on the wall while I tried to work out what to say.

"It seems like the Obsidian Throne is a popular place to holiday at the moment," Thallan said before turning to face Bilvog. "And what brings you here?"

Bilvog cleared his throat and leaned in closer to Thallan. "Well, that is what I wanted to discuss with you. We are here on a rather time-sensitive mission, and I would like your permission to pass through your lands if it is agreeable."

There was a moment of silence, and I heard Nate twitch his wings. The tension rolling around the four of us was so thick that if I clenched my jaw anymore, my teeth would crack. In front of my eyes, all I could see were the people crushed and injured at the Night of Lights. Amos's body laid out on the slab in the library, the weight of the pillar that fell on me and the feeling of the dust that coated my body and throat. This man had done that, and I had to sit here and behave. My eyes blurred, and I was worried for a moment that I would collapse right there.

Before I could spiral too much more, a warm and heavy hand landed on my shoulder. I took a deep breath and got myself under control again. I spared a glance at where Bilvog and Thallan were, but they were talking to each other and hadn't noticed. I sat up straighter and concentrated on my clenched hands in my lap.

After a few moments, I was more in control, and Nate lifted his hand from my shoulder. I turned to Thallan, purposefully ignoring Bilvog, and listened to what they were saying.

"If I'm not mistaken, I would say the two of you know each other, and it might not be friendly. You have both tried your hardest to not look at each other, so out with it. How do you know Bilvog, Gentle dear?" he asked, leaning back in his chair so I would have a clear view of Bilvog. He smiled like the cat who had caught the mouse, and I suppose, in a way, he had.

I cleared my throat. "Yes, I know him," I said before looking Bilvog right in the eyes. I poured every ounce of defiance and anger I had into that look so he would see how much damage he had done. "This is the man we are fighting against. He is the one trying to raise my brother, Dread." Bilvog looked away and I was glad of the small victory. "Do you remember Dread, King Thallan? He killed thousands of innocents before we locked him away. I can only imagine what his plans will be now."

He was enjoying this. Thallan's eyes had a sparkle to them that wasn't there before, and I felt sick he was enjoying this little game.

"Yes, I remember Dread vaguely. So, you want to bring him back? Well, I suppose you will both be after the Crown of Glass?"

Shock passed over Bilvog's face, and he turned to me accusingly. My face must have betrayed my surprise because King Thallan laughed at the both of us.

"Oh yes, I know what you want out of Gleaming Grove. How interesting. I have two groups here who both want the same thing and need my permission to get it. It is a shame you will not find the crown there." He paused for a moment, allowing us to feel rocked for a second time. My stomach dropped, and I wondered how he knew it wasn't there. What were we going to do now? We didn't have time to be searching the whole Other's Realm. We needed the crown now.

"What do you mean it isn't there?" Bilvog asked, some of his deference falling away and showing the gnome I remembered. Thallan looked at him sharply, and Bilvog seemed to realise his mistake. He bowed his head, but I could see the set of his shoulders. He wasn't happy. I had seen that stance multiple times when he was dealing with Ashes and did not agree with something he did.

"I know it isn't there because I have been in the Grove. I know it isn't there because I know where it is." I was sitting on the edge of my seat, waiting for him to tell us where it was, knowing Thallan was enjoying every moment of this. What else would I have to endure to get my crown back? I could see out of the corner of my eye Nate leaning forward in anticipation of what he was going to say.

"I know where it is because it is in this castle. You see, *I* have the Crown of Glass," he stood out of his chair and loomed over us. " I have had it for years. I was wondering if anyone would ever come and retrieve it. It has been quite useful at times. Being able to control a person for a short amount of time has made my life more...fun, shall we say," he said with a smirk.

TWENTY-THREE
GENTLE

We were still sitting at the table, but Thallan had cleared the room of the rest of the partygoers, leaving Thallan, Bilvog, the cult members, Nate, and me. We were sitting in shock at Thallan's revelation, and my mind was churning, wondering what we would have to do to get the crown back. My stomach turned, thinking about him wearing my crown and abusing the power it contained. I had a fair idea who he was using that power on, and I turned to the husk, who was still standing, ready to serve. What terrible things had he made them do, because I knew they would have been terrible.

I tried to sound confident when I said, "well, this is interesting news. And it's good, I think. This will save us from travelling to the Gleaming Grove to retrieve my crown. If I may collect it from you, we will be on our way." My heart was pounding. Would he give it back, and what would be his price? I knew there was no way he would hand it over. He had been waiting for someone to come and get it for a reason.

"Ah well, you see, I have a different idea," he said, standing up and walking around the table. "Do you know what the Gleaming Grove is?" Bilvog and I both shook our heads.

"Essentially, it is a storage area for the hags. No one can enter or take anything unless they have been given permission." He sat in his chair and leaned back.

"So, how did you get the crown?" Bilvog said, asking the question that I was sure was on everyone's mind.

"I found a loophole, and I was able to get in there, and I took the crown. I had heard a bit about it and thought it sounded interesting and I knew it would look good, so I took it," He shrugged, "Unfortunately, the hags didn't appreciate that I managed to get in their vault and they punished me by stealing my wand and locking it in there. I have tried for many years to get back in, but it is sealed up tight." He stood in front of us, looking at us intently. "This is what I propose. I would like you both to go to the Gleaming Grove and retrieve my wand. The first person back here will get the crown. Simple," he said with a gleam in his eye.

"So, you want me to traipse to the Gleaming Grove and collect something of yours, so you will return something of mine?" I asked, annoyed. My hair was floating around my head, and I tried to smooth it back down.

"Well, you were going there anyway. Nothing is free in this world, Gentle. Perhaps it is time you learnt that," he said reaching out as a husk passed him a glass of wine. The sweet smell of it making me sick.

My blood heated at the way he spoke so condescendingly. Before I could respond, Bilvog spoke up.

"How do we know you have the crown? Perhaps we could see it?"

"Of course." Thallan clicked his fingers, and one of the husks walked out of the room.

"What does your wand look like, King Thallan? I am assuming that being the hags' lockbox, there must be many things they are hiding in there. It would make it easier for me to retrieve it if I knew what it looked like," Bilvog asked, and I bristled at the assumption he would be getting the wand. I glanced over my shoulder at Nate, who was glaring at Bilvog, and I wondered if he had taken his eyes off him since he had entered. My thoughts were interrupted by Thallan answering Bilvog's question.

"It is simply a wand made of obsidian," he said, gesturing to the obsidian floor. The black stone was smooth and had a white sheen to it where it shone in the mage light.

Bilvog's face was set in concentration, and I knew he was doing the same as me and wondering how we were going to beat each other at this little game.

The door swung open, and the husk returned holding an item I never thought I would see again. She passed the crown to the king, and he held it up for us to see. My heart practically stopped looking at it. The light gleamed and shone through the glass, making it look like it was lit from within. The tall spikes of the crown were carved with geometric patterns and were sharp enough to stab someone. I knew it would be cool to the touch and when wearing it, it would be light as a feather.

And it was mine.

It was the thing I had given up all those years ago. I had used it to help trap and bind Dread in his prison for what should have been an eternity if it wasn't for the gnome sitting next to me.

Bilvog's eyes were glued to the crown with a look of wonder and hunger on his face. Possessiveness ran through me, and I vowed he would not get the crown before me. There was no way I was letting him give it to Dread, allowing them to use the power that remained inside of it. In all the years I had the crown, I only once had used the mind control powers and that was to trap Dread. My body shuddered to think about what they would do with that kind of power, even if it was reduced after it had been used to bind Dread. I had to get it first. It was mine, and it belonged on my head.

I stood in my seat as Nate moved closer. "Fine. If that is what the price is, then so be it. Are there any more conditions, or shall we move on?"

"So decisive, Gentle," Thallan said with a smile. "But don't be too hasty. I think we have all had a big night and it is time we have a long rest. Morning is soon enough for you both to start on the quest of mine. We shall meet for breakfast, and you can depart after that. We don't want people saying I am a bad host now, do we?" He handed the crown back to the husk, and I watched it being carried out the door and out of my sight once more.

"With all due respect, King Thallan, how am I to trust these two," Bilvog said, finally looking at me with disgust in his eyes, "will not sneak off into the night?"

I cocked an eyebrow. "Us? I would be more worried about you not following the rules. Betrayal seems to come easily to you these days," I said.

"It was your weakness that brought this on. You and your brother and sisters, bringing humans into our realms and letting them pollute and destroy whatever they touch!" he spat back.

"Now, now, as much as I love hearing you two bicker, let's get on with this. There will be guards inside and out of the castle all night, on alert to ensure no one goes sneaking off before I want them to. I would be extremely displeased, and I don't think either of you would like it when I am displeased," Thallan said, and I saw one of the husks standing against the wall flinch.

I swallowed and looked over at Bilvog to see if he agreed. He paled at the threat. Thallan let it hang in the air for a few seconds, letting it sink in before he clapped his hands, calling forward a group of husks scattered around the room.

"Now, ladies and gentlemen. I will let my companions show you to your rooms and we will meet tomorrow morning for breakfast. Sleep well," Thallan said before striding off and leaving us all together. The other cult members came forward to stand with Bilvog, and I took the time to look at them. What sort of people were they that they would give up everything to join Dread and Bilvog? What had driven them to that evil, or were they born with darkness inside them?

They appeared emotionless, but when they turned their attention to Bilvog, I saw a hint of admiration in their eyes. They clustered behind him, and I saw there was one in the middle that was sort of hidden. I hadn't seen their face yet, and whoever it was, was determined for it to stay that way. Their head was deep in the hood, and they stared at the ground the whole time. I filed it away for later and turned to Nate.

I nodded at him and then turned and marched from the room. There was no way I was going to be in the room with

Bilvog and allow him to have any more of my energy. My heels clipped on the stone, and my dress swished, but I still heard him mutter "pathetic" under his breath. I didn't hesitate, but tears sprung to my eyes, and I was glad I was walking away.

As I was leaving the room, something niggled in my mind and wormed its way out. How did Bilvog think he was getting into the Gleaming Grove? If you needed a hag's permission, that meant one of them was against us.

Who was it?

TWENTY-FOUR

NATHANIEL

"**G**entle, I don't like the idea of you staying in here by yourself tonight."

"I will be fine, Nate. We can't leave, and I doubt they will allow us to walk around the castle, so they won't be able to get to me here. Besides, we are going to need a good sleep before tomorrow. This could be our last comfortable night's sleep for a while." She sighed and smoothed the small strands of hair that were always floating around her head due to her wind power. She seemed distracted.

We had made it back to her rooms, and her face was pale, and I knew seeing Bilvog had unsettled her. It had unsettled me, and I didn't have that close of a relationship with him. I had been around when he was Gentle's advisor, but I didn't have much to do with him. I had always thought of him as a kind old gnome, and never once did I think he would be dangerous. Amos had mostly dealt with him. I wished Amos was here now to help. He would know the right thing to do and say to improve this situation.

I was sitting on the couch inside her room while she was getting undressed in her dressing room. I could hear fabric swishing and my face grew hot thinking about the fabric running over her skin. I cleared my throat and tried to focus on what was going to happen tomorrow. The room was neat and tidy, and I saw someone had been in and straightened up since we had gone to the ball.

"Really, it is no trouble. I'll sleep on the lounge. I will get no sleep in my own room if I am worried about you here," I said, hoping to convince her.

I made a note to keep all the things I didn't want them to find tucked away on my body. I trusted no one in this place and since arriving, I was tight with tension. I replayed the story Thallen had told about how he had lost his wand. I knew that story was a lie. The hag didn't take it from him. Someone else did and gave it to the hag. Why was he lying?

Out of the corner of my eye, I saw the silver dress being thrown on the floor, and I winced at the crumpled fabric lying in a heap and had the sudden urge to go and pick it up. Not long after, Gentle emerged in a long, deep purple satin nightgown, and all thought left my mind. Her hair was in waves, flowing to the small of her back, and she had removed her makeup, leaving her skin clean and fresh. Her skin was pale and clear, and she was close to perfect. I didn't think she realised it, but her heart was just as beautiful as her outside.

She had handled that meeting well, especially seeing Bilvog. She was kind and funny, and I hoped to see that side come out of her again. She went and sat on the bed. Immediately, thoughts of laying there with her filled my mind with all the things I could do with her there. I looked away before she saw the desire in my eyes.

She looked at me with a small smile on her face and it was like the sun had emerged from this permanent twilight.

"If that is what you want then fine, but I am sure we will have no issues. I hope you don't snore again. I don't want to waste this comfy bed," she said with a bigger smile.

"Excuse me? Again? I have hardly got a wink of sleep because of the noise you make at night," I shot back, pleased to be joking and laughing again. A pillow sailed across the room at my head, made more forceful by the gale of wind behind it.

I laughed. "Thanks, I'll need that," I said, putting it at the top of the lounge and fluffing it up.

Gentle huffed and settled into her bed. I tried to ignore the satin slipping up her legs as I got up and turned the light off, leaving the room lit by the sunset outside. I stood for a moment and stared out of the balcony windows, admiring the view and thinking about the women behind me. She was everything I wanted and couldn't have. I was her guard, and she was an Ever. I couldn't see a way for us to be together, and I didn't even know how she felt about me. For all I knew, she thought of me the same way she thought of Amos.

I sighed lightly and walked back to the lounge, glancing at Gentle piled under blankets with her eyes closed. I tried to calm my mind for sleep. I stretched and pulled my shirt over my head, letting my wings stretch and bend. It had been too long inside, and they were aching to be free and fly. The air was heavy and stale, and I was restless.

I couldn't stop thinking, and I needed to get out of there and let my wings stretch. I put my shirt back on and walked over to the balcony. As soon as I took in the fresh air, my body relaxed. I flexed my wings and checked the drop below me. The balcony was about three stories high and underneath us was a courtyard that was empty. I climbed up on the railing and hesitated for a moment, looking back at Gentle. From here she appeared asleep, and I worried for a moment for her safety, but she was right. There was no way Thallan would let people wander around, poking into other people's rooms. I checked for guards again and then jumped.

I spread my wings and waited for the wind to catch underneath them. The first gust strained against my back muscles and although it hurt slightly, there was a relief in having the wind lift me. I flapped twice to gain some height and watched the world underneath me. I hadn't spotted any guards yet, so I flew higher. The air was clear and fresh, and a pang of homesickness raced through me for the cold mountain air.

When would we get back there? We had to make sure we got the crown. There was no other alternative. We couldn't let Bilvog win, and while I soared through the clouds, I tried to mentally prepare for our trip in the morning. Gentle would need more support, but I had no doubt she would be able to handle the situation, and we would beat them. I flew around the castle for about fifteen minutes until my muscles started to relax and unwind. I guessed it was about the middle of the night, so I started to head back to the balcony.

I flew down and my thoughts were once again taken over by Gentle. *It's hard to love someone who doesn't love you back*. The thought almost made me fall out of the sky. It settled into my chest and made it ache. It had been a long time since I had been in love, and knowing she didn't love me back didn't change that. I knew I had loved her for a long time, even before this little adventure, but spending this time with her had solidified it. I locked away those emotions in my chest and set my mind on the tasks ahead of us.

I adjusted my wings and continued down, planning to land back on the balcony. After that little revelation, I was distracted, and I didn't see the guards who were hiding in the bushes below me. As soon as my feet touched the railing, something sharp embedded itself between my wings, and I shook them slightly, trying to dislodge it. Around the pain, a warmth spread out, and I had only a moment to look into the room and see Gentle laying in her bed, alone and unprotected.

My body tipped backwards, and I fell three stories, unable to move or flex my wings to break my fall. The air rushed from my lungs, and any sound I wanted to make was snatched away. My stomach lurched as it felt like I was falling forever, and I braced myself for the landing. Surprise flared when I bounced in a net held by some of Thallan's guards, followed quickly by relief that I hadn't smashed on the ground. My eyes were open, but I couldn't move. They dropped me to the ground, and from around the building came a tall, dark figure. King Thallan.

"Hello, Nathaniel. I am sorry to do this to you, but what was I to think when it was reported you were flying around the castle. You could be doing anything. Looking for weak spots, trying to kill my men. Yes, I think it is best you come with me, and away from Gentle and spend a bit of time in my dungeons."

Inside, I struggled and tried to get up, but my body didn't cooperate. Whatever paralytic they gave me was working, and I was helpless. Thallan knelt beside me, and I could smell the wine on his breath. "You know, another thing has been bothering me about you. I know I have seen you before, and it has been a thorn in my side that I can't work out where. Perhaps we need some time alone where I can...study you. Perhaps the answer will come to me."

My body chilled, and goosebumps rose on my skin. I knew what kind of studying he did, and my stomach soured. The thought of telling him who I was made my blood run cold, and my mind raced, trying to figure out how I was going to get out of this. The whole time I had been thinking, Thallan was staring at me. Like he could get to the bottom of my past by looking into my eyes and into my soul.

He smiled and it did nothing to calm me. "I think we have been out here long enough," he tore his eyes from mine and spoke to the guards. "Take him below and make sure he is uncomfortable."

One of the guards walked over and bent to pick me up. He grunted, and I knew it would be a rough trip to the dungeons. I strained my eyes, trying to see the balcony where Gentle slept beyond. Thallan followed my gaze, and when he saw where I was looking, he smiled again.

A fist gripped my heart as I was carted away, unsure when I would see the outside world again.

TWENTY-FIVE
GENTLE

I woke refreshed and well-rested. It had been a few days of roughing it in the forest, and I was so grateful to have a comfy bed again. I sat up and stretched, looking out the open doors to the balcony. It was still twilight, and I missed seeing the sun in the morning. I knew this kind of sky was not for me, and I was dreaming of waking up and looking out over my mountain.

The lounge was empty, and I frowned, surprised when disappointment speared me. I didn't know what I was expecting. Nate probably got up early and went back to his room. My face heated as I remembered the night before when he had taken off his clothes. In the dim light, I was able to see his tanned skin and the muscles bunching underneath it. I had watched him, unable to tear my eyes away as he stretched his beautiful wings. I had only looked away when he had put his shirt back on and walked to the balcony.

I opened my eyes in time to see him fall and then fly off. He had invaded my thoughts as I imagined kissing him and what that would be like. It had kept me awake for a long time as I tried to go to sleep, and I hadn't seen him return.

As I rubbed my face, the reality of the day came crashing into me. I would have to eat with Bilvog and Thallan for breakfast and hope the deal was still on. Seeing my crown last night made me want it more, and no matter what Bilvog said or did, nothing would stop me from getting it back.

I needed to make sure my head was in the game today, no matter how strange that might be to me. All this action sent a zing of electricity through me. I was surprised to find I had been enjoying the adventure and all the things that came along with it. I only hoped I could keep up with the challenge.

I climbed out of the bed, and my feet touched the soft rug, and I was grateful for it. Everything about this castle was hard and unyielding, so it was nice to have some relief in my bedroom. I wondered if one of the husks would be coming to retrieve me for breakfast. I shuddered at the invitation Thallan had given me last night.

With all that happened, I hadn't had a chance to think about him actually asking me if I wanted to become a husk. The thought of becoming one of them made me sick to my stomach, and I wondered if there was a way to save them. No one should have to live like that. My mind shied away, trying to imagine how they were treated here.

I walked to the bathroom and had a quick wash, not knowing what time it was. After I was clean and dry, I stepped into the wardrobe and chose a long magenta gown made of silk chiffon that fell to the floor in waves and was low cut in the front. I ran my hand over the fabric, appreciating the feel of it, knowing I would be back in travel clothes before too long.

I brushed out my long hair and plaited it, coiling it atop my head, giving it the look of a crown. I wanted them to remember who I was and what was rightfully mine. I stepped back and admired myself. I looked like a Greek goddess, and I smiled. I was ready for battle.

While I waited to be taken to breakfast, I packed up my room, knowing we would be leaving soon. Someone had left a backpack and some pants and shirts to help us on our way, seeing how we had lost everything to the pixies. I hated to admit it, but Thallan was being a very generous host, apart from offering to turn me into a zombie. I packed everything carefully, and when I was done, I eyed the wardrobe, wanting to put in some of the beautiful dresses there.

I sighed and closed the backpack, leaving the dresses where they were. I had to get through this, and then I would be back home in my castle, with all my things, doing what I loved. Strangely, that didn't fill me with the same contentment it used to. How did I fill the days again? It was hard to believe I wasn't bored out of my mind. I shook my head knowing once I was home and, in my routine, I would be fine.

At least, I hoped so.

I walked into the room with my head held high and my shoulders back. Inside, my stomach was roiling, and I did my best to try and ignore the nausea that was attempting to take over. Everybody's eyes were on me, and my body tingled with anxiety, my emotions calling forth the wind. I clung to my peace and managed to settle the breeze that had ruffled my dress as I made my way to the seat that had been left empty for me.

I did my best to ignore everyone so they didn't rattle me, but I did notice Nate wasn't here yet. My brow furrowed because I knew he wasn't in his room. I had knocked on the way past, and when there was no answer, I had peeked inside, but the room was clean and tidy, and there was no sign of Nate anywhere. I sat and smoothed my skirts before looking at the people sitting at the table.

Thallan was at the head and was wearing a smirk on his face, and I knew he knew exactly how I was feeling inside. Bilvog sat across from me and he was looking at me with no emotion on his face. I stared back, trying to mirror his look until he looked away, squirming slightly in his seat. For some reason it surprised me he was wearing what he would normally wear, and I was reminded of the many meals we ate together in the past. I steeled my emotions and didn't let them invade my thoughts again.

"Good morning, Gentle. I trust you slept well last night?" Thallan said as he clapped his hands at one of the husks near the door. His hair was tied back in a black ribbon, and he appeared almost cheerful, which was an emotion I hadn't seen from him yet.

I decided to try and be civil. It had always worked for me in the past. "Thank you. Yes, I slept well, although it is difficult to get used to the sun not setting."

"Yes, I suppose that would take some getting used to," Thallan said as some of the husks came in and laid plates in front of us. It was a beautiful spread. Some of the foods I recognised—pears, pancakes, and thickly buttered toast. Some things were new. Fruits of all shapes and sizes and colours overflowed. Pastries and breads were piled, and my mouth watered, looking at the spread before us. Thallan stood and served us himself, and then we all started to eat. I kept my eyes on the room, waiting for Nate to arrive as a ball of worry grew larger in my stomach. Where was he? I couldn't imagine he wouldn't be here when he knew how important this was.

"And you, Bilvog? How did you sleep?" Thallan asked, as he ate, keeping the smile on his face.

"Yes, quite well. Thank you. I have been very impressed with your hospitality, and that should carry some weight, as I have stayed with some of the most important rulers there are," he replied, practically puffing up with self-importance.

I had to forcibly stop myself from rolling my eyes. Thallan must have shared my feelings. His smile turned sarcastic before his eyes went back to the food he was eating.

"Well, I am glad to hear it. I, too, slept well after dealing with a...pest problem." There was a pause, and goosebumps broke out over my skin. Something in his voice made me feel something was wrong, and I couldn't shake the shadow that fell over me.

Thallan turned to me, "We were speaking about the mission you will find yourself on shortly. We will provide a pack with supplies, of course, seeing how yours was lost, and you will all leave at the same time. I would ask that any violence happen outside of my kingdom. I don't need the bad press you see," he said, talking around the food in his mouth, and I shuddered with the easy way he spoke about us hurting each other. Bilvog appeared unfazed.

"Now I would like you to go to the Gleaming Grove, retrieve the Obsidian wand, and the person who hands it to me, will be the one to take the crown home. I understand there are more people in Bilvog's group, but that was poor planning on your behalf there, Gentle," he chided me, making my blood boil.

"I had one question for you, Bilvog," I said, steeling myself to look him in the eyes. "How do you plan to get into the Gleaming Grove?" I had been turning it over and over in my head all night.

He smiled at me. "Now don't you worry your pretty little head about it. I have my ways."

I smiled back, knowing he wouldn't answer my question. My mind turned over and over, and I didn't like the conclusions I was drawing.

Where was Nate? I needed him here to help me navigate this. I was no good at all this double talk, and I had grown to rely on him. I had to ask, and I cleared my throat.

"I can't help but wonder if anyone has seen Nate this morning?" My voice was strong, and I was relieved when it didn't wobble or break. The emotions I had pushed away were bubbling up my throat, and I was holding onto them by a thread.

Thallan looked at me with pity in his eyes, but it wasn't quite right. My heart was beating faster knowing whatever he was about to tell me, I wouldn't like.

"No, I haven't seen him today, but I did see him last night. I am surprised you don't know what happened. I assumed he would have spoken to you beforehand," he held his hands out in front of him and looked at Bilvog with a mask of concern on his face. I gripped my fork tighter until my knuckles were white, and throughout the room, a sharp, cold breeze was cutting through the tension. By now, the thread snapped, and any control I had on my power was gone.

Thallan turned back at me. "Last night, one of my guards brought it to my attention someone was flying around the castle. When I made it to the roof, I could see it was Nate and...well, I am sorry to be the one to tell you this, but he was flying off, and it seemed to be in the direction you arrived to us," he watched me like a wolf, eating up every morsel of betrayal, fear and worry that was flying through me.

My heart stopped, and I was frozen. The food in my stomach turned sour and threatened to come back up. Was this true? My mind refused to believe it, but I had seen him fly away last night. How could he do this? How could he leave me here, knowing how important this was to save our realm and potentially the world? Bilvog was staring at me, radiating smugness. I shrunk away. Here was a person who had betrayed me, but something told me Nate wouldn't do that. So where was he?

"Now, now, Gentle," Bilvog said, "I must admit I was surprised when I saw you here with Nathaniel and not Amos. He would have been much more capable," he looked between Thallan and me.

Something sharp stabbed into my chest. Sorrow crashed over me, and it was like I was falling apart right here at this table in front of some of the most dangerous people I knew. I dropped my fork, and it clattered to the ground, the noise startling me and making me jump in my seat.

Before I could bend over and pick it up, I heard bare feet walking quickly behind me. I flinched as one of the husks bent over and picked up the fork for me. She glanced at me, and her lavender eyes were trying to send me a message. When she passed me the fork, she squeezed my hand before she turned and walked back to the wall. I could see violence in Thallan's eyes as he looked at her.

I felt fear on her behalf, and that shook loose the stupor I was in. She had risked her safety to try and help me in some small way, and I committed her eyes to my memory. I would not waste it. I breathed deep, letting it flood my body and wash everything away as I looked at Bilvog. I tried to convey all the contempt I had for him, letting the last few months show in my stare.

"Amos would have been here if it wasn't for you and your fanatics. The bomb you planted for the Night of Lights killed him." I surged to my feet, leaning over the table. "You did that. You killed the man you used to call a friend!" I spat at him.

He flinched, but he recovered quickly. Before he could speak, Thallan stood. "Let's not let emotions get the better of us. You have a busy day ahead of you. I recommend you go back to your rooms, where you will see food has been left for you, and you will meet at the castle gates in an hour." His face darkened, and he stared at us both in the eyes, sending a chill down my spine. "One of you will bring back my wand. Or it won't only be the crown I will be holding onto. Go."

I stood and walked out with as much dignity as I could while trying not to fall apart.

TWENTY-SIX
GENTLE

I stood at the front gate, between the giants holding up the castle, and I felt like I could relate to them. My face was clean and clear of any trace of the crying I had done once I had made it to the sanctuary of my rooms. I was wearing the travelling clothes I had worn to the castle, except they had been freshly cleaned and mended, and a pack was strapped to my back, weighing me down. I had checked it for anything strange but all I had found was food, a blanket, and a dagger. I had put the dagger in my pocket hoping I wouldn't need it, but sure I would.

I pulled my long braid over my shoulder and played with the end. I looked around, alone. The crushing weight of what I had to do and what had happened was pressing on me, and it threatened to leave me in a puddle on the stones. We had lost all our things, Bilvog was here, trying to beat me to my crown and Nate had left me to deal with it all alone.

Thallan walked out of the front doors with some of his husks, and Bilvog and his followers were behind him. I turned and stood tall, faking my confidence. I reflected there was a time when I didn't have to fake it and I missed that version of me. Bilvog walked past Thallan and came to stand near me while four of his cult members followed.

"Good morning, Gentle," he said, wearing his own backpack.

"Good morning, Bilvog," I replied, looking away from him and towards the sky.

I could feel his eye looking up at me, "I'm afraid Nathaniel isn't going to sweep in and rescue you. I must admit, I was a bit surprised when I heard you were the one going on this adventure, knowing you like to play it safe, but I always thought you were stronger than you or your family gave you credit for." His eyes seemed to soften before shuttering again. "Ah, King Thallan wants to speak." He turned and walked abruptly towards Thallan as I stood there stunned, with tears pricking my eyes. Bilvog believed in me more than some of my family.

I allowed myself a moment of affection for him, remembering how important he had been to me. He had always been one of my supporters since I first became the Ever of the Air and I had been able to rely on him for anything up until a few months ago.

I blinked the tears away and let the pain of betrayal come back to a simmer. It was dangerous to feel anything but anger for him. He killed my people and was trying to raise Dread. There was no room for softness when it came to him. I walked to Thallan, keeping my eye on Bilvog's cult members. They watched me with obvious disdain, and I stared back. I was sick of giving up. They lowered their eyes before me, and a small thrill went through me at the victory.

"I see we are all gathered. Now, in a moment, you will be off on your task. Now, to remind you of our deal. Whoever hands the Obsidian Wand to me will get the Crown of

Glass. Now it is fairly straightforward. Continue heading east, and you will cross the Nothing. You will likely have to spend the night there, which is why we have provided you with blankets. On the other side of the Nothing is the Gleaming Grove. I will expect to see whoever is left in three days. Do not disappoint me. If you try to run, we will find you, and you will not like the consequences. Now I think that's it. It's all fairly obvious, so off you go. Bring me what I need, and I will give you what you need. Good luck." He nodded at us, turned, and walked inside, leaving us alone.

Bilvog turned to his followers, determination on his face, and they stalked off. I looked again at the stone giants and wondered how I was going to do this. *You can do this, Namara. You have to do this. Aeris Isle is relying on you; don't let them down.*

I wondered where Nate was. Why had he left? I thought we were getting on well, better than well, actually. I didn't look too closely at the feelings that were trying to tell me there might be more there than I wanted to admit. I wasn't a fool. I had admired his quiet strength and good looks for many years, but being alone with him, hearing him laugh and seeing how he was when he relaxed slightly, I had grown to more than admire him. I stared up at the skies again and wondered what had made him leave me and if he really made that decision himself.

I sighed and looked towards where Bilvog and the others had gone, and I followed them towards the tree line where they had disappeared. I needed to be on my guard. I would be fooling myself if I thought we were all going to travel in peace. It was every man for themselves, and I needed to be alert. I headed into the trees after them, formulating a plan.

I emerged from the trees and immediately stepped onto hard-packed, dusty earth. One foot was on grassy green land, and the other was on a wasteland. There was a clear line between the two like they were two different worlds. I was amazed, but I didn't have time to sit and admire the landscape. I had to move and get as far as I could from Bilvog.

I had managed to skirt around them in the forest using their larger group against them. They were noisy and slow, and I was able to keep track of them, while I travelled through the forest stealthily and quickly, but I knew they weren't too far behind me. The forest had been slow and difficult. The ground was covered in a clinging vine that seemed to stick to you, tying you up and making it hard and tiring to get through.

I had saved my power, hoping the Nothing was desert-like, and I was right. I extended a small stream of power to create a wide strip of air to kick up the dust, and I started to run. I wanted to use my air power to create a dust storm to obscure Bilvog's view and slow him down a bit, and it seemed like it was working. The question was, could I keep it big enough to obscure me but small enough I didn't use up all my power.

Before long, my breath was sawing through my lungs, and my chest was heaving. My eyes filled with grit and the hot air was oppressive and felt like it was trying to suffocate me. Unfortunately, I had vastly overestimated how long I could run. Despite feeling like I was dying, I kept moving my legs, knowing if Bilvog and the others caught up to me, I would be in big trouble. Five against one was not good odds.

Behind me, my dust storm was doing its job and I smiled, knowing Bilvog would be annoyed at the delay. I slowed my run to more of a jog and kept going, keeping track of my power levels. So far, so good. I tried not to think about what would happen when I needed to stop and sleep and instead kept jogging east through the wasteland that was the Nothing.

Now that I was confident I was ahead of them a bit, I took in my surroundings. The Nothing was a very fitting name. There were no trees, no water, and no animals anywhere. To my right, I could see the viney forest extended into the distance, and I wondered if I should head into there to sleep under the cover of the trees. To my left, there was nothing apart from a few boulders and mounds sticking out of the ground, but I was too far to really see what they were.

I paused for a moment, and dug my water bottle out of my pack and had a drink, being mindful not to drink too much or spill any. I let my dust settle and checked behind me, half expecting to see Bilvog and the others, but they weren't there. I checked my power supply, and I was sitting about half full. I took a moment to decide what my plan was for the rest of the day.

My legs ached, and my chest hurt, but I decided to run a bit more to try and get as far ahead of them as possible so I could have a few hours rest before going again tomorrow. I sighed and apologised to my body, and started to jog again.

After about an hour, I was worn out. I had been running or jogging for hours and I could no longer convince my legs to move faster than a walk. I had a blister on my heel, and I had been putting off healing it, wanting to save my power for the dust storm, but it was time to rest, and I could have cried with relief when I did send a small stream of healing to it.

I took in my surroundings, and something caught my eye. I had been so focused on looking forward that I hadn't noticed what was rising out of the sand beside me. Curiosity got the better of me, and I limped over, my brain trying to make sense of what I was seeing. Sticking out of the sand were two hands, from the wrist up, with their fingers outstretched and pointing to the sky.

Hanging from the wrists were two chains joined together like handcuffs. They were the thickness of my body, and I wondered what they were carved out of and why they were out here. I walked around them, and a nagging suspicion rose in the back of my head. Were these...real? I stared with my mouth open, unable to comprehend how a creature this big could end up with its hands sticking out of the Nothing. I wondered if the rest of it was under the earth and if I was standing on the body of the giant.

I tore my eyes away from that mystery and continued east, keeping an eye out for a good place to rest for the night. Bilvog would have to rest at some time, right? After another couple of hours walking my body was worn out and screaming for a rest. I decided to head into the trees where I could get more cover. When I crossed the line between the Nothing and the trees, I sighed under the shade. I dreaded what my skin must look like after travelling for hours in the setting sun, but I pushed that from my mind. Even though the sun was setting here, it was hotter in the Nothing, more like the Bleak Wilds desert that Ashes lived in.

I decided the best thing would be to stay towards the edge of the forest, not wanting to venture too far in and encounter the creatures that called this place home. The trees here were not multicoloured like the other forest we walked through. These ones looked like normal trees but were covered in bell-like nuts that tinkled quietly when the wind blew through them. I had been hearing the noise all day, wondering what it was, and now I knew. It was soft and subtle but beautiful, and I wished we had them in Aeris Isle.

I picked a few of the bell nuts and put them in my bag, hoping maybe we could grow them or maybe learn more about them, and found a tree to climb. I wanted to be higher up so I could keep a look out and see if Bilvog caught up to me. I also wanted to get out of the sticky vine that made walking so difficult.

I found one and settled in the tall branches that made a natural hollow I could nestle into. I opened my bag and took another drink and dug out some of the fruit and bread that had been packed for me. I was starving and sore and sad, and I ate in silence, thinking about all the problems piling up around me. The bombs, finding the wand in Gleaming Grove, getting back with it without running into Bilvog, making Thallan keep his deal, getting home, and last but not least, Nate.

What was I to do about Nate?

Was he still here?

Would he return so we could get home together, or did he find his own way home?

I pulled my knees up close to my chest, rested my head on my knees, and rocked back and forth while I tried not to fall into the yawning nothing that had opened up inside my body. All I wanted to do was fall in or drink my potion and give up.

While I had been moving all day, I had kept it at bay, but now it all came rushing back, and I didn't know how I was going to keep going. I took a deep, shaky breath and lifted my head, looking out over the Nothing. There was no sign of the others and I put a mark in the positive column. Unbidden, Amos's words came back to me, *you are much more than a pretty face. You have steel within you. Do not bend.* I blinked back tears and stretched out my legs. I had to do this. I needed to find the steel within me to make Amos proud.

In the last few months, I had fought cultists with Gloom, visited and bargained with Bella, travelled and survived the Others Realm and dealt with King Thallan of the Obsidian Throne. I had travelled to the Nothing and came face to face with Bilvog. I could do this. All I had to do was get to the Gleaming Grove, retrieve the wand, and give it to Thallan, and I could get out of there. If Nate was there, then fine. If not, he was the one who left so he could make his own way home. I put the backpack behind my head and settled in for a few hours of sleep, trying to stay positive.

Tomorrow would be a big day.

TWENTY-SEVEN

NATHANIEL

In the dungeons, it was cold and dirty. The black stone that made up the castle above ground also made up the walls below, but it was not as smooth and polished. Here, it was rough and dirty, covered in slime from the constant moisture that dripped down it. The ground was covered in dirt and bones and disintegrating scraps of fabric left behind by some other unfortunate prisoner. There were no windows or a bed in the room, and I dreaded the thought of sleeping on the cold, dirty floor, but I would to keep my strength up.

So far, no one had been here to deliver food or water. After I had been brought here, I was knocked out, and when I woke, I guessed I had been down here for at least a full day. Gentle might have already been out in the Nothing for a full night without me. My mind wanted to spiral, but I held it in check. I needed to stay calm and get out of here.

I looked at the green-coloured water dripping down the wall and knew if I drank it, I would probably end up sicker than if I didn't. My body was cold and cramped, but I pushed the discomfort out of my mind and focused only on what I would have to do to get out. *I must get to her*, was a constant mantra in my head. Gentle can handle herself, but I knew how bad things could get here. Plus, if Thallan and Bilvog were to join together, no one would be safe.

I stood up and rattled the bars on the cell, hoping that since the last time I did it, one of them had loosened. Unfortunately, they were still solid. I sighed and walked a couple of steps to the other side of the cell and back again. Being here was like ants crawling all over my skin. It had been a long time since I was locked in here last, but it felt like yesterday.

If I squinted, I could see myself as a small child, huddled and covered in blood, broken feathers littering the floor while I tried my hardest not to sob too loudly. Back then, I had only been in here for a night, and I was scared for myself and my parents, knowing what I was going through was to punish them. I wanted to be brave for them, and I wanted them to be proud of me.

I closed my eyes and rustled my wings, reminding myself I was no longer a child, and I was free, and the bodyguard of one of the fairest, kindest beings I had ever met. I smiled a little, knowing my parents would be proud of me today.

My thoughts were disrupted by the door at the top of the stairs opening as light poured in, illuminating the miserable place I was in. The same guard that had found us in the swamp walked in as serious as ever. He looked me over, his brown eyes not missing a thing, and I stood tall, ignoring his stare.

"He's contained," he called back up to the door, and I waited to see who was going to enter.

King Thallan walked with a plate of food in his hand, and I tensed on impulse. He walked slowly and deliberately, his footsteps echoing on the stone and in my skull. His clothes were perfect, and his hair was neatly tied back. He wore an imitation of a smile, and I ground my teeth, trying to keep the disgust off my face.

"Well, Borthox, it is nice to have one of the Alanti in here again, isn't it? It has been a while longer than I would like." He sighed and looked around the other cells as I tried to prepare for what was to come.

"You might wonder why I have been capturing Alanti and keeping them down here. It is simple, really. I once had one here when he was a boy. Unfortunately, he wasn't old enough for the colour to appear in his wings, so I don't know what they ended up being. It would make him much easier to find," he muttered as he walked closer to the bars of my cell. "Because of him, something was taken from me, and I want revenge if I am honest." He pinned me with his dark purple eyes, and I stared back, defiant. "The first time I saw you, you were familiar to me. I don't know if you are the boy I was looking for, but I intend to do everything I can to find out." By the end, he was practically whispering, and stupidly, I stepped closer to hear him.

Like lightning, his hand shot out, and he grabbed me around the throat. My eyes widened in shock as I clawed at his hand, which was like a vice cutting off my air supply.

"If you are that boy, the things I will do to you will make you wish I had caught you and killed you earlier. I have only wanted two things in this life. To retrieve the item that was stolen from me and find that boy that took it."

I was gasping for air, trying to pry his hands off me. I would not allow myself to die here. Gentle needed me, and I had to make Amos proud. Dying here in this dirty cell would not accomplish that. Unfortunately, he was stronger than I thought, and I couldn't even loosen a finger.

Thallan ignored my struggles and continued, "I am about to achieve one of those things. I would love to achieve the second as well." He flung me away, and I stumbled, my chest heaving as I tried to control my breathing and stop my head from spinning. I glared at him and thought of all the things I wanted to do to him if I had got my hands on him. Ripping him limb from limb seemed like a good start.

"I don't know what you are talking about. This is the first time I have been here," I ground out, lying through my teeth and hoping he couldn't see through me.

He smiled at me and said in a cheery tone, "Right, well, that's all I have to say. Here is your breakfast. By now, Gentle and Bilvog should be getting closer to the Gleaming Grove. I expect they had a hard night out there in the open. By the way, if you are wondering what I told the beautiful Gentle, I may have told her you flew off and abandoned her."

My stomach fell to the floor as I imagined what that might have done to her. Not that I thought she was overly attached to me, but I knew she couldn't take another betrayal. It had broken something in her when Bilvog turned against her and the others, and now, with Amos gone, I wasn't sure how she would take it. I had to get out of here.

"Let me out of here! I'm not that boy! Let me go!" My anger had overridden sense and though I knew he wouldn't be reasoned with, I couldn't control myself. I grabbed hold of the bars, wanting to rip them from the wall.

"I'll be back to see you soon, Nathaniel. Now you have a long, hard think. I wouldn't want you telling me lies and passing the consequences onto Gentle. She is going to have a hard enough time facing Bilvog and his followers in this little race. I would hate for her to return and find you have gotten her in trouble." He turned and walked away, and I shook the bars behind him, roaring my anger into the cold space. Spit flew from my mouth and Thallan paused a moment before carrying on. Borthox remained emotionless and followed him out, and I wondered if he was part husk as well.

The heavy iron door closed with a creak and a bang, and I was left in darkness after Borthox took the lantern. I rattled the irons again in frustration and leaned against the back wall. Gentle was out there travelling across the Nothing and I was stuck in here, useless. I put my head into my hands and closed my eyes, hoping when I opened them, I would be somewhere else.

I don't know how long I stayed like that, but I was startled out of the silence when I heard the door creak open. I jerked my head up and stood, wanting to be ready for whatever was about to happen. Who would it be that came down to torture me? I vowed I would not break. No matter what they did to me, I would not give away the information I had inside. I heard light footsteps coming down the stairs, and my eyes widened when I saw who it was.

TWENTY-EIGHT
GENTLE

I could see the end of The Nothing. In the distance, the dirt and dust stopped and another woodland began. I could have dropped in relief. My legs were aching, and I was dirty, tired and fed up. I was also worried about the fact that since I had made it to the Nothing, I hadn't seen Bilvog or his followers. I would have thought I would have seen them at some point. Where were they?

I shook off the worry, and with an extra boost of energy, I jogged to the edge of the Nothing and stepped under the canopy of bell trees. Instantly the air on my skin cooled and I realised how hot it was out in The Nothing even without full sun. I walked through, savouring the soft grass underfoot and the smell of flowers and dirt. I was over-whelmed that I had made it, and I had to narrow my focus on the small things so I didn't collapse and cry. I reached up and unbraided my hair, instantly relaxing. I shook out the sweat-soaked strands and promised myself as soon as I got back to Aeris Isle, I was going to have a long bath and a hair treatment.

I was walking and wondering when I would come across the Gleaming Grove when I stopped still. There in front of me were more trees, but they had one big difference. All the trees were covered in liquid silver. It was covering every trunk, branch and leaf of the trees in a circle about twenty metres wide.

My mouth hung open, and I wondered what else I was going to come across in this place. I walked around the outside of it and confirmed it was a large circle of silver trees and grass, and the rest of the woods appeared normal. I made it back to the start, realising now I had to walk through because this was surely Gleaming Grove.

I reached out a trembling hand between two silver trees and stretched out into where the trees changed to silver. As it passed between them, there was a slight resistance, like I was pushing my hand through jelly, but after a small hesitation, it did eventually push through. When I pulled my hand back, it was normal and unharmed. I gritted my teeth, moved my pack, and stepped through to the place where the hags hid things they didn't want people to find.

It took a moment for my eyes to adjust. All around me were almost invisible shelves laden with items. There was so much I could hardly get my eyes to settle on just one thing, so instead, I studied the structure I had walked into. All around me were the silver trees, but they appeared transparent. I was standing in a hut-type building. I reached out and touched the wall that was fading in and out of my vision and was surprised when it was solid. I let my eyes follow the wall around. The building was huge.

My stomach fluttered when I realised I would have to search through this place to find the wand, and from what I could see, there was no organisation. I checked behind me and to the outside, and as far as I could tell, I was still alone. I smiled a bit, realising I had done it. I had actually made it to the Gleaming Grove and was standing somewhere I didn't think many people had ever before.

Pride rushed through me at the things I had done, and I wished Nate was here to tell him that maybe Amos was right. Maybe I was more than a pretty face. Thinking of Nate made my smile drop, and for the hundredth time, I wondered where he was. There was an ache in my chest, and I didn't want to look too closely and identify why it was there. Now was not the time to be examining my feelings for a certain personal guard.

I smoothed my hair and dropped my bag near the door to give my aching shoulders a rest while I walked through the strange building, trying to keep my mind on the task at hand. The only logical thing was to begin at the front and move through each room, knowing I would find what I needed quickly so I could get out of here and retrieve my crown.

I walked to the fading shelves and scanned the items. Luckily, there were small labels on all the items, and I sent a silent thanks into the world. This would make my life a bit easier. I picked up the label in front of a small glass ball that had silvery smoke swirling around inside. The small spidery script was hard to read, but after squinting a bit, I deciphered it.

"Antigravity Sphere. When broken, gravity will disappear for thirty seconds. Ember Norwood, March 1864."

I put the sphere back carefully, wondering what Ember would want with an antigravity sphere. She was a kitchen hag and usually kept to creating powerful foods. I shrugged and moved on to the next item, which was an old, stained and yellowing sack. As I leaned closer to get to the note, I caught a sniff of it, and I had to cover my mouth. It stunk old and stale and like urine. I turned away, but curiosity got the better of me, and I picked up the note and read it from as far away as I could.

"Bag of rats. Infinite rats live inside and can be pulled out one by one or can be tipped out all at once. Allard Mortem 1795."

This made sense, and I wasn't surprised the creepy necromancer mage, the only male in the coven, would have something like that. I moved on quickly and skimmed over the rest of the items, paying attention to all the wands I could see. I noticed that, strangely, there was no dust or smell in the building. Some items smelt when you got close, I found out the hard way, but the rest of the place was clean and tidy. I wondered if they came here to clean or if it was enchanted.

After what felt like hours, I was no closer to finding the wand. I had looked at at least fifty wands and still couldn't find the one I wanted. As the minutes ticked by, the fluttering in my chest got faster and harder. I had to find it soon. I had been lucky so far, and I had made it here before Bilvog, but I couldn't be here when they arrived. My stomach dropped, and a thought slithered in.

Had they been here already?

Had they somehow managed to get around me while I was sleeping and were already on the way back?

I knew Bilvog had powers, not that he told people, but with Dread on his side and possibly a hag, I had no idea what to expect from him or his new followers. This could all be for nothing. Before I let my thoughts spiral, I decided

I needed to check this place and not let my imagination get the better of me.

I kept searching and pushed away all negative thoughts, focusing on the positive, and after another few hours, I found it. I was standing on a stool in one of the back rooms, and there it was. It was a long black wand made out of the same stone Thallan's fortress was made from. It tapered at one end but otherwise had no markings or anything. It was a black stick of rock and nothing special. I read the sign in front of it:

Obsidian Wand. Using this wand will rip the personality, and agency from a human or creature permanently. Camilla Crimson, year not recorded."

So, Camilla took this from Thallan. I wondered if she had seen the future and thought it would be good if he didn't have it anymore. If that was the case, I had to agree with her. I felt sick about handing this back to him when he was planning to make more husks. How could I give it back, knowing he was going to ruin more lives? He said the women had to agree to it, but I found it hard to believe any would do so willingly. I held it in my hand, and it was light, too light to bring such destruction to people's lives.

Was it worth handing it over so I could have the crown?

Were my people more important than the people living here?

No, I didn't think so, but I had the opportunity to save a lot of people by stopping Dread. If he got out, he would start up his crusade to entrap, enslave and kill humans and us all over again, and I couldn't let that happen. The only way to stop it was to get the crown back and use it to destroy him.

I ran my hand through my sticky hair and studied the room around me. Such a waste. In this building there were thousands of artefacts that could be used to help us in so many ways. The hags had them sitting here and going to waste. With all the things in here, we could save our people and stop Thallan. We could use it for good and not evil. A shiver tiptoed up my spine as I thought of what the hags could do with this loot. They were already powerful, especially when together, but with all these items. If they decided to use them, they would be unstoppable.

Unfortunately, I could only take one item out. I looked at the wand. I had to do what I came here for. Essentially, the plan had not changed. Come to the Others Realm and retrieve the crown. That was my mission. That was how I was going to save the most people. I put the sign back for the wand and made my way back through to the front door, careful not to knock anything over and picked up my bag. I put the wand in my pocket and braided my hair again, preparing for the long walk back. I had a drink and put the bag on my back, reminding myself of why I was here, what I had to lose and what I had accomplished.

After this, no one could say I was just a pretty face. Not even me. I made a promise to myself that I would come back and help the people Thallan had trapped with this wand once I had saved my realm. I just had to hope it wasn't too late. I thought of the woman with the lavender eyes that had strengthened me at breakfast yesterday and vowed I would help her and the others like her.

With my body infused with a new energy and my spirit hopeful, I stepped out the door. I felt the resistance again, but this time, it was less inclined to let me through. I kept pushing, and finally, I was released. I checked my back pocket, making sure the wand was still there and walked through the trees towards the Nothing.

"Hello there, Gentle. How nice to see you here."

I froze as Bilvog and his cult members stepped out from behind the trees they were hiding behind. I stared into Bilvog's eyes.

"Now if you don't mind, I'd like you to hand over the wand, and we can all be on our way," he said, the other cult members spread out before me.

"You coward. You have been waiting out here for me to do your dirty work." I laughed humourlessly. "I don't know why I am surprised. You have turned into a rat, after all."

His face turned red, and he stepped closer, the others also moving towards me. I studied them in their brown robes, with the same symbol tattooed on their bare heads. None of them had a shred of emotion on their faces, and that scared me most of all. They would truly do anything.

"What I am doing is for the greater good. I really thought you would understand. Humans are a plague on this world and their own. They do nothing but consume and destroy. How many habitats and species have been lost since they arrived? How many of our people have suffered because of them? It is time someone did something!"

I couldn't believe I was really hearing this, that he truly believed the hate he was spewing.

"You could join us, Gentle. I have always thought of you like a daughter and I hate to see you on the other side of this. You know I am right. Come and join us. The two of us will have to convince Dread it is for the best, but we can do that together. Please, it doesn't have to be this way. Come with us." He held out his hand, and I looked into his eyes, shocked. He truly believed I would go with him. He thought he was right, and I would betray my family and people by siding with him. I took a step back.

"You're mad! There is no way I would ever join the two of you. What you want to do will bring more destruction, not peace! You are going to try to enslave a whole group of people. How do you think that is going to work? Sure, we have magic, but they outnumber us a million to one. What about the good humans out there? The ones that create art and help us and want to make the world a better place? What you are doing will hurt our people more than it will help them, and I pity you that you don't see it. Now get out of my way." I picked up the wind around us and used it to buffet the cultist back so I could get through. I was so angry I wanted to get out of here. Before I could go far, Bilvog sighed.

"I must admit it was a long shot, but it was worth a try. I really wish you had come with me because now you truly are one of the enemies. Never forget I gave you the chance to join the winning side, for what is to come will change the world." He nodded at one of the cultists standing next to him, and the others rushed towards me. I barely had time to think before a fist came flying, connecting with my cheek.

Pain exploded, and I yelled out. I flung my arms out, wind exploding from my fingertips, and they were all pushed back a step. I had a few seconds to collect myself before they came at me again. I crouched and brought my fists up, hoping to get a few hits in before they killed me.

My heart was exploding out of my chest, and my cheek was screaming in pain as I lashed out wildly, trying to hit the first man who rushed at me. I missed, and he smirked at me, punching me in the stomach. The air exploded out of my lungs with a grunt, and I bent over, trying to suck the air back into my body. While I was bent over, someone reached out and plucked the wand from my back pocket. I whirled around in a panic, but before I could make a grab for it, someone kneed me in the face.

My nose flattened against my face, and my eyes instantly watered so I couldn't see anything. Blood and snot were pouring from my nose, and I sobbed, knowing how pathetic I must look. How easily I was defeated.

"Tsk tsk tsk. That was almost too easy, Gentle. Are you sure you don't want to change your mind? Now you know what it feels like to lose?" I could see Bilvog's brown shoes standing in front of me through my tears, and I summoned all my energy and grit, lifted my head, and spat a large gob of blood at him. I missed his face, but it did hit his lovely, clean white shirt, and I felt a second of satisfaction.

He yelped and stepped away, looking at my blood on his shirt in disgust. "Now that wasn't very lady-like." His face twisted into something cold and evil, and my heart stopped, waiting to see what he would do next. Would he be the one to kill me?

He reached over and grabbed my plait at the back of my head and pulled me forward roughly. I was taken back to seeing Lilly in that basement, being dragged around by her hair, and I lashed out, trying to trip him or scratch him. In my panic, I couldn't direct my wind blasts effectively, and all they managed to do was kick up more swirling dust and leaves around us. But I would try anything to get away from this monster I once called friend. Nothing worked. He pulled until my plait was stretched tight from my head, my neck exposed. "You, come here. Hold this," he said to one of his followers.

A lady with wild feline-like orange eyes came and pulled my head back further, straining my neck painfully. Bilvog pulled out a knife with his good hand as a smirk spread across his face, and he stared into my eyes.

"When will you learn that we will win? You have failed, and now you will pay for your behaviour. You have brought ruin to your family. I have the Staff, and I will soon have the crown. You are nothing. What are you doing here? You weren't made for adventure. All you are good at is sitting in your castle wearing pretty dresses and playing princess."

He took the knife and held it to my neck, making me freeze. This was it. I had disappointed everyone, and now I was going to die in the Nothing. I bared my teeth at him. I would not go down mildly. If he wanted to kill me, he would have to work for it. Despite having the knife at my throat, I reached for his face, trying to claw his eyes out and managed to scratch one side of it. He grunted in pain as three small lines of blood dripped down his face. He reached up with the black and shrivelled hand that had been hit with Amelia's disintegration. Seeing his own blood on it, he roared, leapt forward, and sliced with his knife.

I waited for the pain and blood and death, but I did not die. I turned my head as much as I could and saw what he held in his hands. My braid. He had cut off my hair. Despair filled me, and tears streamed down my face.

"I thought that might hurt. Now, I think you have been beaten enough already," he leaned in close, knife back at my throat. "I want you to tell your brothers and sisters what will happen if they continue to go against me," he shook my golden braid in front of my face, and I helplessly reached out for it. He snatched it out of my reach and stood.

"Let's go."

I watched as they walked away, and through my despair and sadness, another emotion was building. I was weak and in pain, but somehow, I managed to stand. Wobbling, I held out my hands and poured every emotion into my power.

I unleashed.

The power of my blast knocked everyone over and formed a dust storm around me. The little specks of sand peppered me and them, but I didn't care. I could hear them screaming as they were trapped inside of it, and I hoped the sand was stripping the skin from their bodies. I could make out their shapes in the storm, and I watched as, one by one, they disappeared. I could hear them running, but with no more strength to follow them, I collapsed onto my knees and watched them run. Bilvog reached out his hands, and one by one, they vanished. It seemed he had picked up a few new spells.

I lay on the dust, bringing my hand to my head, and a sob escaped my raw throat. All that was left of my hair was a few inches all over. Everything that was me seemed to empty into the pit that had opened in my chest. All the pain and betrayal I had been pushing down came roaring back and I let it.

Nate. Bilvog. My family. I let all the disappointment and shock crash over me like a wave and I welcomed it. I was tired of trying to put on a good face and act like I had no feelings, so I let them all empty out.

I was done.

I closed my eyes, bleeding, broken, and aching all over, inside and out, and gave up.

TWENTY-NINE
NATHANIEL

Exhaustion weighed heavily on my back. I had been flying for hours, and my muscles were screaming. For the hundredth time during my mad flight over the Nothing I thought of the husk with the lavender eyes who had freed me.

She had approached my cell on eerily silent feet. At first, I had stepped back, wondering if Thallan had sent her, but after a second of looking into her eyes I could see she was frightened. She did not speak but reached into a pocket of the black satin dress she was wearing and brought out one silver key. She held it out to me through the bars, and I took it, noticing it was wet. With what little light was coming through the door at the top of the jail, I could see it was blood. She held a finger to her lips and held up five fingers.

"Five? People? Seconds? Minutes?" I asked until she nodded at minutes. I reached through the bars and clasped her hands before I could think and said, "Thank you. Are you safe? Do you want to come with me?" I had no idea how I was going to get myself out, let alone her, but she had risked her life to save me, and I owed her the chance to be free.

She shook her head sadly and pulled her hands from my grasp. There was such a look of resignation and sadness that I knew she understood what would happen to her if caught. I was impressed and touched by her bravery and wanted to tell her that, but she was gone before I got the chance. I saw her slip out of the door and close it almost all the way. I felt the weight of the key in my hand and thanked her again silently, hoping I would see her again.

Waiting the five minutes was torture, but when it was up, I put the key into the lock and held my breath as I turned it. What if it was the wrong one? Or worse, a set-up. I froze, wondering if she had been sent here and if this was all a trap. I didn't think it was. She had seemed genuine. Plus, when would I get this opportunity again?

The lock was stiff, and it took a moment for the key to turn, but it did. I opened the cell door, flinching with the loud screech it made on the rusty hinges. There was no way no one heard that. I took the stairs two at a time until I was hiding behind the door waiting until I heard boots running down the corridor towards me. I waited until they were inside and then slammed the door closed behind them. I lunged out and smashed one of the guards' heads into the wall, and he crumpled to the ground.

The one in front spun around and launched a series of punches and kicks that had me on the backfoot immediately. I was not ready to fight. I hadn't eaten or drank anything, and I was stiff from being in the cell and not moving. He landed a few blows, and I shook off the pain, pushing it deep as I blocked the rest of his blows. I managed to get a few good punches in, and one landed with a satisfying crunch in his face.

While he was dazed, I spun him around and wrapped my arm around his neck, cutting off his air supply. After a minute he slowed and then eventually flopped against me. I laid him down and wasted no time searching their bodies for weapons. Both had daggers, and one had a sword, which I took and headed back up the stairs.

I walked out into the hall on high alert to any sound. Using snatches of memory from when I was a child and from when they took me, I made it out of the dungeons and onto the main floor. I had to make it to a window large enough for me to jump out so I could fly away. I rustled and stretched my wings. I needed to get some movement into them in preparation for flying, but I knew it was going to hurt.

I made it to the end of the hall and then up a flight of stairs. Up ahead, I knew there was a large sitting chamber, and if I could get there, there were large windows along one wall. I had to get there and hope it was empty. I crept along and stayed low and to the shadows the wall mage lights cast.

I reached the open sitting chamber and ran to one of the windows. I pushed open the shutters and could have laughed in relief when they opened quietly. I was on the first floor, and I stepped out onto the window sill. I scanned the sky and roofs of the castle and couldn't see anything. I flapped my wings and grimaced when the tight muscles strained, but I kept going.

Eventually they were loose enough that I crouched before pushing up with my legs. My wings flapped, and with great effort, I was finally in the air. I tried to stay away from windows, but it wasn't long before I heard shouts of alarm coming from all directions. I gritted my teeth and flapped harder, trying to find a thermal to help me rise faster.

Something whizzed past my ear, narrowly missing a wing. Guards were shooting crossbows at me. I flew higher, hoping I would be out of their range and after a while, I was clear. I orientated myself and flew east to find Gentle.

Hours after my escape, I was aching all over my body, and all I wanted to do was rest, but I needed to get to the Gleaming Grove. Every beat of my wings sent sharp pains into my back and through my legs. I tried not to think about the fact that once I landed, I likely wouldn't be getting back up. I distracted myself by looking out over the Nothing. It was split into two by a strange strip of forest that seemed to be...ringing?

Dotted throughout, I could see lumps and bumps coming out of the sand, and my eyes grew wide when I noticed it was a pair of knees, a hip, and hands. A giant had been buried here. I didn't want to believe what I was seeing, and as much as I wanted to go and investigate, I had my mission, and I had to stay focused.

My mind kept going around and around, worrying about Gentle and thinking about the realisation I had. While I was locked up in the cell, there wasn't much to do except think, and one of the only things on my mind was how my feelings had deepened. There was no denying it. I was in love with Gentle. I knew it had been sneaking up on me, and I was now ready to admit it to myself, if not to her. I knew it was wrong and against the rules, but for once, I didn't care about the rules.

This was bigger than that.

I tried to pinpoint the moment I fell in love with her, and I think it was when I was in the library with Amos's body, and she had treated me like a human. For once in my life, I didn't feel like I had to be the strong one. Normally, crying in front of someone would have been unthinkable, but in front of her, it was alright.

In the distance, I could see another little pocket of forest that seemed to be shining, reflecting the little bit of sunlight that was in the sky like a mirror. That must be the Gleaming Grove. I flew closer to the ground, my muscles twitching and wobbling as I got closer to the forest. My heart stopped and restarted double time when I saw there was a person lying near the tree line. I landed hard, my wings giving out as they drooped on my back. I grit my teeth and ran the short distance to the body. My footsteps sent sparks of pain through my whole body, but I didn't care because I could just make out the figure lying on the ground. Gentle.

With a burst of energy, I didn't think I was capable of, and I sped forward. "Gentle!" I called, praying she would move. I could see a stain around her that could only be blood, and I could hear my heart pounding in my head. I reached her and fell to my knees, ignoring the pain and my wings dragging in the dust.

"Gentle, are you alright?" I asked, softly cupping her head. Her hair was gone, and her face was covered in blood. I could see her nose was squashed against her face, and my heart broke for her. The smell of blood was strong and I tried to cut myself off from it before it made me panic. Who had done this, and where were they now? I knew I should be up looking for them, but there was no way I was going to leave her side.

After what felt like a lifetime, Gentle stirred and opened her bruised eyes to look at me.

"Nate...is it you?" she asked, with her brow furrowed. I could see she was confused, and I wondered what Thallan had told her about my disappearance.

"Yes, it's me. What happened?"

Her eyes dimmed, and she looked away from me. "Bilvog. I got the wand, but he took it from me. I failed." A tear dripped from her ruined nose and onto the dust.

"Are you hurt anywhere else?" I asked, trying to calm the wild surge that went through me at Bilvog's name. What else was that gnome going to do to her? I ran my hands down her body, feeling for any injuries and to reassure myself nothing was broken. She seemed fine physically, but I waited for her answer before I tried to move her.

"No, just my face and my hair." Her voice cracked on the word hair, and another bit of my heart cracked.

I put my arms under her knees and back and lifted her. I walked into the cool of the forest and out of the heat. My body shivered as the sweat on my skin cooled. Even though there was no real sunlight, The Nothing was definitely hotter than under the trees. I tried to ignore that she was limp in my arms. It was like her spirit was broken. She had lost some of the spark that filled her with life, and it scared me. Her arms wrapped around my neck, and she tucked her head into my shoulder. Ahead of me I could see a pocket of trees that were silver, and I was intrigued but I put all my focus on Gentle.

I went back and picked up her bag and brought it to her, digging out the water bottle and opening it.

"Can you sit up?" I asked her.

She grimaced, and her body tensed as she pushed herself up to lean against a tree. Her hands wrapped around her stomach, and I saw her flinch slightly.

"Here, have a drink."

She held it up to her face and cringed when the bottle touched her lips, but she took a sip.

"What happened here, Gentle?" I asked, trying to keep my panic in check. Even though she said she was alright, my mind refused to believe it.

When she turned her face to me, her eyes were hard and unflinching. "Where were you? You left me alone," she said, hurt in her voice, and even though it wasn't my fault, the blame settled in my stomach. She sat up straight and tense against the tree.

"That night in your room, I went for a fly, and Thallan caught me. He gave me a drug that paralysed me and took me to the dungeons." I ran a hand through my gritty hair, waiting to see her reaction. "I only just managed to escape, and I flew as fast as I could to get here to you."

Her eyes didn't soften as she stared at me.

"You have to know I would have been here in a minute if I could have." I couldn't stop myself and I took her hands. Something in my body was telling me this was one of the most important moments in my life. I had to convince her I would never leave her. I didn't think I could ever come back from that in her eyes, and I never wanted to be the one that caused her pain.

"Why would Thallan want you locked up? He has been interested in you since we got here. Why?" she asked as she reached up to touch her hair and winced as she realised it had been hacked off.

Surprised by the question, I hesitated a moment. I hadn't told anyone about my past here, and I wasn't sure I wanted to. It was in the past, and I didn't want to think about it any more than I had to. I opened my mouth and closed it again, trying to work out the words to tell her. I decided to tell her the basic truth, with none of the gory details.

I cleared my throat and sat back, releasing her hands. "I grew up here. I was taken from Aeris Isle when I was small and brought to the Others Realm. My parents were caring, and I was treated well for the first few years. Then things changed. When my parents were not around, people would treat me cruelly. I was only five or six at the time and couldn't defend myself. My parents saw this and wanted to get me out of there.

"The problem was, my parents were one of the senior people in Thallan's court, and there was no way it would go unnoticed if we left, and they didn't know if another realm would accept us. They had stolen a child and left a changeling in my place." I sighed heavily, trying to block out the people in the court who had hurt me. "Eventually, they managed to take something from Thallan and used that to buy their way into Aeris Isle. I think he suspects I may be the Alanti they tormented, and now he wants revenge."

"What happened to your parents?" she asked, her eyes softening.

I swallowed the lump in my throat. "They died not long after we arrived in Aeris Isle. Before they died, they asked Amos to take me in, and he did."

"I'm sorry. That sounds awful. No wonder you wanted to avoid Thallan when we were travelling. Did he find out it was you? Are you in danger from him?"

"No, he didn't find out, but if he ever did, I definitely would be in danger." I stood and stretched my aching legs, looking around for somewhere to rest for the night, knowing neither of us could make it across the Nothing in the state we were in. Plus, I wanted to put some distance between Gentle and the questions she was asking.

"Wait," she said, and I closed my eyes, knowing what she was about to ask. "What did your parents take from Thallan?"

I turned around and looked at her. "They took the Obsidian wand and gave it to Bella." I said softly, "I only found out about it when I was asking Amos about my parents years after they died...or, to be more accurate, were killed. Thallan found them and had them murdered. He is still looking for me, and I can only imagine what he wants me for."

"So that's why Bella acted like she knew you. How long have you known her?" she asked, leaving forward, warming to the story. "And the wand said it belonged to Camilla. She must have got it off Bella for some reason."

"I only met her once, but I hardly remember it. Amos took me for the first time after I had been asking about my parents and the memories I had of Thallan's castle. She told me what had happened, and I pretty much avoided her after that. I didn't want to have anything to do with her in case Thallan ever came looking for her. As to why it said Camilla had it, who knows? They probably share all the stuff in there," I sighed, glad to be speaking the truth but still wanting to change the subject. I had never told anyone about my parents and the wand and I found it strange to speak about it so openly. "Anyway, you didn't tell me what happened here. I am guessing this is the Gleaming Grove," I said, pointing to the patch of silver that stained the trees.

She withdrew again. "Yes, that's it. We could go and rest there, I suppose. I know he won't, but I hate the idea of Bilvog coming back."

"Coming back? How long ago did he attack you?" I asked, holding out my hand to her.

"I don't really know how long, to be honest. I sort of gave up after he attacked me, but judging by my magic level, it must have been a few hours. He would still be running across the Nothing. Didn't you see him?" Her hand was warm and smooth beneath mine. My heart sped up a little as I held it carefully before letting it go.

"No, I didn't see anyone unless you count the giant that seems to have laid down and never gotten back up."

"He must be able to hold his invisibility for long periods of time then," she said, furrowing her brow.

"Wait. He can turn invisible?"

"Yes, him and all his followers. Certainly up's the stakes a bit, doesn't it?" she said.

"It definitely makes things interesting, that's for sure." I walked towards the silver trees and stepped through into a room with no walls. Every surface was loaded with items and descriptions, and I wondered how long it had taken Gentle to find the wand in here. I could see shimmering walls and doors, and Gentle was standing at the one that led outside, shaking her head at me.

"What's wrong?" I asked, opening the door.

"I can't get in there," she said, looking like she was standing in a glass box. "I have already entered once. Maybe that's all the hags will allow. I'll have to stay out here." I walked out the door to stand next to her and tried to walk back into the house, but I was locked out as well.

"Wow. Those hags really need to have a garage sale. It is packed in there," I said, smiling, trying to lighten the mood.

She smiled back, but her heart wasn't really in it. I held out my hand, trying to reassure myself she was alright, but I knew she wasn't. There was something broken inside I wasn't sure I could reach. She took my hand and held it lightly.

"Let's find somewhere to rest for the night. We will have a big day tomorrow trying to catch up with Bilvog."

THIRTY

GENTLE

Nate's hand was warm and strong, and I savoured each point of contact. When I had woke up bloody and broken, I thought he was an angel, and my heart skipped a beat. He had never left me, and he came back. In that moment of realisation, it was him, a wound inside of me knitted back together, and I rose, a small bit, from my despair.

We walked through the forest on the edge of the Nothing, listening to the bells in the trees until we found a nice, flat, grassy area to rest for the night. Nate unpacked my pack and laid out the few supplies I had. A blanket, a water bottle, a portable mage light and a small amount of food. He laid out the blanket carefully while I stood and watched, feeling numb. As much as I was excited to see him, having him here made my failure all the worse. Now I had to fail with an audience.

Aeris Isle was his home, too. What did he think about me having the means to save it and then losing it? I didn't dare ask him because I didn't think I wanted to know, plus he seemed a bit talked out after telling me his story. My mind still struggled to wrap my head around the fact he was stolen and brought to live in the castle with Thallan.

I wondered what things they had done to him for his parents to risk stealing the wand. I couldn't imagine Thallan would be very forgiving. His parents must have loved him a lot to do that, and I was glad. He was a man worthy of love.

"Here we go. You sit here for a minute, and I will go and get some wood for a fire and see if I can find anything safe to eat. Will you be alright by yourself for a bit?" he asked, concern in his eyes.

I looked around at the small camp he had created. "I'll be fine," I replied, trying to convince myself—and him—of that fact.

He nodded. "Okay. I'll try and find some more water as well to clean up. Won't be long." He walked off into the trees, and I waited until I could no longer hear or see him before I buried my face in my hands. I winced and held in a cry when I touched my smashed nose. I took jagged breaths, reached to the bottom of my power, and held my hands above my nose. My nose got warm, and it tingled before I heard a loud crack.

This time, I did cry out as it righted itself. I had enough power left to dull the sharpness of the pain, and I was grateful for the relief. I sat and gave myself a moment to get my body sorted out before taking a drink. I closed my eyes as the water slid down my dry throat, and I had to stop myself from drinking the whole lot in one go.

Once all my pressing needs were done, I no longer had anything to keep me distracted, and my brain turned straight to what I had been holding back.

What are you doing here? You weren't made for adventure. All you are good at is sitting in your castle wearing pretty dresses and playing princess.

The words came back to me, and tears sprang to my eyes because I knew Bilvog was right. Even though I agreed with him, it did nothing to dull the sharp pain of betrayal and shame that filled me with his words. I was hopeless, and now I had lost the one thing that could have saved everyone. I sat and made myself lift a shaking hand to what was left of my hair.

I held back a sob as I brushed the short strands that were no longer than my hand. All my hair, gone. I knew it was vain of me, but it was one of the only things I was proud of and had become one of the things I defined myself by. I hated the thought of looking in the mirror and seeing what he had done to me. I ran my hand through it, and it felt like Bilvog had taken a bit of my soul. What good was I now? I had no brains and no beauty.

At that moment, Nate returned. He had taken off his shirt and was carrying berries inside of it. It was so full they were practically tumbling out of it. My stomach rumbled, but I didn't care. He was smiling at me, but it dropped when he saw my face.

"Gentle, what's wrong? Are you okay?" he said as he placed the orange and red berries on the ground. I watched a few roll away, uninterested. All the anger over my attack came roaring to the surface, and I snapped.

"No, I am not okay. I am an idiot. I have lost the artefact, been attacked, failed to protect my people." With every point, my breathing was getting shorter and shorter. "And we are stuck in the Others Realm." My hands and voice were shaking, and I couldn't take in a full lungful of air, but I kept on going. "Not to mention, my evil brother is rising, intent on killing us and most of the non-magical world population, and I am ugly. I am vain, and all my beauty is gone, and I am useless. Totally useless." It felt like someone was sitting on my chest, and tears started leaking out of my eyes. I clutched my chest, my heart beating wildly.

Nate sat in front of me and took my hands. His mouth was moving, but I couldn't hear what he was saying. I could tell he was taking deep breaths. I kept my eyes on him and eventually, I was able to focus,

"Deep breaths. Come on, one more."

I tried to listen to the sound of his voice and follow his directions, and after a few minutes of intentional breathing, I started to feel better. I took notice of the things I could see around me, like the silver trees, the red juicy berries, the stars and moon above me and the beautiful pink of the sunset sky. I noticed what I could hear. The pounding of my heart beating a rhythm, the tinkling of the bells growing in the trees and the sound of small insects flying through the air. I could smell the grass we sat on, slightly musty and dirty.

My breathing slowed, and my head was no longer spinning. I sat for a few more minutes, collecting myself, while Nate went and picked up the berries that had escaped his shirt. He sat across from me and separated the berries for us to eat silently. I peeked at him and wondered if he was going to say anything about my outburst or ignore it. The back of my neck tingled in shame at exploding at him. I had always prided myself on being kind, and I was embarrassed

I had spoken so harshly to someone who had done nothing wrong.

He started to eat, and after my stomach rumbled, I ate as well. I was on edge and nervous, wondering what he was going to say about all this. Looking at him, he seemed like he didn't have a care in the world, and I didn't know what to make of that. By the time we finished eating the berries, the rawness of my hunger was gone.

Nate cleaned up, still silent and sat opposite me. I was practically jumping out of my skin, waiting to hear him speak. Would he condemn me for being foolish, or had his anger been growing? I couldn't look him in the eyes, and I kept my attention on my crossed legs, waiting for him to say something.

After a moment, I felt his hand on my chin as he lifted my head and made me look at him. My now short hair was in my eyes, and he brushed it behind my ear with a surprising tenderness. Despite my reservations about what he would say, my heart sped up at his touch, and I could look nowhere else but his bright blue eyes.

"You are one of the best people I know. You speak to everyone with kindness, even if you don't receive it from them. You care and love your people enough to travel to another realm to retrieve something that *might* save them. You laugh when they laugh and shed tears when they are hurt. You are kind, positive, funny and a joy to be around. Losing the artefact doesn't mean you have failed. You have survived King Thallan and the Obsidian Throne, which very few people can say. We will find another way to win this battle, but I will not hear you talk about yourself like that." He looked away for a moment.

My heart was beating fast, and tears were pricking my eyes from the kind words. A glow had started to spread through my body. He turned back to me, and his face shone with emotion like he had removed a mask. My body stilled as I waited to hear what he would say that caused such a change in him.

"The reason everyone loves you," he swallowed, "the reason *I* love you is the beauty that is on the inside. Not what is on the outside. You are the most amazing person I know. You inspire me every day to smile and be happy. Never doubt you have a strength no one else has."

He was breathless by the end of his speech, and I stared at him, convinced he could hear my heart pounding. Uncertainty and vulnerability were all over his face, and I forced my mouth to move and break the silence. Unfortunately, my brain couldn't focus on anything other than those three words.

"You love me?"

Sitting as close to him as I was, I knew he wasn't breathing. Noticing that made me realise I, too, wasn't breathing as I waited for his confirmation. I tried to convince my body not to jump the gun as it began tingling and warming with the possibility that my feelings were being reciprocated because, at that moment, I knew it with certainty. I loved Nate.

He swallowed. "Of course I do. Why wouldn't I? You have shown me compassion, laughter, and friendship more than anyone else. Even growing up with Amos, there was something missing. With you, I feel like I have found it." He lapsed into silence as I absorbed what he said.

I took a moment to arrange my thoughts before I took his hands in mine. They were warm and rough, and touching them sent tingles to my soul.

"I am so glad to hear that." I swallowed, my mouth suddenly dry. "Because, well, I feel the same way." His eyes widened. "I think I have for a while, actually. I have always admired that you do things the right way and not the easy way. You're reliable and responsible, and I'm realising as I say this, it doesn't sound super romantic," I said with a giggle.

He smiled at me and squeezed my hand.

"But these things mean a lot to me. I am an Ever, and even though I have let it slip, I need someone who can rule by my side. Someone who can deal with the problems as they arise and help me. I can't think of anyone else I would want to do that with. You are perfect and amazing, and I am madly in love with you." I reached up and cupped his cheek and waited to see what would happen next.

Nate leaned forward and gently put his hand on the back of my head and pulled me forward. We moved until our foreheads were almost touching. I kept my eyes open, not wanting to miss anything. I had been dreaming about this for a long time, and now the moment was here, I didn't want to waste a second of it.

When I felt like I couldn't take it anymore, he leaned forward, and his lips brushed mine softly, gently. My whole body tingled at the contact like I had been electrocuted from within, and all thoughts fled from my mind. I savoured the feel of our lips touching and kissed him back. I couldn't catch my breath. It was everything I dreamed it would be, and I knew I would never be the same. This kiss had changed me, and I couldn't get enough.

It wasn't long before passion threatened to overtake us when our noses bumped, and pain exploded in my face. I gasped and pulled back gently, touching my nose. Nate had a dazed look on his face, and I giggled. He shook his head and smiled back at me.

"I have dreamed of kissing you for years, and it was better than I ever could have imagined. However, I never imagined you would have a smashed nose. Are you alright?" he asked, reaching forward and putting his hand on my knee.

"I'm fine. I'll heal it tomorrow when I have my power back. For now, I think I would like to get a nice rest and see what tomorrow looks like." I looked at him, shy. "Would you like to lay next to me tonight?" I asked in a small voice, surprised at the fluttering in my stomach. It was so strong I felt like the butterflies were about to lift me from the ground and fly away.

"I would love that. Here, let me help you up." He reached out and took my hands and pulled me to standing.

We stood for a moment, holding hands and looking into each other's eyes, and for the first time since Bilvog had betrayed me, I knew I had someone I could rely on. Nate had helped me through all this. Visiting the hag, travelling to the Others Realm, flying, and finding me today. I knew no matter where I went and what happened, he would be there by my side. I stood up on tip toes and kissed him again, pouring all my love and trust into it, and he wrapped his arms around my waist, making me feel safe and cared for.

We broke apart and I led him to the sleeping bag he had settled on the ground. His wings were drooping, and the end feathers were dragging on the ground, making the light blue feathers dirty and brown. He was exhausted after his mad flight over the Nothing, so I laid down, and he settled in behind me.

His arm was wrapped around me, and I snuggled in, hardly believing we were here together at last. I savoured the warmth and contact and smiled, but exhaustion took me, and I fell into a deep sleep, listening to Nate's steady breathing behind me and the bells tinkling in the trees.

THIRTY-ONE
NATHANIEL

I dreamt I was back in the Obsidian Castle dungeons.

It was cold and there was a constant drip from the walls that smelt like old stale water. In the corner of the cell was a bucket for my toilet and I was ashamed to say I had to use it, and no one had emptied it for days. I looked at my hands at the bent and broken fingernails I had bitten and pulled off. My wings were white, not the blue they are today, and I was all alone without my parents again.

Tears fell from my eyes, and I gripped the bars of my cell that were coated in something that looked a lot like dried blood. I rested my head on them, willing my tears to stop, knowing they would do me no good. The door opened at the top of the stairs, and every muscle in my child's body locked as I waited to see what sort of torture would be rained down on me today. I unconsciously ruffled my wings as the air kissed the bare skin where my feathers had been plucked out for one of the ladies to decorate her dress. Would they be coming for another lot or something worse?

The light was brighter than usual, and it blinded me as I covered my eyes and squinted, wanting to face whoever it was eye to eye. I wanted to show them I wasn't afraid even though I was literally shaking. The person walked towards me, and I could hear the tap, tap, tap of their shoes on the stone floor. Their silhouette was getting closer, and my jaw clenched, causing my teeth to ache.

The person came into view. The door closed behind them and the bright light was gone, and my vision started to adjust. Right when I thought I would see the person who had come to take me, I was startled in the real world, and I was ripped from my sleep and shocked awake.

"Sorry, I didn't want to wake you, but I have made a decision." Gentle looked at me with her short hair in her face. She tried to tuck it behind her ear, but it fell right back out again. I could see the sadness and frustration written on her face, but she ignored it. I rubbed my eyes and sat up. My whole body ached from the day of flying, but I was already stronger and ready for the day.

"What did you decide?" I asked as I leaned in and gave her a peck on the cheek. I had to make sure last night wasn't another sweeter, nicer dream. She blushed slightly but didn't pull away.

"We need to go after Bilvog. We need that crown. I have been awake for a while and worked out if you could carry me and fly us there, I can make it easier with the wind, and we might still get there in time. They would have had to rest last night, and we will be flying faster. I think we can do it. We can get there. Do you think you can carry me? I know you were exhausted from yesterday."

I stretched out my wings to see how they felt. There were a few aches, but nothing major. "If you are helping with the wind currents, then yes, I think we might have a good chance. But it will be close. Are you sure you want to see him again after what happened?" I was concerned she might not take to dealing with him again so soon. He had ripped away a part of her, and that could do some terrible things to a person.

She stood up and began to pace, touching her nose, which was still black and bruised. "Yes, I know I can do it. I have no choice. I have to get that crown and I will do anything to do it. Aeris Isle is depending on me. It is time I stepped up and protected my people. The first thing I am going to do when I get back, with the crown, is tell all my advisors I am back in charge. For too long, I have played the pretty hostess, and I am sick of it. I am ready to be a leader, and a leader has to do things they don't always want to do. We have to get the crown."

I sat and stared at her for a moment. Here was a woman who had always had the best of things easily. Now she was in stained, bloody, torn clothing, with her hair having been hacked off. She was dirty and dishevelled in a strange land, and she was still planning on facing the person who had betrayed her the worst. I would do anything for her. She had stolen my heart, and I never wanted it back. There was steel in her gaze, but underneath it, there was a small speck of uncertainty.

I stood and took both her hands. "I will follow you anywhere. We will face Bilvog, Thallan, Dread, and anyone else who comes along and threatens the people we love. I am with you all the way, always."

Tears welled up in her eyes, but she didn't let them fall.

"Right then, let's go. We don't have much time to catch up." She started to clean up, and I stopped her.

"If I am going to carry you, we will need to leave as much as we can here. Only take what you can't be without. The less weight, the better."

"Oh. That makes sense." Frowning, she went through her bag. She pulled out the water and leftover berries and set them aside. She continued digging through the bag and eventually pulled out her hairbrush.

"I suppose I don't really need this anymore, but I can't leave it behind." She ran her fingers through her short hair and smiled at me sadly. I kissed the top of her hair and tangled my fingers in there.

"It will grow back. You are still the most beautiful woman I know. How is your face today? Have you healed it yet?" I asked, looking at the mottled colour from the bruise.

She shook her head. "No. I need to save my powers for the trip. We are going to need all the help we can get to get there in time, if it's even possible. I will have to look like this for a little longer," she said with a small smile. I smiled at her, loving the way it warmed me from within, and we gathered our things, making a pile for someone to find one day.

As we were doing that, I glanced over at Gentle, and pride filled me. She was a different woman from the one that arrived here. She was stronger, braver, and less self-focused. She had a new determination in her, and I was proud of the way she had adjusted and was willing to keep going, even when it was hard.

When we were ready to go, I cradled Gentle up in my arms and unfurled my wings, testing them out. I prepared myself mentally, knowing the journey ahead would be a hard one with Gentle's extra weight, and I was still tired from the day before, but I had to do it. Gentle's air power would make it easier, and I hoped that would be enough.

I flapped my wings a few times and told Gentle to hold on. Her arms tightened around my neck, and I squeezed her tighter to my body. I jogged and let the wind lift under my wings, and we were airborne. I faltered for a moment with the added weight, and we dipped a little. I adjusted my wings and leaned into the updraft of the wind, and we were rising again.

"Oh, I was a bit worried there for a moment," Gentle said loudly so I could hear.

"So was I, but we will be fine now." I smiled at her and continued to climb. We were flying into the sun, leaving the moon behind us. The sky was a purple-pink colour, and it was one of the most beautiful ones I had ever seen. It was a sharp contrast to the place where we were going. In my mind, I was turning over and over all the different things that could go wrong and all the things we could do to prevent them from happening. I knew there would be no easy way to get the crown.

Even if we beat Bilvog and got the wand off him, there was no way Thallan was going to give us the crown with no conditions. No matter what angle I looked at it, we had nothing to bargain with except one thing.

My stomach clenched, and my brain rebelled. I would lose what I had just gained, but I would do it. I would do it for Aeris Isle, for the other Evers and for Gentle. I would do anything I could to make her happy and stop Dread from rising. I had lived with and suffered at the hand of evil. I would not let anyone else go through that if I could help it.

For the rest of the flight, I tried to think of other ways to bargain, but nothing came to mind. I watched the Nothing fly past with its giants reduced to bone sticking out of the sand. I flew hard and fast in a straight line, keeping an eye out for Bilvog and his cult members, but there was no trace of them. Were they already there? I tried to calculate how long it would take them on foot and realised that because we could fly in a straight line and avoid all the obstacles on the ground, we could do it. All these thoughts were occupying my mind on the long flight helping me to keep my mind off my tiring body.

My arms, back and wings were aching, and I worried I might possibly not make it. The wind helping to push me along was a blessing, but after the long flight yesterday and the extra weight of Gentle, the hours in the air were taking its toll. Every beat of my wings sent shots of pain through my back and down my legs, and I knew my wings did not have the strength they usually did. I held Gentle closer and grit my teeth knowing there was no way I could stop and let her down. If she was finding a way to keep going, then I would, too.

We flew for hours.

Just when I thought I couldn't make it, the rough, empty landscape changed, and ahead, I could finally see trees and signs of life. We were getting there. By now, the pain in my back and wings was eye-watering, and all that consumed me was stopping and resting. Gentle had stopped using her air power to save some for when we arrived, and I no longer had the lift I had before, making it harder and harder to inch forward. We cleared the Nothing and were flying over the trees. We had flown all night, and the Obsidian Throne was close, but there was every possibility we would no longer make it.

"We are almost there. Can we make it?" Gentle asked, echoing my thoughts.

"I don't know," I said, the strain in my voice evident. I watched her frown with worry. "I am struggling, but we should be alright," I said, trying to convince her and myself.

"Set me down, and we can walk the rest of the way." She watched the ground as it passed us by slower than before. I gritted my teeth and commanded my muscles to keep going. I had permanent cramps in my back, and it was seizing up, no longer able to beat my wings to keep flying.

Gentle started to move, and she reached around my shoulders to touch the top of my back. I was about to ask her to stay still so we didn't fall out of the sky when a warm breeze brushed over my skin. Wherever it touched, it calmed me, and some of the aches were released, allowing me to move a little easier. My wings moved with more smoothness, and the rhythm evened out, allowing us to climb a little higher.

"There. That should keep us going for a bit longer," Gentle said as she settled back in my arms, wrapping her arms gently around my neck.

"Did you heal me?" I frowned as we rose higher, keeping my eyes on the castle. "You should be saving your powers. You know it won't be easy there."

"I know." She shrugged. "But I also know I won't be able to do it without you, and I need you to be able to move and fight. You are no good to me if you are a broken heap on the ground. I have enough power left in me for what is to come."

I smiled despite myself. "A broken heap, hey. That's not nice. True, but not nice. We will be okay. Is there a plan? Or are we going in hoping for the best?"

She tried to put her hair behind her ears again. "The only thing that matters is we get that crown any way we can. I will do anything to keep Bilvog from winning," she said with determination written all over her face. The castle was getting closer, and I focused on where the best place would be to land. We had to get as close to the audience room as possible. I knew Thallan would want to make a big spectacle of getting his wand back, and he would have everyone in there to watch.

As I flew closer, I kept my eyes open for any danger, knowing I likely wouldn't be welcomed back with open arms after my escape. Out of the corner of my eye, I saw a glint in the setting sun. I dived to the left and heard a gasp from Gentle as an arrow whistled past my ear.

"Was that an arrow?!" Gentle asked, her voice a lot higher than it usually was.

"Yes, it was," I grunted. "I'm guessing they weren't happy about me escaping the dungeon." I dodged another arrow and flew close to the ground, hoping to use the walls as a bit of cover as we made our way to the front door.

"Drop me here," Gentle yelled over the shouting we could now hear from the soldiers who were gathering at the front entrance.

"What? Are you crazy?"

"No. They won't hurt me, and I'm not going in without you. Trust me."

I looked into her eyes, and against every fibre in my body, I landed and set her on the ground. She jumped up, arms outspread in front of me and shielded me from them. Her body was tiny in front of mine, but still, she stood tall and proud. Her face was fierce, and I knew there was no way they were getting through her if she didn't want them to, impossible as it may have appeared.

"We are here to see King Thallan, as he directed," she announced in a clear voice.

The guards held their weapons at the ready, and I, too, was ready to pull the sword I stole and join the battle if it came to that. There was movement at the back of the crowd, and when the Others parted, Thallan's head guard, Borthox, appeared. Borthox was still wearing his impossibly clean, black uniform, and he seemed exactly the same as the other times I had seen him. He stared at us with no emotion, a coldness leaking out of him.

When he looked up, his dark eyes looked deep into me, and all the happiness I had felt earlier with Gentle was syphoned out of my body, and I was now empty. He waited a moment before speaking.

"Of course, Lady Gentle. But I am afraid your friend is not as welcome as you are. He will have to answer for the crimes he committed against us earlier." He snapped his fingers, and the ten guards standing behind him surged forward.

I drew my sword.

THIRTY-TWO
GENTLE

I was shaking like a leaf standing in front of Nate, trying to stare down the guards in front of me. Looking at Borthox, a shiver licked up my body, and he appeared empty to me. I steeled my spine and dragged up whatever courage I could muster, held out my hand and said, "STOP!"

My voice was strong, and I was relieved there was some power behind it. Borthox swung his stare back to me, and whatever courage I had found vanished. Sweat had started to form on my upper lip, and every cell in my body was telling me to run away. What had happened was that I was now having this reaction. He had always made me uncomfortable before, but not like this. Cold malice was coming off him in waves. I swallowed and spoke to him.

"You will not be taking Nate. He has done no wrong. You were the ones who broke the rules of hospitality by drugging and imprisoning him with no proof of any wrongdoing. Then King Thallan lied and told me he had left me." I took a step closer, settling into my anger now. "You are the ones in the wrong here, and you will be making it right with him by letting us pass."

I stared at him, and the muscle in his jaw ticked, but he held up a hand to the other guards who were watching us expressionless. Nate was at my back, tense and silent and all I wanted to do was turn around and run into his arms, but I had started something here I needed to finish. Something solid settled in my soul, and when I poked at the strange emotion, it felt like confidence. A different confidence to the one I usually felt when I got dressed up and hosted parties.

This was a confidence in my ability, in my brain that wasn't there before. For one of the first times, I had thought clearly and got us out of a situation that could have been extremely bad. I chanced a look behind me. Nate looked at me, and I could see his sword was still drawn, and lines of strain bracketed his wary eyes, but when our eyes met, he gave me a small smile and a nod and warmth flooded me again. I turned back around as the guards moved in front of us, and a new, stronger Gentle took a step to follow.

My eyes scanned the audience room, my heart in my mouth, taking stock of who was in the room. People and creatures filled the room, and it was hard to find Bilvog and the other cultists among them. Thallan was sitting atop his Obsidian Throne, looking out over the crowd and laughing. I stood on tip toes, trying to see the front of the room, but there were too many people in the black stone room. My body was shaking again, and I was terrified Bilvog might have already given him the wand, and all this would be for nothing.

My eyes snagged on someone on the edge of the room. A man in a brown robe bent over, looking at me. His hood was pulled forward, so I couldn't see his eyes, but I knew he watched me. Borthox and the other guards walked in between us and when I glanced back again, the man had moved. Before I could find him again and try to work out why I felt dirty all of a sudden, Thallan's voice boomed out.

"Welcome, welcome! How the plot thickens! Here we had a clear winner, until a moment ago, our other team arrived at the eleventh hour! Exciting times." He was practically vibrating in his seat with glee and my stomach curdled at the joy he was taking from this. How did I get caught up in this? The only consolation was he hadn't received the wand yet.

I walked through the part in the crowd Borthox made until I was standing in front of Thallan on his throne. His grey hair was straight and neat, with the sides pulled tight and tied at the back. His deep purple eyes were lined in a green shimmery eyeliner, making them seem otherworldly, which he was. His deep green suit was tailored and showed off his tall, muscled body, but there was no attraction to him. Only fear.

Behind him were his husks in their practically transparent robes, looking beautiful and emotionless. All of them ignored us but one. The husk with the lavender eyes who had tried to help me at breakfast was looking right at me. The look in her eyes was urgent, but I had no idea what she was trying to tell me. I tried to work out what she could be warning me about, but nothing came up. I had never spoken to the husk, so I had no idea. The fact I couldn't work it out made my scalp prickle, and it was another worry to add to my list. I looked away and tried to centre myself.

The eyes of every being in the room were on me like little pinpricks digging into my skin. I dug deep to find the confidence from earlier, but it was fluttering, just out of my grasp. Next to me was Bilvog, and I pinned him right in the eye.

"I must say, I am surprised to see you here. I thought we had beaten the drive out of you," he said quietly, hiding his weakened arm inside the rich red robe he was wearing. His beard was threaded with gold thread and small silver bells that tinged softly when he spoke. I used to think they were cute, but now they grated on my nerves.

"I wanted to thank you, Bilvog. Having you viciously attack me has brought a few things into focus for me. I now know what I want, and it isn't to be a doormat anymore. I intend to rule." I stared into his eyes and let him see the new me.

The one that had emerged like a phoenix and was ready to take action and look after my people the way they should be. I was going to fight, and not only when it was convenient or expected. I was going to fight every day to keep the world from falling into the clutches of Dread, even if it meant fighting people I loved and respected. I let it all shine through, and I saw Bilvog pale slightly. "I will crush anyone that stands in our way."

Bilvog cleared his throat. "Yes, well, we will see about that. Dread was the most powerful Ever and he is well and truly on the way to full health. Once we have the crown, we will have two artefacts to your none, and then we will see who will be crushing who."

He shuffled on his feet as I continued to stare at him. Something inside of me changed and I made the decision he could no longer hurt me. I had finally accepted that he had betrayed us, and there was nothing I could do about it. It was time to let it go and get on with stopping him. My thoughts were interrupted by a touch on my lower back. I turned around and saw Nate.

"Well done, Gentle. Now let's get that crown."

Thallan's voice boomed out before I had a chance to reply. "Now we are here to return the Crown of Glass to the one who hands me the Obsidian Wand. Both groups are here, but I see no wand. Don't tell me you have failed? I would not be pleased." The crowd that a second before was whispering and chatting quietly suddenly went silent. I swallowed as I suppressed a shudder.

Bilvog spoke up, "Don't worry, King Thallan. I was indeed successful, and I have retrieved the wand for you." He bowed low, reached into the pocket of his robe with his good hand, and withdrew the wand. A small gasp echoed through the room as people recognized it, and the atmosphere changed. There was tension and a...fear in the room. The people gathered had realised King Thallan now had the means to make new husks, and it might end up being them.

Thallan's eyes got big, and they glinted with possessiveness as Bilvog held out the long black stone wand towards him. I could see it all play out in my head. Bilvog would pass Thallan the wand and he would give him the crown, and all would be lost. The fact that Bilvog had the Staff of Thorns and then the Crown of Glass filled me with horror.

I imagined the things he could do with the crown, being able to control people's minds, even for a few minutes, could change the course of a battle or prevent one altogether. He could make people kill themselves or, worse, give it to Dread, and he would take over the world if he had the opportunity. I couldn't let that happen. Before Bilvog could hand it over, I stepped in front of him and the outstretched wand.

Thallan snapped back to reality, and his eyes met mine. They were hard and unforgiving as he said, "Is there a reason you are preventing me from getting what I want?" His voice was quiet and filled with violence. The room was silent, and waiting to see what he was going to do with me.

I tried to swallow the lump in my throat and talk around the fear that was thickening my voice, "Bilvog is a liar. He didn't even go into the Gleaming Grove. I am the one who retrieved the wand for you. He attacked me to take it. He is deceiving you." My voice filled the space, and I was proud it only wavered slightly. Thallan stared at me for a beat, and my brows furrowed, wondering how he was going to react.

He laughed. I recoiled in shock. It only took a short delay, but the rest of the gathered people started laughing along with him. I turned around and people were pointing at me and laughing. A wave of heat washed over me as my face got hot. I wanted to melt into the floor and get away from all these people mocking me.

Nate stepped forward, anger written all over him as the people pressed in closer to me. He lifted his sword and made a growling sound to warn them off. I saw Thallan's guards pushing through the crowd to get to him. He held out his arm to keep me back, and I hid behind his strong body, scared about the turn of events.

"STOP!" Thallan roared from behind me.

The crowd froze. At first, I thought he had used magic, but then they started to move back, making the power he had over them evident.

"Now, Gentle. Do you think I care that he took the wand from you? All I am worried about is who gives it to me. That was the deal. Now, I can see you have been through some trials. Your beautiful hair is missing, and if I'm not mistaken, you have two black eyes. While I think it is abhorrent to destroy such beauty, the bruises will fade, and your hair will grow. Go back to your realm and rule, or you can always take me up on my offer. I have the wand." He raised his eyebrows at me as he motioned to the wand Bilvog was still clutching in his good hand. I needed a way to get it out of his hands and into my own. I stepped forward again, hoping to reason with him.

I bowed deeply, hoping my show of respect might help my cause. He leaned back in his throne and stroked his bare chin, looking at me intently.

"King Thallan. I think it is important I explain to you what will happen if Dread were to rise." I prepared myself to talk about the brother I had tried to forget for the last one hundred and fifty years.

"Dread was my brother, and I saw firsthand what he was capable of."

Bilvog stepped around me in an attempt to interrupt, but Thallan held up his hand to silence him. "Let her speak. Let us see if she can change my opinion," he said with a grin I didn't trust. Bilvog sniffed and bowed stiffly before stepping back, allowing me to continue.

"Dread was a terrible person. He was powerful and cocky and only thought of himself while convincing others he was doing things for their benefit. He had plans to take over the human realm and use the humans as slaves or kill them outright. He had no sense of compassion or empathy, and if he were to be released, it would be devastating." Thallan's expression had not changed, and I knew I was not doing a good job. He didn't care. I tried again.

"He would round up the humans in the Evers realms, men, women and children, line them up and shoot parts of their bodies with his withering power." I looked at Bilvog, knowing he knew exactly what I was talking about. Amelia had done the same thing to him in our battle in the mansion. He kept his head lowered, but I saw him move his withered hand further into his cloak as his cheeks reddened.

"It was excruciating pain, and he would make them stand outside as the withering power slowly passed through their body, eventually killing them. We could hear the screams, and it was terrible. It is a sound that will never leave me." My voice cracked as I recalled the sounds those people and children made. All for being human and for no other reason. Tears sprung to my eyes as I tried to block out the sounds, but it was hopeless.

Thallan was looking at me and a hush had fallen over the crowd. "Please. Give me the crown. We need to stop Bilvog from raising him. It will lead to only destruction." I hated the pleading tone of my voice, but there was nothing else I could do.

"Dear Gentle. Your story has moved me." I didn't trust him for a second, but searching his face I could see nothing to reveal he was lying. Hope fluttered in my chest, and I tried to put a lid on it, knowing there must be a trick somewhere, but...what if it worked. My heart was beating thinking about holding my crown in my hands. It was once my most valued item, and I had worn it every day. I rarely used the mind control powers but wearing it had made me feel like the ruler I once was.

Was that what had been missing from me? Had giving up my crown all those years ago caused me to fall back into the unassertive and passive person I had become? If I was honest, since we all decided to track our items, in the back of my mind, I had been hoping putting it on my head would change something in me. I would revert back to the leader I once was. I waited, holding my breath for him to continue.

Thallan turned around and snapped his fingers at the lavender-eyed husk, and she turned and walked out of a door at the back of the room. "Your story is sad for those humans he tormented, but I myself am guilty of doing much worse, and to people I actually like." The smile he turned to me was predatory, and my stomach dropped. I had failed.

Bilvog's chest puffed up as he took a step in front of me. I hung my head and tried to ignore the emptiness that was filling me. Nate moved forward and held my hand, and it was the only thing that was warm in my body. I let him see my devastation and apology in my eyes. He stared back with no disappointment, just sadness.

"I'm sorry," I whispered to him, stepping closer to his protection. "I tried, but it was no use. He was never going to give it to me."

"I know. You did an amazing job. People here were moved, something I have never seen here." He cupped my face and I leaned into it, ignoring the people talking around us and took the comfort he was giving. His eyes shone with love, and I wondered how I had never seen it before and how I had lived without it.

The door at the back of the room opened, and the lavender-eyed husk walked in with a box covered with a pink velvet cover. The crown. I stepped aside and watched as Thallan made a slicing motion with his hand and silenced the room once more. I was hollow as I watched him take it from the husk.

"Thank you, Calas. Ah, here it is." He pulled the velvet off with a flourish, and my hands ached to hold the crown when I saw it again for the second time in one hundred and fifty years. It hadn't aged a day, and I could practically feel its weight on my head.

My short hair started to rise and swirl around me as my power stirred. I didn't bother smoothing it down. What was the point? I had lost, and now I had to watch my greatest enemy take one of the things that could have saved my family and world. Nate squeezed my hand, and I stared at the floor, unable to look at the crown any longer.

"The Crown of Glass. Here it is, Bilvog. Time to exchange so we both get what we want and then I want all of you gone. I'm tired of your faces." He held out the crown, and Bilvog bowed again, his grovelling making me sick. He stepped forward with the wand and held it out in front of him. I couldn't help myself and I looked up. I had to see the moment it was gone.

Right before they exchanged the magical artefacts, Nate muttered, "I'm sorry, Gentle. Forgive me."

Before he let go of my hand and surged forward. He ate up the few steps and stood between Thallan and Bilvog so they couldn't exchange the items. Irritation flitted across Thallan's face, and Bilvog's twisted in rage.

"What are you doing?" he hissed.

Nate ignored Bilvog and kept his eyes on Thallan. "You captured me, drugged me and imprisoned me all because you thought I was the Alanti that caused you to lose your wand."

"Yes, I did, and I do not apologise for that. This is my realm, and I will imprison whoever I feel like when I want to. You!" He pointed at a woman in the crowd who appeared to be wearing a necklace of human toes strung around her neck. Her yellow hair was piled up and cascading to the floor creating a train behind her, as the black scales that covered her dress shimmered in the mage light. She looked shocked as she realised he was pointing at her.

"Arrest her! Take her to the dungeons. I don't like her dress," Thallan demanded. Immediately, the people around her stepped away, and Borthox and another guard were there, and she was whisked away. I was shocked, and my face grew hot with anger. What kind of ruler was Thallan? How was he still the king?

"I know, believe me, I know," Nate said, and cold washed over me as I realised what was going on. I gasped, but before I could step forward and stop what he was about to do, he continued. And he said the words I dreaded and made my heart stop and leap into my throat.

"Well, this time, you were correct. I am that Alanti changeling."

THIRTY-THREE

NATHANIEL

"My parents were Rabdos and Mattia, and we lived here until they escaped to the Evers Realm, where you tracked them down and had them killed. I am that Alanti and I want to trade my life for the crown."

My hands clenched as I waited to hear what he would have to say. I heard Gentle gasp behind me, but I didn't dare turn around and look at her, knowing I might not go through with this. Giving her up after I had found her made my heart crack, but I had no choice. I had to stop them from raising Dread, and this was the only way to do that. It was the only thing I could do that I knew for sure he would take. Thallan had been searching for me, and I hoped I was the one thing he would not give up.

"You? Ha! I knew I would find you eventually." He sighed and stared at me with a cruel smile on his face.

I knew what that meant, and my whole body quaked remembering all the things he put me through. My parents' faces flashed in my mind, and I pushed them from view, not wanting to imagine the disappointment they would have felt. Their deaths were for nothing. They had died to save me, and here I was, offering myself up to the monster they tried to protect me from. My thoughts were broken by Thallan speaking again.

"I have waited many years to find you. Because of you that hag took my wand, and I was left with the husks I have and not able to make more." He walked towards me, prowling like a cat that had caught the mouse. I held my ground not wanting to give him any satisfaction seeing me afraid.

Because I was.

Inside, I was shaking and trying to keep the panic that was beginning to rise and was threatening to bubble over. I clenched my teeth and tried to ignore the tightening in my chest. By now Thallan was standing in front of me, and I noted we were the same height. I always thought he was taller.

"I have you now, my little winged rat. You can't believe how long I have wanted to find you. No one has ever bested me. You and your parents were the only people to ever evade me, and you saw what I did to them, didn't you? They didn't look much like your parents when I was finished with them."

The room was silent. The people gathered, hanging on his every word. I had never seen my parents' bodies after Thallan's men had gotten to them, and I was acutely re-lieved right now. I heard my parents' names whispered, and I knew there were people here that had been around back then. Maybe even been the ones to torment and torture me. My blood heated, and I clenched my fists harder.

"You can do whatever you want to me, but give Gentle the crown and let her leave untouched and safely. Then I am all yours. I know you have been waiting to get your hands on me. Here is your chance." I fluttered my wings for effect and saw his greedy eyes run the length of my blue feathers.

"You unveiling yourself has changed things," he said as he turned and walked back to stand in front of his throne. He sat and looked us over. Gentle appeared next to me and took my hand, squeezing it almost painfully.

"How could you do that? There is no way I am allowing you to sacrifice yourself to these people."

I bristled. "What do you mean? I am doing it for you. You can take the crown and get back to Aeris Isle. Forget about me. I can do this, and I want to do this for you," I hissed back, praying she wouldn't do anything stupid to wreck this plan. We were interrupted by Bilvog stepping forward again, wand in hand.

"King Thallan. While I am surprised to hear about Nathaniel's history, I don't see how it changes our deal. You said the person who hands you the wand will get the crown. Here," he said, reaching out his arm as far as it would go without getting into Thallan's personal space. "I have the wand. Take it, and let's finish this." Frustration was evident in his voice, and Bilvog's cult members were starting to approach, making me tense.

Thallan appeared deep in thought, but I knew it was an act. He already knew what he was going to do. He liked to drag out the dramatics of it and the crowd was eating it up.

"You are right, Bilvog. That was our deal, and while I could easily change my mind and get out of it by having someone take the wand from you, I will honour it." He looked at me. "It was foolish of you to come in here and offer yourself up. While I have been searching for you, now I have you. I find my anger has cooled over the years. Also, not giving your precious Gentle the crown will hurt you the most, I think, so I am inclined to do just that and give it to Bilvog here. Guards!" He clicked his fingers, and as before, the guards materialised from nowhere, and I was grabbed.

Someone yanked Gentle's hand out of mine, and I exploded. I threw my elbow back and managed to break one of their noses, and blood sprayed out as he yelled in pain. Before anyone else could grab me, I got low and swept my legs out, knocking one of the guards over before I stomped on his stomach, winding him as he curled into a ball on the ground. I stood and held up my fists, waiting for the next guard to approach, but there were none left. I chanced a look at Gentle and saw she was alright before a sharp pain ripped through my wing. I cried out and craned my neck, trying to see what had happened.

Out of my left wing, a large crossbow bolt was sticking out of it. The pain was so intense I had to grit my teeth to stop it from overpowering me. I needed to stay alert and in this room. I couldn't afford to leave Gentle here with these people. I spun around and held my hands in the air, hoping to calm the situation. The guards that were left grasped me and held me still. I was breathing heavily as I tried to ignore the shooting pain in my wing. I tried to move it, but it was stiff. The bolt must have gone through a muscle, and I tried not to let the panic overwhelm me.

"That was quite a show there, Nathaniel. I knew Amos had trained you well, but I didn't realise you were that good. Shame it is all about to come to an end," Bilvog said, wearing a smug smile on his face. I glanced around at the crown, helpless, hoping someone else would come and, by some miracle, stop this from happening.

I was out of luck.

None of the people gathered could think for themselves. They knew the consequences of disobeying Thallan. There would be no help from them, and I couldn't blame them. I knew the pain and evil he was capable of firsthand.

Bilvog once again held out the wand, and I knew this was it. As soon as Thallan took it from him, he would have to give Bilvog the crown and that would make it harder to get. We needed all these artefacts if we wanted to avoid another time of despair with Dread killing innocent humans. I watched and it was in slow motion.

Thallan swaggered towards Bilvog, greed in his eyes. Bilvog had a smug look on his face, and it seemed like his whole body was vibrating. I swallowed and thought if there was anything I could do to stop this, but there was nothing. The hands gripping me tightened like they could read my mind, keeping me rooted to the spot.

Bilvog reached out, and Thallan's hand was getting closer and closer. I closed my eyes, not wanting to see the moment the wand was handed over. Right before I closed them, a gust of wind swirled around the room. Hair and clothing were flapping and snapping in the wind, and it was difficult to keep my eyes open against the onslaught. I tried to shield my eyes, but my arms were held tight.

Ahead of me, Gentle stepped out next to Bilvog. Her hands were outstretched, and she was pale, but she was every bit the Ever. She radiated power and beauty, and my heart stopped as I watched her throw her power around one of the most powerful rulers I had met. Thallan's lips were pulled back from his teeth, and his grey hair was whipping about his head. Bilvog's grip on the wand was tight but I could see he was struggling to stand and was losing his balance. Gentle continued to move forward until the gale was so strong I could hardly see from the tears that were torn from my eyes.

Then, the wand was free.

It blew out of Bilvog's hands, and I watched his eyes widen as he scrambled, lost his balance and face-planted on the cold black floor. Thallan tried to grab it but was too slow as it landed on the floor and skidded to land in front of Gentle. My heart was beating wildly as she bent over and held the Obsidian Wand in her hands. The wind died which allowed what she said next to be heard by everyone.

"I accept your offer. You can turn me into a husk for the crown."

THIRTY-FOUR

GENTLE

My stomach was roiling, and I worried I was about to throw up on the floor at Thallan's feet. I swallowed my nausea and tried to process the fact I had just told Thallan I would be a husk and submit to him. There was no way he was going to refuse me now. This was the one way I could *guarantee* we would get the crown.

The wand was hard and cold in my hands, colder than it should have been, and as I ran my thumb over the rough surface, I did my best to not think about the fact I was holding the thing that would take away everything that made me, me. I would be a shell of myself. Tears pricked my eyes as I thought of the people I would leave behind.

Had I been too hasty?

I shook my head and swallowed. Think of the people I would be saving. They are why I agreed to this. I would do anything for the people in my realm and my family. I was only one person, and if Dread got the crown, potentially millions of people would die. My life was no more important than theirs.

The crowd around us was moving and talking, wondering what was going to happen next. I took my time composing myself, silently saying goodbye to the people in my life. Gloom, Enduring, Ashes, Awe, Crescent, and Amos. I didn't know what I would retain after becoming a husk, but from what I had seen, it wouldn't be much. I sent them a silent message of love I knew would go unanswered. I lifted my eyes, and Nate looked back at me. He was standing in front of me, and his face was all hard lines, but his eyes were in turmoil.

"You can't do this. I won't leave you here with him," he said roughly as he took my hands and stepped closer. Everyone else in the room seemed to fall away, and I was with only him. This would probably be the last time we would have together, and there were things I wanted to say. I stared into his eyes, wanting him to know I was focused only on him and wanting the truth of my words to shine through.

"Nate. I love you. I have admired your strength and resolve for years, and I never thought in a million years I would be able to say those words to you." A tear fell from my eye and left a wet trail down my face, but I still didn't wipe it away. "You are the best thing I ever could have hoped for, and although we have only just found each other, I will carry your love with me. I will not let this wand take it from me. For the next hundred years, while I am here, I will be thinking of you and your love, and that will be what gets me through. My heart beats for you, and I am yours." A tear slid down Nate's cheek as my voice broke at the end.

"Please, don't do this. I can't live without you. You are my everything, and I can't go on without you," he pleaded.

I reached into the pocket of my pants, pulled out the vial of gold swirling liquid, and pressed it into his hands. "You will need to take this to get back. Get the crown to the others as quickly as you can. Don't try to stop me. I have made my decision, and I need you to promise me you will save my people. They need you." A sob escaped as I tried to ignore the tearing of my heart. All that was left there was a sharp pain I knew was now permanent. A pain I would never escape, even if I forgot the cause. I focused on his face, memorising as much as I could. If I was going to remember one thing, it would be him.

I took my hands from his and stepped aside, wiping my nose, unwilling to draw this out any longer. Once I was out of the bubble of me and Nate, the noise of the room reached me. I turned as the people gathered were milling about whispering behind their hands about what I had done. Most of them were glad to have a new husk serve them, while others spoke about what they wanted to do with me once I was empty.

I shuddered and blocked them out, walking to stand where Thallan and Bilvog were arguing. The rest of Bilvog's cult had gathered in a tight circle around him, keeping an eye on what was happening. I pushed my way through them, feeling the roughness of their robes against my skin. The feeling was far away and foreign to me and I welcomed the numbness that was slowly settling into my body.

"She stole it! You saw what she did. You can't give her the crown. I had it!"

Bilvog's face was red and blotchy, and the bells were ringing in his beard as he shook his head and gestured with his good hand. My body was trembling, walking into all the hate and violence that rippled in the air between the cult members, Bilvog and Thallan.

"I never touched the wand. I think you need to remember where you are gnome. You are in my castle and my realm. I don't think you want to threaten me."

Bilvog's mouth snapped shut, and a sliver of fear crept into his eyes.

Thallan turned to me. "I am tired of this. I should have had the wand in my hand an hour ago. Give me the wand, and I shall turn you into a husk, and your Alanti will be allowed to leave. As much as I hate to give him up, I sense he will be foolish enough to return to rescue you. I will scoop him up at a later date. Right now, I want the wand and you."

I hesitated a moment, knowing this was it. I turned and looked at Nate, who had a haunted look on his face. I gave him a watery smile, trying to seem okay with my decision, and he gave one back, even though his whole body appeared to be in pain. With my heart beating so hard I thought it might explode, I turned to Thallan and held out the wand. For some reason, I was compelled to look at Bilvog. He was watching me with a strange mix of shock and...sadness.

"You did this. I hope you can live with yourself knowing what I had to do to stop Dread." I said sadly, the anger draining away.

"I must admit I am surprised. I did offer you a place with me. As much as we don't agree on...certain things, I am sad to see it end like this. I hope your people are worth it."

"They are. I will do anything to stop Dread."

"Are we done?" Thallan asked with a sigh. "Let's get this over with," He clicked his fingers, and the husk holding the crown approached. I took a second to admire the crown I would never wear again as he held it out to me. I stretched out my hand and waited for him to take the wand from me.

It was done in the blink of an eye.

The wand left my hand, and the crown was in front of me. I reached out and touched its smooth surface, and a smile lit my face. Touching my crown after all these years was like coming home. The power was nestled in it, ready for me to use. I held it in both hands and flicked my eyes to Thallan. He, too, seemed like a starving man holding food in his hands. It made me sick to think what he was going to do with that wand and what evil he was going to spread. I lifted the crown to my head.

"Uh, uh, uh. None of that, Gentle," Bilvog said, and Thallan's head snapped to me. I cursed under my breath and scowled at Bilvog. "I don't think King Thallan would appreciate you trying to use the crown's mind-control powers on him, do you?"

"No, you are right, Bilvog." He watched me as I lowered the crown.

"Can you blame me?" I asked with my chin held high. Nate was standing next to me, and I drew strength from him and his presence. "You can't truly think I want to be a husk."

"No, I know you don't, but you have made a deal, and you will honour it." He raised his voice and spread his arms wide, including the restless crowd watching our show. "We all know what happens to those who break their deals, don't we?"

The gathered crowd clapped and hooted, and I nearly had to cover my ears from the noise. They were beginning to whip into a frenzy, and my whole body tingled, and nervous energy sizzled through me. I was suddenly aware these people were other beings and could do a lot of damage, especially since my magic was now completely depleted.

After a moment, Thallan called for silence and turned his attention to me.

"Now, the moment I have been waiting for. You will be the jewel in my collection Gentle. No one will ever match your beauty, despite the hacked-off hair and black eyes. You will be by my side for the rest of eternity, and people will admire you forever. You will never grow old, and your beauty will be with you forever."

Once, that might have been appealing to me, but now, after this adventure, I found it no longer was. I would happily lose my beauty if it meant I could go back and take up the reins of Aeris Isle and rule and protect my people like I was meant to. My face heated as I thought back to my past and how I had acted. I wanted to go back and change that, but I never would.

I handed the crown to Nate and gazed into his eyes one last time, taking the image with me. I stepped forward and stared into the cold, crazed eyes of King Thallan of the Obsidian Throne. I lifted my chin, squared my shoulders, and stared at him defiantly.

He held up the wand and said words I couldn't understand. I had a moment to think of my loved ones before a shot of black flew from the wand and hit me in the chest. It was oily and wrong as it spread throughout my body. That was the last thing I knew before I fell.

THIRTY-FIVE

GENTLE

I felt like I was falling for years. The foreign black magic slithered through my veins and invaded every pocket of my body. In my mind, there was like a scream that was erasing any thought I had and leaving me black. I desperately tried to grab hold of any memory I could and not let it erase it all, but it blanketed them all and left me hollow. I felt something essential to my life being sucked out.

Right when my last thought leached from my body, I heard a small laugh in the back of my mind. "Not today, dearie. I own a piece of you, and I won't give it up so easily." Whatever was leaving my body stopped and sprung back, and everything came flooding back to me. I sucked in a deep painful breath, and my open eyes became seeing again, and I saw Nate leaning over me, worry filling his face as he said my name over and over again.

I blinked and studied my body, trying to work out what happened. I probed my mind for the black blanket that had covered it, but it was gone. I had my memories, and my eyes watered in relief. Something was missing, though. I struggled and managed to sit and look around at the people gathered. All were looking at me expectantly, but I had no idea what they wanted of me. Nate helped me to stand, and

I looked at Thallan. He was like the cat that got the cream, and my skin crawled.

I continued to probe my body to see what had changed, but from what I could tell, I was the same. I still had my memories and free will. Had the wand failed? Thallan looked at me and held out his hand, but I didn't move. I waited for the compulsion to walk, but there was none. Something had gone wrong, and I sagged in relief that I wasn't a husk.

I glanced at my hands and got a shock. My hands were no longer the pale, smooth skin I was used to. They were now freckled and had small scars dotting them. They didn't look like an old lady, but they had definitely aged and were not the perfect hands I was used to. My clothing hung off me in certain places. My hips were no longer as full, and my breasts seemed smaller.

"What happened? I look...different," I said to Nate.

"Your memories? Do you still have your mind?" Nate asked me urgently, cupping my face, panic in his eyes.

"Yes, all that is still there, but I feel different. My body is aching, and I look different, don't I?"

Nate also sagged, and a smile spread across his face. "Who cares. You aren't a husk. That is all that matters." He pulled me close and hugged me, and I took in his scent, thankful I didn't lose the memory of it. I was here, and I was okay.

"What the HELL is going on here?" Thallan roared.

I jolted apart from Nate and came face to face with fury. Thallan's face was pale, and his eyes were like thunder. His whole body was rigid, and my stomach dropped looking at him. This was not going to be good.

"Why didn't it work? What did you do? It was working, but then, all of a sudden, it stopped. What happened to your beauty? I didn't get it, and it is obviously gone, so WHERE IS IT!"

My heart stopped at his words, and I froze in place. My beauty was gone? I looked at my hands again and that's when it sunk in. He didn't get my memories, but whatever had stopped that from happening didn't stop my beauty from being taken from me. My chest was getting tighter as I tried to work out what that meant for me now.

The rest of the crowd was moving in closer to see what had gone wrong, and my mind was racing. The bodies and the voices of those gathered were pressing on me and I clutched at Nate's hand.

"We need to get out of here now," he said, and I heard him unscrew the top of the potion bottle.

I grabbed the crown from his hands, needing to know we had it and waited for the potion to do its thing, hoping it would work before Thallan reached us or the people surrounding us crushed us. I glanced around frantically, trying to keep my eyes on everyone at once, knowing I could do nothing to stop them. I was weak from whatever the wand had done, and I had absolutely no power left. I was beginning to feel lightheaded, and all the faces were starting to blur in front of me. I clutched the crown in one hand and Nate's arm in the other, hoping they would anchor me and keep me holding on a little longer.

The sounds in the room had reached a clamour in my head, and I couldn't tell who was speaking, but one voice cut through them all.

"Hold on. Here we go!" Air rushed over us as the potion took hold and began to whisk Nate and me out of the Others Realm and back to Aeris Isle. I had one moment to look, and I saw Thallan screaming, face red as he clutched the wand and tried to fire at me again. I cringed into Nate and stared at the people we were leaving in the audience hall. Bilvog was yelling at his cult members, and they all looked furious.

All except one.

The one I had seen earlier was staring at me. His hood was still pulled forward, but whoever it was, was watching us. I strained and tried to turn my head to see who it was as my mind prickled with awareness. I knew them, but it was out of my reach. Before I could look anymore, we were gone.

THIRTY-SIX

NATHANIEL

I clutched Gentle with all my strength, not willing to let her go. My body warmed as the potion took hold, and we sped through the sky. The Others Realm began to fall away, and I tensed as the people in the audience room yelled and threw goblets at us as we rose. I didn't relax until we were high enough for them to be tiny dots and then nothing.

I gripped tighter when the strength of the wind threatened to rip Gentle away from me, reminding me what it felt like when we arrived. I pulled on Gentle's arm, trying to get her in front of me so I could hold tight, and she climbed up my body to help. My wings were pressed against my back, almost painfully, but I sighed in relief as Gentle wrapped her arms around my neck and her legs around my middle. I hoped it would be as quick a trip as it was getting here, but there were no guarantees.

My mind was churning with everything that had happened since arriving in that audience chamber. I had revealed myself to Thallan, Gentle had offered herself, and I had come close to losing her. Her short hair had lost the golden shine it once had and was now a dull blonde colour. I knew she would be disappointed about her new appearance, but to me, she was still the most beautiful woman I had ever seen.

I gripped her closer, and a tightness I didn't know I had in my chest since arriving in the Others Realm seemed to loosen. We were out of there and going home, and we had the crown. We had done it. I smiled and buried my head in the crook of Gentle's neck, and waited to land.

It didn't take long before I could see Aeris Isle rushing up at us. My stomach launched into my chest as we neared Gentle's castle. The mountains were snow-capped, and the waterfall was full and gushing down the mountain. Alanti and Pegasi flew in the sky, and we passed through one of the many spires of the castle. The floor of Gentle's ballroom rushed up at me, and I tensed, hoping we would stop before landing again. Luckily, we did, before falling in a heap on the stone floor with an oomph.

"Ahh!" I looked up at the sound and saw four Alanti surrounding us.

"Oh, it's you. You are back! We have been standing here since you left waiting." Relief filled Otton's voice. His and his deep brown eyes ran over our bodies, looking for injuries, and when he saw none, he helped us to our feet. The huge grin split his red beard in two, and I couldn't help but smile back at him. We were home.

"Lady Gentle, are you alright?" he asked as she swayed slightly on her feet. I held out my arm to steady her, concerned about her after all she went through. Otton frowned and looked at her. "You look different, Lady. Do you feel alright?" he asked. Gentle jolted in surprise and ran her hands over her hair, which for once wasn't floating around her head.

"I'm just tired. Can you please tell my advisors I have returned? I'm going to my room, and I will see them in the meeting room in thirty minutes." Her voice shook, but she was firm.

"Well, I was told to take you right to the meeting chamber when you returned, Lady Gentle," Otton said, twisting his beard around his finger. I opened my mouth to tell him not to question Gentle, but she beat me to it.

"Thank you, Otton, but I have just been transported from another realm. I am exhausted and dirty, and I would like to freshen up before I must recall our entire trip. The council will wait, and I will be there when I see fit." She stepped around him and stalked off. I grinned, unable to help myself.

Otton hesitated a moment chewing his lip and looking back and forth between us, caught between following the orders of the council and Gentle. "Go on then, go and tell them. While you are there, can you tell Theo I have returned, and I would like him to be present in the meeting chamber as well? Also, you better send some messages to the other Evers and let them know we have returned with the crown. Thanks, Otton. It's good to be back. Oh, how long have we been gone?" I asked, knowing time worked differently here and in the Others Realm.

"It's been two days, sir. It's good to have you back. I'll tell them now. Come on, men," he said to the others, and I gave them all a nod and wave as they followed after Otton. I sighed, relieved to be back where I belonged and that time hadn't been blown away from us. A few days gone was fine. It could have been years, and that would have been a disaster. I walked towards the door, planning to follow

Gentle to her room. When she looked in the mirror, she would need a little support.

The castle was busy, and every person I met welcomed me home with smiles and cheers. I acknowledged them all, aware I was the new head Alanti, and I needed to act a certain way now. Plus, I was happy to see the familiar faces. I had never been so grateful to be here, where people were kind and thoughtful and not treated with cruelty. These people had hardly known conflict, and I was acutely glad about that. It needed to stay that way, and it fuelled my need to protect them all in the battles to come.

I made it to Gentle's room, and I stopped in my tracks at the doorway. Gentle was standing in front of her full-length mirror and staring at her reflection. She stood out in her room, which was an explosion of colour. I hesitated, wondering what her reaction was going to be. Her eyes met mine in the mirror, and I stepped in and closed the door, not wanting anyone else to hear what she was going to say. I tried to read the expression in her eyes, but it was guarded, and I couldn't get a read on them.

"I look different," she said quietly.

THIRTY-SEVEN
GENTLE

My brain was trying to process what I had seen in the mirror. I had lost my...spark. I had dulled. It was hard to put my finger on exactly what had happened. My features were the same; I still had my bright blue eyes, but they were missing the sparkle. My hair was still blonde, but it was dull and less bouncy. My skin was still clear, but it was uneven in places. I was not the "beauty" I had always been told I was. I was sad, but I had to admit, I was dealing with it better than I thought. A few weeks ago, this would have broken me. Now, I was upset something had been taken from me, but I knew it wasn't the end of the world. I was still the same Gentle I had always been, I had only lost some of my sparkle.

Nate appeared at the door, and I turned to him, hands shaking. What if he didn't love me anymore? What if he no longer wanted to be with me now that I didn't look the same? He was standing in the doorway, and I waited until he had closed the door before speaking to him. My heart was beating wildly, and I was starting to sweat, worried I would get an answer I wouldn't like.

"I look different."

Nate crossed the room and stood in front of me. He didn't touch me; he stood there and watched me.

"Yes, you look different, but at least you aren't a husk," he said, smiling lightly. I agreed with him, but I didn't smile back. There was too much anxiety in my body to joke around. I needed to find out what he thought of me now.

I looked at our feet. "Is it bad? Do you—" I swallowed. "Do you still love me?" I asked, more exposed than I thought I had ever been before. The silence was overwhelming, and tears crawled up the back of my throat. After what seemed like an eternity, he lifted my chin so I was looking into his blue eyes that were so like mine.

"I love you more than the air I breathe. You are the beat of my heart, the blood in my veins, and I would tear the world apart for you. I don't care what you look like because I have only ever loved you for what's inside. Every minute of every day, you have shown kindness, patience and humour, and you brighten up a room by stepping into it. There is nothing in this world that could be more beautiful than you, and I will never stop loving you until I die."

I shuddered and let the tears fall from my eyes. How did I get so lucky to have found someone like Nate? He fell in my lap, and I would be forever grateful to have him in my life. I tilted my head up, and our lips met in the sweetest kiss I had ever had. He wrapped his arms around me tightly and held me close as I laced my hands behind his neck.

With his kiss, he made all my doubts vanish. In that moment, I knew I could do anything, and no matter what had come before, I knew he would be by my side for always, and I would be loved unconditionally. We stayed like that for a while, revelling in our privacy and the newfound assurance I had discovered.

Finally, we pulled apart and smiled at each other.

"So where do we go from here?" Nate asked.

"I'm going to change out of these gross clothes and fill in the council on what we learned." I steadied myself. "I'm also going to let them know I am taking over the running of Aeris Isle, and that you and I are together and remind them you are the new leader of the Alanti and my personal bodyguard. I don't think they will take it very well. They don't do well with change. I am fairly certain we will lose a few of them, and that worries me." I frowned and stepped out of the warmth of Nate's embrace.

I walked to the wardrobe and opened it up, sighing in happiness as all my fluffy, tulle-filled dresses practically exploded out at me. I might have changed inside and out, but one thing had stayed the same, my love for big dresses. I flicked through them knowing what I chose had to show the change in my outlook. I wanted to look strong and confident.

"Sounds like a bold plan. I will come to the meeting with you, but then I will have to return to the Alanti House so I can see my men. Otton said it had only been two days since we left, so that will work in our favour. We are in for a fight ahead, but at least we have the crown," he said, picking the crown up from the vanity where I had sat it. "I think you should wear this when you go."

I stopped, my mouth going dry. I had wanted to put that crown on my head long before we needed it to stop Dread again. I had missed its weight for many years, but was I worthy of it now? I had been so apathetic to the rule of Aeris Isle. Should I wear the crown? I took the gown I had chosen and went into the bathroom to clean myself up and get dressed.

"I'll be back in a minute," I called through the door, putting off the moment I would have to accept the crown and wear it on my head.

I stripped off and had the quickest wash in history before sliding into the gown I had chosen. It was a deep, red colour made out of the softest smoothest satin fabric. It was tight to my body and flared out gradually at the bottom. The wide shoulder straps dipped into a sweetheart neckline, and although modest, it made a statement. I was confident and serious. I picked up my mother's brush and brushed my short hair, which looked like a bird's nest. We had had a rough few days, and I was sad to see the state of my once beautiful hair. I dried it and brushed it smooth. I would need someone to come and cut it better, but for now, it was passable.

I stared at myself in the mirror. "You can do this, Namara. It's time to stand up and be the Ever you once were."

I opened the door and stepped out, the fabric swishing around my feet.

"Gentle. You look beautiful," Nate said, and I blushed.

"Thank you. I'm hoping it will make me strong enough to stand up to the council. They might be older men, but they are stubborn." My stomach was fluttering, and I couldn't stop knotting my fingers together.

Nate took my hands in his. "You will be fine. You deserve this, and you have always been a good leader. This will be for the better you will see. Should we go?" he asked, gesturing to the door.

"Yes, let's go," I said, trying to hype myself up. Before we left, I took the crown from the table Nate had sat it on. I held the cold, smooth glass in my hand as my skin warmed the surface of it. It was light, and I tried to steady my breathing as I lifted it to my head. It slipped on and fit like a glove. I closed my eyes and savoured the weight that was foreign and familiar all at once. The magic swirled through it, waiting for me to use it. The thought crossed my mind. Maybe I could use the mind control power to help the council accept the changes easier, but I brushed it off. That was not the way I wanted to rule. I took Nate's hand, and we headed out, ready to change the way Aeris Isle was ruled forever.

"It's so good to have you back, Lady Gentle, and with the crown. We are all very proud of you," Lomano said, his white clouded eyes looking at me. The others nodded, some with more enthusiasm than others. We were back in my meeting room, and I was on my glass throne, planning what I was going to say. It was slightly chilly because I still didn't have enough power to warm the air. Nate was standing beside me, closer than Amos ever did, and I was grateful. A few eyebrows had risen when we walked hand in hand, but so far, there were no comments.

"Thank you Lomano." I stood and smiled at the seated council. "We went through quite an ordeal to retrieve the crown, but as you can see, we have it, and it will be one more weapon we have against Dread." The council applauded lightly, but there was tension in the air. They knew something was coming, and they knew they wouldn't like it.

"While we were away, I came to realise something. I am going to be taking a more active role in the running of Aeris Isle." The council shuffled in their seats.

"I know that for a long time, I have left the running of my realm to you, and I have taken a back seat. Well, that is going to change. I will now be picking up my crown and ruling in a more active role. I appreciate all you have done for this realm and for me, and I will need your help going forward as I take up the reins. The good news is you will have more free time and less of an active role in the management of Aeris Isle."

I waited for their reaction, knowing I hadn't articulated it well but hoping I got my point across. It took a moment before Vasair stood, his wispy hair fluttering in the cold breeze coming through the open window.

"I am sure my other council members agree with me in congratulating you on your new sense of responsibility. But I'm not sure you are aware of what it takes to rule a realm. It is not an easy thing. Do you think you can handle it?"

It was a valid question, even though I bristled at the insinuation.

"I understand it will be an adjustment, and I won't be doing it alone. I am hoping I will have your support to guide me, but I *will* be ruling from now on."

"Are you sure? Your strengths lie in socialising and connections, not in complaints and logistics," Vasair spread his hands and looked at the nodding members, and my stomach twisted. He had such a smug look on his face that my anger peaked. "Perhaps you should leave that to us. We have the experience after all and have been doing it well for the last one hundred years."

"I agree, but I am the Ever. As I said, I appreciate you have been doing my job and have been doing it well, but I no longer need you to. I will be taking control, but you are more than welcome to stay as my advisors. Otherwise, you are welcome to leave, but I hope you stay." I looked around to include everyone in what I was saying. "I hope we can work together to make Aeris Isle stronger and better than it ever has been."

I couldn't tell from the faces in front of me if my plea had worked. Even though I wanted to take control, I did value their wisdom, and I knew I would need their help to run this kingdom. I smoothed the slinky fabric and my hair in my nervousness. The men were talking to themselves quietly, and worry slid through me. If they all left, I wasn't sure I could do this. Vasair was shaking his head angrily, and my stomach sank.

After what seemed like forever, Vasair spoke, "We have spoken, and I don't know how this will go. I am sorry, Lady Gentle, but myself and Tagour, we can no longer stay here. We have...doubts about whether you can run the kingdom effectively." Tagour stood, and his blond combover ruffled in the breeze.

I stared both the men in the eyes. "Thank you for all your service. Aeris Isle would not be as secure as it is without you. I am sorry you feel that way, but I will prove you wrong. Goodbye."

I turned away from them as they stood and walked out the door. I started to sweat, shocked that I had stood up to them, and I tried to calm myself before turning back to the other men.

"Right. Well, thank you for staying. I am proud to have you on my council, and I know we will make Aeris Isle a strong, beautiful, and fair place to live. Now we had best move on to other matters. We learned a lot in the Others Realm, and I am afraid we may have made another enemy. I think it best we gather the other Evers and discuss our next actions. Lomano, please send messages to my brother and sisters informing them we are going to host a celebration of our return with the crown. I want their advisors here as well so we can work out our plan and what we are going to do to stop Dread and his cult from taking over."

The rest of the meeting continued, and all the plans were set. Now, we had to make a plan for the rest of the artefacts.

THIRTY-EIGHT
GENTLE

The music filled the ballroom and made my body want to dance. Candles were scattered throughout, big blobs of wax holding them in place as they dripped down the side. The sky was midnight blue with tiny pinpricks of stars scattered all over. I couldn't stop looking at the sky, glad it was not the perpetual twilight of the Others Realm. At the back of the ballroom, tables were practically overflowing with food and wine, and there was a beautiful smell of jasmine in the air, winding around everyone.

I smiled at the people gathered, watching them as they danced and chatted among themselves. Laughter filled the room at times, and it was nice to see everyone having a good time. At the back of the crowd, someone caught my eye. A person bent over double was lingering in the doorway, looking through the crown.

When our eyes met, I realised it was Bella. I smiled and crossed the room to greet her. "Bella, what are you doing here?"

She looked up at me, and gave a cheeky smile, "Ay, dearie, I heard you were back. I can see you were successful." She lifted her eyes to the crown on my head. "It's nice to see my potion worked. I was worried there for a moment..."

"You were? You didn't tell me that," I said with a laugh.

"Well, why would I? That would be bad for business." She cackled loudly, drawing the attention of a few partygoers.

"Yes, I suppose it would. Would you like to come in?"

"No, dearie, I won't stay long. I just wanted to pop in and make sure you were alright." She squinted at me, staring intensely. "I can see you look different. Lost a little of your spark. Lucky that's all you lost, eh. I did my best to keep you safe, but sometimes sacrifices must be made."

"What do you mean?" I asked as a thought niggled in the back of my mind.

"Well, I knew what kind of man King Thallan was, and I knew as soon as he saw your beauty, he would want you, so that's why I took some of your essence. The tear, blood, and hair you gave me stopped him from sucking out your soul because I had a prior claim to it. You can thank me later. Right now, I'm going to head home. I have a rather large order of charm potions to prepare for tomorrow." She turned to leave, and although my head was reeling with the information she had told me, I stopped her, bent over, and gave her a hug. The smell of herbs was almost overwhelming.

"Thank you," I whispered in her ear.

"You're welcome, dearie. But remember, you owe me now," she said, winking at me.

I smiled and let her leave as I turned to the crowd, thankful for the old hag. I would worry about owing her later. Not tonight.

My siblings were scattered throughout, and their advisors were huddled in groups around the outside, likely discussing our meeting earlier. I had filled them in on all that had happened in the Others Realm. Thallan trying to turn me into a husk, Bilvog attacking me and my suspicion there was a hag actively working against us. I had kept the hooded man to myself for now. I was still trying to work out who it was. My announcements got the reaction I was expecting. Awe was angry, Crescent was silent, Enduring cried, Gloom was practical, and Ashes was in denial. By the end of the meeting, we had a plan. If you could call it that.

"I think the most important thing is that we recover the artefacts. It's the only way we know to stop him," Enduring said. Her melodic voice was beautiful. "Do we know where they are?" she asked.

Kennock, the leader of Gloom's guards, spoke up, "We know he has the Staff of Thorns, Gentle has the Crown of Glass, but the Chalice of the Sea, the Hourglass of Time and the Cloak of Stars are unaccounted for. The Sword of Light is still in your possession, I believe Awe."

"Yes, I still have it. And believe me, no one is going to get it. It is hanging in my personal chambers, and no one gets in there."

"Are you sure it is safe? Your personal chambers don't seem very secure, knowing the many women you have traipsing in and out of your bed," Ashes said with a crooked smile.

"Well, obviously, I don't have them in my bedroom. I have another room for that. Even though I like...companionship, I do like my peace and quiet as well. I'm not entertained every night. The sword is as safe as it's going to get. Plus, I like having it hanging on my wall," he said with a shrug.

"I still don't know what those symbols mean on the cult member's head, but I know they have power. I just can't figure out what. Shayde and I will keep working on them," Crescent said, nodding to her advisor standing behind her.

"That's good," Nate said, standing by my side. "Looks like we are all working towards something. I think, on the top of our list should also be to investigate if one of the hags has turned against us. How did Bilvog think he was getting into the Gleaming Grove?"

"Wait, did he actually go in there? I thought he stayed out," Gloom pointed out.

"He didn't go in, but he was definitely sure he could," I said. "He told King Thallan he could go in and get the crown, and the only way to do that was to have a hag's permission. It's worth looking into, I guess." Everyone nodded, and we lapsed into silence, caught up in our own thoughts.

"Plus, now we have Thallan to worry about. Do you think he will be a problem in the future?" Kennock asked.

"I'm not sure," I said, fiddling with the lilac-coloured sleeves of my dress. They were long and loose and were beautiful but could get in the way. "Who knows what happened when we left. They could have formed an alliance and still be there for all we know. I think we need to keep him in the picture as well. We don't want to underestimate him." We discussed a few more things, but by the end of the meeting, we were happy with our decisions. The main thing was getting those artefacts before Bilvog. They were the only things we knew that would work. We would have to figure out how we were going to use them later.

Before we left for the party, Gloom stood. "Gentle. While we are here together, we wanted to tell you something. We are all very proud of you." I stood up straighter as tears pricked my eyes.

"You have told us a bit of what you went through there and I must say we are all impressed with how you handled yourself." Everyone smiled and nodded at me, and my throat tightened.

"We know you took Bilvog's betrayal harder than the rest of us, and after he attacked you, you could have left and given up, but you didn't. You kept going and beat him and King Thallan. We are so proud of you, and we knew you could do it. Well done and...we love you."

By the end, tears were pouring from my eyes, and I was warm inside. It was amazing to know how my family felt about me. To be honest I had always believed myself less than the rest of them. It was nice to know they were proud of me, but more than that, I was proud of myself. I had done something I didn't think I could. Many times, I had wanted to give up, when attacked by the pixies, falling in the bog and especially when Bilvog attacked me, but I didn't. I stuck it out and did what I had to to save my people, and no one could take that away from me. Not the advisors that had left or Dread himself.

The party began, and we started to mingle. Tonight was a celebration. I wore the crown on my head with pride and defiance. We had done it. I danced with Nate in the middle of the dance floor, surrounded by my friends and family. We were quite the pair. Nate was wearing a deep purple suit, and his wings were gleaming in the moonlight. His blond hair had been brushed, and he looked gorgeous. My lilac dress brushed the ground as it billowed around me. The beading on the bodice caught in the candlelight, and although I had lost my glow, I felt like the most beautiful woman in the world. I had the love of my family, a wonderful man, and I loved myself.

I was ready to take on anything.

I was ready.

THIRTY-NINE
BILVOG

The room was dimly lit.

The usually cold room was hot and stuffy, filled with the members of the cult, their bodies pressed together, leaving little between them. Their numbers were growing. Dread would be pleased. As I walked in the narrow walkway the members had left me, I reminded myself to walk with pride.

I had done this. I had gathered loyal people to pay witness to what was about to happen. Powerful people from every realm were gathered and willing to sacrifice everything for Dread. And I had done that. Of course, to do it, I had to do some hateful things, but when the history books were written about this moment, they wouldn't remember those things because *I* would be the one to write them.

My shoes clipped on the stone floor, and my black robe dragged along the floor, collecting dust at its hem. I could hear whispers throughout the room, but I couldn't hear what they were saying. The fingers on my withered hand twitched as I worried they were talking about my failure in the Others Realm. I pushed it from my mind and focused on what I was here to do.

I walked up the steps of the stage that was at the front of the room. My knees ached, and I held back my wince. I was level with the stone bench that had been brought in, especially for tonight. It was black, and as I ran my hand over it, I was thankful I had thought to ask King Thallan for it. I had convinced him Dread would appreciate it and see it as a sign of partnership. I hoped I was right because I didn't want King Thallan as an enemy. He was a dangerous man, and I was glad to get out of the Others Realm and be back here in our hideout in Toleran.

The room was quiet now that I was on the stage. I looked down at the body that was lying on top of the slab, pale and cold. It would do. It was the body of a mage that had died and was perfect to be the vessel of Dread. In life, his hair was curly and black. His skin was tanned, and he had green eyes. The most important thing was that he wasn't a human. I walked around to the other side so I was overlooking the gathered cultists. Red robes and bald heads looked up at me as I spread my arms wide.

"Welcome, and thank you all for coming to this momentous occasion," I said, putting authority into my voice and soaking in their rapt attention. This is what I was made for. Commanding people and taking control.

"Tonight, we are going to witness the greatest leader of all time rise and rule once more. Dread was banished and trapped, thought never to return, but with the help of your magic and dedication, we will see him rise again."

Applause broke out, and I let a small smile grace my lips. Once it was quiet, I reached into my black robe and pulled out the soul knife. The bone-handled blade was heavy with souls, and my stomach did a flip as I held it out for everyone to see.

"With this knife, I will fill Dread's new vessel with enough souls to bring his back from where it was sent by his family. He will be reborn in this body, strong and vital, ready to lead us into a new age!"

I raised the hood of my robe and waited until everyone else had as well. I brought the blade down, steadying my slightly shaking hand and traced the ancient rune onto the vessel's stomach with the soul knife. As soon as the rune was finished, a bright white light filled the room. Everybody had to shield their eyes, and I heard gasps and shouts of alarm.

Finally, it died down, and when I looked at the rune, it was gone. The mage's skin had warmed from pale white to a golden brown colour. I watched as the chest rose and fell slightly, and the fist that had been gripping my heart loosened. It had worked. Dread was back. I sat the now light knife on the table and looked at the cultists looking at me with wide eyes.

"It is done. Dread's soul has been successfully put into this body before us. Well done everyone. It is with your help and sacrifice this has happened. Now go and celebrate. Dread will need his peace to rise again." I could see a few people hesitate, but they all filed out. I focused on my breathing and listening to the sound of the footsteps of the crowd on the stone floor. I needed a minute to gather my thoughts. I needed it to sink in that I had done this and that Dread was going to rise again.

I busied myself, packing away the soul knife into its box and taking off my robe. I had removed the bells from my beard, and the silence unnerved me somehow. I turned back to Dread's new body and let myself think about how things were going to change. I had been his faithful servant and uprooted my whole life for him. I had done things for him that I didn't even want to think about sometimes. But, I had also failed him. I hadn't managed to get the crown even though I had held it in my hands. He would not be pleased. I needed to think of a way to get back in his good books and get the other artefacts—fast.

Something caught my eye, and I looked at his face.

Dread's eyes were open.

He was back.

Do you want more of Gentle and Nate?
For a bonus epilogue, visit this link now
https://dl.bookfunnel.com/fug2jmrsaa
If you enjoyed this book, I would sincerely appreciate it if you could take the time to leave a review. It would mean so much to me!
Just for you, I have the first chapter of Book 3 of The Evers Saga, Awe's Awakening.
[Please keep in mind it is an early draft and things are likely to change in further edits :)]

Awe's Awakening

Ailis

I pushed open the heavy door, wincing as it screeched on the old iron hinges. I stood inside the room and huffed out a sigh, turned around and kicked the door that had given me so much trouble. I added *"oil door"* to my growing to do list and stepped into my brand new house.

Standing in the dining room, I pushed on the wooden door to make it close again and looked around the room. It already had furniture and it was all covered in white sheets, like fat little ghosts squatting on the floor. There was a large fireplace near the front door and I could already see my cauldron hanging there, swinging on its chain. I pulled off a few of the sheets and clouds of dust filled the air and my lungs, making me cough. This place really needed a good clean. A thrill zinged through me and I smiled, running my finger across the back of the chair I had just uncovered. This was my house and I got to clean it. After being isolated and held in the same house for years, being out was like filling my lungs for the first time.

I took a few moments to remove the rest of the sheets from the ground floor furniture and open the curtains. Specks of dust danced in the air, caught in the light. I opened the windows and a beautiful fresh breeze blew through making the dust dance. The trees outside were green and I could hear the stream that ran through the woods, just a few minutes away. I couldn't wait to start to add my touches on this house, do readings, and really settle in.

There was a knock at the door and my bubble popped. The reality of my situation came crashing back. I wasn't here to make friends. I was here for a job and I knew that once it was done I would be right back to Shadowstone Burrow to serve Camilla until she saw fit to release me. I swallowed the lump in my throat and walked back to the front door, pulling it open and cursing as I dragged it across the stone floor.

Standing on the threshold was Camilla Crimson, the hag of Ceplar. Maybe she shouldn't be a hag. Hag implies old and crotchety and Camilla was anything but. She was the newest member of the coven and she was all about making an impact.

She was wearing a gothic style red satin dress that clung to her curves in all the right places. Her long black hair reached down past her hips and her long nails were painted bright red. She really stuck to the theme. On her head was a long black lace veil that covered her face at all times. I had never seen under the veil and it drove me mad wondering what she looked like under there.

"Ailis. What do you think of your new house? It was all I could get on such short notice without causing too much suspicion," she said, her voice husky as she walked in, careful not to touch anything. I knew if I could see under her veil her nose would be wrinkled. After spending a hundred or so years with her I didn't need to see her face to know what she was thinking.

"Thank you Camilla. This will do nicely," I said.

"Nicely? I should think so, considering you have never had a house before. I thought you would be more grateful."

I could never win with her. "Of course I am grateful. It will make my job much easier." I said, trying to inject the right amount of sincerity into my voice.

"Good. Now. Let's go over the job again." she said, perching on the edge of the wooden dining chair that I had uncovered for her. I sat opposite her and tucked a red curl behind my ear. My face was emotionless as I tried to hide the emotion I was feeling inside. Camilla wasn't a fan of emotion.

"Thank you. Please, what am I to do while I am here?"

"You already know a little bit, but basically you are to pose as a fortune teller, which shouldn't be too hard with the talents I gave you. While doing that you are to keep your ears open about anything to do with the artefacts. Especially the Sword of Light. Dread is growing impatient and wants these artefacts as soon as possible. Bilvog appears to be on the outs with Dread at the moment so this could be my chance to squeeze my way in." She said the last bit almost to herself. I knew she had been waiting for Bilvog to fail so she could get in with Dread and it seemed like she had got what she wanted. Good news for her, bad news for me. There would be no chance of failure. I clenched my hands under the table.

"Once Awe has heard of you, he will come. You are exactly his type and he will be sure to pursue you." She leaned in close and through the veil I saw her eyes blink. The sweet smell of roses filled my nose and I did my best to hide the shudder that ran down my back. "You will do your job. You will need to stay focused. Find out where the Sword of Light is and tell Tyrus. He will sneak in and retrieve it. Do not let any *feelings* get in the way of this mission. If you ruin this for me, you will never be free."

I could not repress the next shudder that travelled down my spine.

"Yes, mistress."

"Good." She leaned back and tried to look more relaxed. "I made sure there was a spare room here for you to do your fortune tellings, and a room for Tyrus to stay. You will have to come up with a reason for him to be here. A brother maybe? Or perhaps a lover would be better. Give Awe a little competition. You two can work that out." She said, waving her hand, while she glanced around the room looking for an escape.

I nodded, hoping she would be satisfied with that and leave. I was lucky. She stood and dusted off the back of her dress before she turned to the door and stood there. After a moment she cleared her throat and I jumped up to pull open the door, wincing again as it scraped the floor.

"Now Ailis. The most important thing to remember is that you don't know me. I have gone to great lengths over the years to keep secret who my girls were that I have been training and I don't need you revealing yourself and throwing suspicion on us. Stick to the plan and get that sword. Or you will be mine forever." Without saying goodbye or waiting for an answer, she turned and walked away into the cover of the trees, disappearing and leaving me alone. I sighed and walked back into the house leaving the door open.

For a moment I stood here and watched the shadows from the leaves on the trees dance across my feet. I needed to get this right. My freedom was at stake and I would not let anything get in the way of being free from Camilla.

I pulled the notebook out of my pocket that I never left home without and flicked to the front page. *I am resilient in the face of challenges.* I repeated it a few times to remind myself I could do this. All I had to do was befriend Awe and find out where he kept one of the most powerful artefacts in the land, and then give it to his enemy. I could do that, right? I shook my head and put my notebook back into the pocket of the linen pants I was wearing.

I went to the back of the house where the laundry was and found cleaning supplies in a cupboard. I filled the bucket with water and soap and carried it to the sitting room and started to clean the house. It was time to settle in, and pretend I was a normal woman, moving into her first home.

Pre order Book 3 of The Evers Saga now!

About the author

Brooke is a fantasy author from Australia who loves a yarn. She was often told in school she talked too much, but she is putting that to use writing stories and tales she loves. She loves enchanted forests, a slow burn romance with a hint of enemies to lovers, folk tales and myths.

She dreams of visiting Scotland and Ireland, but until then, she will look for the fairies and Good Folk between the pages of her books. She spends her time with her two sons and partner watching monster trucks, playing video games and staring out the front door day dreaming.